FORBIDDEN INSTINCT

The Summer Park Psychics
WANDERING SOUL
WHISPERING HEARTS
LINGERING TOUCH
THE SUMMER PARK PSYCHICS OMNIBUS

Other Works
CRAFTING A WRITER'S LIFE: Building a Foundation

Coming Soon

The Blades of Janus
PERIHELION

Cygnian 7
DORN
BRON
TARN
ROM

Lar: A Scifi Alien Warriors Romance

Cygnian 7
Book Three

Cassandra Chandler

Copyright Page

You are a good person! You know that stealing is wrong. Remember, eBooks can't be shared or given away. It's against copyright law. So don't download books you haven't paid for or upload books in ways other people can access for free. That would be stealing.
And you're better than that.

Lar: A Scifi Alien Warriors Romance
Cygnian 7, Book Three
Copyright © 2022 by Cassandra Chandler
Print ISBN: 978-1-945702-91-4
Digital ISBN: 978-1-945702-90-7

First eBook edition: March 2022
First print edition: March 2022
10 9 8 7 6 5 4 3 2 1

cassandra-chandler.com
P.O. Box 91
Mission, Kansas 66201

Chapter One

Harbor, Kansas
Sol System - Planet 3
Earth:

Sophie jerked back as the blade hummed through the air, heading straight for her neck. She blocked it at the last moment. Her sword emitted a shower of sparks as it collided against the other energy weapon. The impact jolted Sophie all the way to her elbows, making her fingers tingle painfully. She shook her hand and gripped the hilt tighter as she staggered back a few paces.

Thank God I'm wearing the Cygnian wristbands, she thought as the tingling receded.

The wristbands were generating a reassuring pale golden light that coated her body, forming a protective shield. Sophie felt a surge of strength course through her muscles from the special augmentation she had activated. Otherwise, her weapon would have fizzled out under the impact.

Her adrenaline spiked as she twisted to keep her

opponent in her line-of-sight. Her heart beat faster, echoing in her ears like the beat of a sound system with the bass turned up too high. As she waited for an opening, she wished she could say her adversary was doing the same, but all she *had* were openings.

She gulped in gasping breaths. Sweat dripped from her chestnut and sun-streaked hair under her collar and ran along her spine, making her skin prickle. She resisted the urge to squirm as it rolled below the waistband of the jeans she had borrowed from her sister, Becca. Every joint and muscle in her body ached.

I have to be better than this.

Light flashed over the milky-white crystal of the opalescent walls of the *Arrow's* training room, but she maintained her focus on the fight. Her sneakers squeaked on the polished crystal floor, making her wince. She ignored the dull ache in her rear-end that reminded her of the consequences of hitting the unpadded surface of the training room floor. Rolling her neck to ease the tension in her shoulders, she noticed how her opponent's eyes followed the movement.

Sophie decided to take advantage of his distraction and charged, lifting her weapon above her head. She brought her sword down with all her enhanced strength, even though she knew it would have little effect.

Her opponent parried her attack, easily knocking her blade away. Sophie spun around, hoping for an opening.

Of course, her strategy didn't work. The clash between the two swords engaging created another shower of sparks that danced outward in a brilliant, blinding display of light. This time, her opponent didn't put any effort into pushing her away. They ended up nose-to-nose.

Her sun kissed nose to his very blue one.

Her deep brown eyes to his warm golden ones.

Her panting breath to his soft smile.

He is so gorgeous...

It was so easy to get distracted by Lar when he was near her—especially when they were sparring. She never felt more alive. Her skin tingled, her heart raced. Even when they weren't sparring, she felt like she couldn't quite catch her breath.

She only wished she could catch his attention. His cobalt-blue skin gleamed like the crystal walls around them. Her fingers twitched with the desire to touch him and explore the abundance of muscles that covered his body. His eyes were glowing like twin suns on a summer day, warming her soul as he returned her gaze. His hair fell down his back in dozens of indigo braids and a thick beard hid what she guessed was a jaw strong enough to match the rest of him. She wondered if he could sense her attraction or even shared it.

Stay focused. Think of Hayley.

Sophie repeated the chant. Hayley, her best friend in the universe, was out there somewhere, alone and at the mercy of the Tau Ceti—or worse. Unbidden memories pushed through the wall she had erected around them.

Tau Ceti Epsilon Base
Ceres Dwarf Planet
Sol Asteroid Belt
Two days earlier:

The taste of scorched popcorn and bile filled Sophie's mouth as she slowly woke up. Her back ached. She was lying on something cold and hard. What was she doing on a cold metal table? She had been about to start a sisters' movie night with her older sister, Becca, and her youngest sister, Amy. Becca was still out on her walk, but Amy...

Amy!

Pain pierced Sophie's brain right between her eyes as she jolted upright. She clenched her eyes shut, pressing her forehead with the heels of her palms, and tried not to throw up. As soon as the nausea began to pass, she looked at her surroundings. The room she was in was small, with grayish-brown metal walls. She was sitting on a bench that was attached to one of them. There was a toilet in one corner, along with a sink.

"Gross," Sophie murmured.

She stood slowly, gripping the bench as her legs wobbled beneath her. The room felt like it was spinning.

She kept one hand on the wall as she tried to learn more about where she was and what had happened. The walls were completely smooth except for the outline of a door. There was a small rectangle etched in it at about eye level and a larger one at waist height.

Her stomach sank. She had seen doors like these in Amy's favorite crime shows. Prison doors.

Amy wasn't here. Something had happened to her. The memories trickled in as Sophie's head cleared.

Three men had broken into their house dressed in silver catsuits like something out of a 50's B sci-fi movie. Hayley's ex-boyfriend, Dean, had been with them, dressed considerably better, but he had morphed into some sort of shapeshifting monster. The men in silver had fired an alien-looking weapon. They had... They had shot Amy!

Sophie's stomach roiled and her heart sped up in her chest. Her skin prickled painfully. Amy was hurt, and Sophie had no idea where she was. She didn't know where she was herself. She had to escape and find her younger sister.

Sophie carefully studied the walls. There had to be an access panel or a control switch to open the door from inside. Her vision was still bleary from sleep and the drug they had used to knock her out. She rubbed her eyes to clear them and surveyed the room again.

On her third pass, she found a small rectangle etched into the metal near the door. Its outline was barely visible, but there was a spot that was scratched, as if someone had been trying to pry it open. Sophie ran her fingertip over the spot, feeling the roughness of the abraded metal. The edge was even raised a bit there. All she needed was something strong enough and flat to pry it open further.

She glanced down at her charm bracelet. They hadn't taken it, thank God. She didn't know what she'd do if she lost it. She hugged her wrist to her chest, thinking of Hayley. They always said their matching charm bracelets kept them connected, no matter what. Now it was going to help get Sophie out of this.

She unhooked a flat, solid charm and started picking at the spot where the panel was scratched. Her hands were shaking. She wiped her sweaty fingers on the back of her jeans and took a deep breath. Then another. When she felt calmer, she started working on the spot with her charm. She didn't know how much time she had before someone or something came through the door. It felt like it took forever, but eventually she wedged the charm into the tiny gap between the panel and the wall.

"Yes!"

Her heart raced faster as she managed to get her fingernails behind the panel and pry it a little farther out of place. Her nerves were so tight, she could barely breathe. Something jabbed against her fingers, and there was a flash of light on metal. Sophie yelped and flinched, dropping her charm. The panel snapped back into place with a tink.

"Dammit!"

She looked down at the offending item that had caused her to lose her progress and her brain just stopped. She couldn't understand what she was seeing. Her heart felt like it was lodged in her throat as she bent down and picked up the charms. Both of them.

The one she had been using to pry open the panel made sense. The other didn't. It was a half-heart charm with "Fs VAR" engraved on it. Sophie's hands were shaking as she brought up her bracelet and found the charm she had bought for herself and Hayley that year for their birthdays. Sophie held the half-heart charm she had found inside the panel against hers, where "BF 4-E" was engraved.

They matched up perfectly. Sophie had special-ordered them so that the charms would be an absolutely unique pair. This had to be Hayley's charm, but she had told Sophie that it was lost in the mail and she hadn't received it. That had been months ago.

Sophie staggered to the bench and sat down, her head spinning and tears burning in her eyes. She held up the charms side-by-side, trying to figure out what it all meant.

Only one thing made any sense at all. Hayley had been here. They had kept her prisoner.

The door swung open and Sophie quickly slid the charm into her pocket. A man entered wearing yet another sci-fi costume, this one bronze with odd fins on the shoulders. He told her he was one of the three alien soldiers who had broken into their house. Tobek. He brought her food and water, and what she needed most of all—hope.

Hayley had made a deal with him to try to keep Sophie and her family safe from Dean. That's why Tobek had purposefully thrown off his fellow soldier's aim when the other man, Jaxa, had fired at them. Tobek didn't know why Dean was interested in Sophie's family, but now, he was her only hope of finding Hayley.

That was until the next time Sophie saw Tobek—being carried into her cell, held aloft by his throat in the grasp of an enormous man who turned out to be Kral, crown prince of the Cygnians.

Unless it was Dean in disguise. Unless it was another trick.

Kral was followed by Becca and two of Kral's warriors, Bron and Lar. Sophie didn't believe it was a genuine rescue until she saw Lar.

Instinctively she sensed she could trust him with her life, her heart, her everything. It was as though she had known him forever. She could feel him, knew that he was telling her the truth. He was the only person she could trust.

"Sophie? Are you ready to continue?"

Lar's gentle voice snapped Sophie back to the training room. A continuous pulse of energy raced up and down her spine. It spread out to her limbs, making her fingers tingle almost painfully. Lar's gaze was so bright, her eyes burned. How long had they been staring at each other? She lifted a hand and rubbed her temple, trying to get her bearings.

Breathe, Sophie. I'm on the Arrow. *Deep breath. I'm with Lar. Breathe. I'm safe. Just breathe.*

She felt calmer. While *she* was on the *Arrow*, Hayley was not. Sophie had to find her friend. There was no one else who even knew Hayley was missing. She couldn't afford the luxury of a nervous breakdown until Hayley was safe.

Hayley needs me to stay focused. After she's home, then I can have a total meltdown. Right now, I need to learn everything I can to get her back.

If Sophie answered Lar with words, they would start talking and she might let something slip. No one could know about Hayley. Not when there was a shapeshifting alien mercenary targeting Sophie's family who could take anyone's form.

Just the thought of Dean finding out that Sophie was on to him was enough to make her stomach sour. If he found out she knew about him, she would lose the only advantage she had. She would lose her only chance to find out what he had done with Hayley.

"Sophie?" Lar prompted again, his voice even softer, her name like a caress.

The only time he let them be close was when they were sparring like this. Sophie wasn't ready for that closeness to be over. The prospect sent her spiraling back toward the panic she had just clawed her way out of. She answered by lashing out with the leg closest to him, wrapping her knee around his in a move that should have knocked him off balance and thrown him to the floor.

It didn't work. It did, however, send frissons of pleasure racing up and down her spine. Her skin rose in tingling goosebumps, her heart beat faster, and her mouth went dry. Heat pooled low in her belly. He was still standing so close.

Lar cast a strained smile at her and her stomach did a flip. His eyes glowed brighter and she felt some kind of rumbling vibration emanating from him. It permeated through her muscles, relaxing and arousing her at the same time. She leaned closer, their blades touched again, emitting a crackling sound.

"That might work on a human, but not on me," he said.

He pushed against her sword. With her leg still half-wrapped around his, she lost her balance and fell backwards, landing hard on the crystal floor. Pain lanced through her body as old bruises were joined by new ones.

Lar stood above her, still smiling that gentle smile of

his. "You need to remember that your opponents will not always be human. Find their weaknesses. Exploit them."

"That doesn't sound very Cygnian," Sophie said.

He shrugged. "You're from Earth. We need to work with what you have."

He extended his hand toward her. They had never touched—not like this. Her heart leapt frantically in her chest as she reached for him. She was about to take his hand when his eyes widened and he suddenly stepped back, his gait stiff. He winced as if he was in pain.

What had just happened? Sophie scrambled to her feet, humming the control note for the wristbands that would deactivate all of their current functions. Her sword vanished with a fizzling sound.

"Are you okay?" she asked.

"I'm fine." He smiled at her, but she could see the lines of strain around his eyes.

Something was wrong. Something he wasn't telling her about. She reached out to him again. "Are you sure?"

Before her hand could connect, he turned away, moving out of reach. He deactivated his energy blade, his back toward her.

"You're very good with a sword," Lar said.

Was he trying to break the tension of that strange exchange with humor? It didn't seem like him. Cygnians might not even have a similar idiom in their culture. Sophie decided to let it pass.

"I dated a guy in college who was super into fencing," she said. "I really liked it, so I kept training after we broke up."

A stronger wave of vibration hit her. She gasped as it delved through her muscles to ring in her bones. The shivers down her back turned to prickles, like all the hair on her spine was standing on end. She rubbed her arms to make the fresh—and less than pleasant—goosebumps go away.

"Thanks for helping me learn how to use these Cygnian wristbands," she said, trying to distract herself as much as anything else while the vibration subsided.

"You're pushing yourself very hard," Lar said. "Not even Becca is training as much as you are or studying our ways with such intensity. It makes me wonder... Why are you?"

Sophie shrugged. "Well, Becca and Kral have other things to do, if you know what I mean."

Oh, damn. Did I say that out loud?

Lar arched a dark blue eyebrow. "I suppose you have a point."

She pinched her lips together to keep from embarrassing herself further with a quip about Becca having access to two "points" thanks to Cygnian anatomy. Apparently, Cygnians were fairly similar to human men, only times two. Sophie felt her cheeks heat, knowing they must be beet red. She hoped Lar would assume it was from their sparring and not the erotic thoughts she couldn't get out of her head.

Oh, but that is a nice setup, she couldn't help wickedly thinking.

"You still haven't answered my question," Lar said.

How could Sophie get out of this? She looked away, trying to think of what to say while her mind spun. She wished she could tell him the truth.

Because my best friend is out there somewhere, being held captive either by the sadistic scientist who ran the secret Tau Ceti base in our solar system or a Scorpiian mercenary. Rescuing her is my highest priority even though I know there's a war going on and everyone is needed elsewhere. I just have to keep trying to find her no matter what and do whatever it takes to bring her safely home.

Her heart sank as she thought of what would happen next. If Sophie told Lar the truth, he would tell Kral. Then Kral would tell Becca and who knew how many others. The more people who knew, the better the chances were that Dean would find out. Heck, one of the people they told could actually *be* Dean. He had tricked Sophie into thinking he was Hayley for months. Sophie couldn't even trust her dog anymore.

Her eyes filled with tears at the thought. She missed spending time with Dash so much, and knew Dash must feel the same. If it really was her dog, she hated the thought of how it must be confusing and hurtful to Dash that Sophie was keeping her distance. They hadn't done her agility practice or anything.

Sophie hadn't been able to even be near Dash. Instead, she was relying on Nuar's Earthling soulmate, Lian, for help. Thank goodness Lian had her Saint Bernard, Ed, for Dash to hang out with and knew how to care for a dog. Sophie would be relying on Lian to care for Dash during the next part of her personal mission.

She sniffed and blinked to clear her eyes. "Listen, I actually... I need to talk to Rom. Is he around?"

She gasped as a wave of hurt and betrayal rippled through her. Where had that come from? She didn't understand why she would feel that way. She must be more messed up from her ordeal than she realized.

For a second, she swore she saw Lar's lip curl up in a sneer. Did he not like Rom? They were in the same prism. She was still learning about their group, but she thought that meant they were all connected somehow, on a deep soul level. She supposed they didn't necessarily have to like each other, but Lian had described it as "kind of an epic bromance between seven Cygnian dudes."

"I would take care when dealing with Rom if I were you," Lar said, his words coming out a bit stiff. "He is... I believe the Earth word of your region is 'a player.'"

Sophie laughed. She could totally see that, with Rom's smoldering violet eyes and soulful smile. But Lar was the only Cygnian who held her interest. He was the one who made her heart beat faster just by walking into the room, the one who made her feel better, even when it seemed like everything was hopeless.

"I'm not in any danger there," Sophie said. "I just... I was just going to ask for his help with something." As soon as she figured out how to ask without giving away her secrets.

Rom was the Cygnians' pilot, and Sophie needed to get back to the Tau Ceti base on Ceres. Back to where she had been held prisoner by Dean and his minions. Back to where they'd held Hayley.

"Perhaps I can assist you instead," Lar suggested. Again, his eyes widened, as if he had surprised himself with his offer. His jaw snapped shut with a clack.

If he could be the one to take Sophie back to Ceres, that would be perfect. She felt safer with him than with anyone she had ever met. If they were alone together, she might even be able to tell him about Hayley, if she swore him to secrecy first. He seemed like the kind of person who kept his word. Sophie liked that about him. If she was honest with herself—and she usually was—she liked everything about him.

If only he felt the same way about me.

Chapter Two

An intense impression of desperation was emanating from Sophie. Lar could sense it. It had been building ever since he and the others had rescued her. At times, she was almost frantic with it.

He... could relate.

The urge to touch her lit a fire beneath his skin. His need burned him, consumed him, and stretched the limits of his control beyond anything he thought he could withstand. The plates along his spine ached constantly from his desire to comfort her. The muscles on either side were two lines of agonized tension. A steady vibration pulsed out from his spine plates, even when clamped firmly against his back—his muted mating call to her.

My vow is to Kral. My word. My bond. Till the day I die, I must hold him above all others.

Lar's hearts seized painfully, their alternating beats so close to matching Sophie's. The thump of them taunted him with a glimpse of unity that he could never achieve. A tightness spread through his chest, robbing him of breath. He resisted the urge to rub the area. Instead, he held himself as still as a statue, his muscles tight and his expression fixed. He couldn't let Sophie know how much her presence affected him. If he did, she might leave.

As much as it pained him to be this close to her, the thought of being parted was more than he could bear. It would take him to the ground if he let slip even a moment of his self-control. Sophie needed him. He could feel it, the way her heartbeat picked up whenever she saw him. The way her fear retreated in his presence.

The iron grip on his hearts eased. The first breath he could take, he gave to her.

"Tell me," Lar said. "What is it you need?"

Now she was the one holding her breath. She stared at him, her perfect lips parted, and her rich brown eyes fixed on him with indecision. Some of her long dark hair had fallen forward during their sparring. His arm twitched toward her. It would be so easy to brush it back behind her ear, to run his fingers through that silky hair, to pull her against him and crush her lips to his.

His groin tightened, his cocks responding to his thoughts. The Earth-style clothing he wore would only do so much to hide his reaction to her. He tightened his control further, willing his body to stop. His claws extended as the pressure within the rest of him built.

"You can't tell anyone," Sophie said. "Swear it."

Her odd request surprised him, a welcome distraction from his longing and pain. What was it that was so important to her? He would never know unless he swore. He briefly closed his eyes—yet another oath binding him. He prayed to the Maker that he would not regret this oath as much as he did the first.

"I swear," he promised.

Sophie bit her lip and shifted her weight from one foot to the other. She glanced behind him at the open door to the training room. Her eyes filled with worry and a slight plea.

Stepping closer to him, she said, "I need to go back to Ceres."

"Ceres? Why?"

"I can't say."

He could feel its importance to her. His hearts raced along with hers. Her eyes were wide with a longing of her own—a longing not related to him. At least, not directly.

"The Tau Ceti base was destroyed by the Cygnian queen's personal warship," Lar replied with a frown. "There's nothing left."

"You don't know that," Sophie insisted in a low, frustrated voice.

Her anger and desperation washed over him, making his spine plates start to rise despite his best efforts. Every cell in his body was prepared for action, ready to defend her against whatever threat she perceived. He thrummed with the need to make her feel safe, his muscles twitching, begging him to take action. He wasn't certain that the threats she felt were real, though.

He knew the Tau Ceti were absolutely a threat to everyone in the Sol system and beyond, but the feelings coming from Sophie were immediate. It was as though she was still in the cell with her captors. As if they were hurting her in this moment.

"I'm sorry," she said, looking away. "I just... I need to see for myself."

That made sense enough, but he knew there was something deeper beneath her request. He could feel it. Another might be fooled that this was her truth, but she couldn't fool him. He was her soulmate.

A surge of pain stabbed through his hearts as he admitted their connection to himself. His hearts clenched again, agony like a fist with hundreds of protruding needles crushing them in a grip as strong as the gravity near his home world. For a moment, he couldn't breathe.

He had to breathe, though—for her. He had to help her, even though he felt as if he was being torn apart. She needed him, and whether he was ready to admit it or not, he needed her. Even as that realization formed, he remembered his vow.

Kral comes first, he chanted in his mind. *Kral above all others. He would want me to help Sophie where he could not.*

The pain slowly subsided. Sophie was Becca's sister, and Becca was Kral's soulmate. If he knew that Sophie was struggling and had reached out for help, Kral would want whomever she approached to support her. He was not breaking his vow to Kral. If anything, he was keeping it by agreeing to assist her, he reasoned.

"I will take you," Lar said.

A wave of shock, hope, and gratitude flooded through him. Sophie's emotions were so strong and pure, he could almost become drunk on them. His heartbeats quickened again at her jubilation.

"You will?" she exclaimed. Her eyes widened, and a huge smile graced her lips. "Oh, thank you! Thank you!"

She leapt forward and threw her arms around his neck. Her feet dangled above the floor as she clung to him. Lar felt as though he had grabbed hold of the ship's plasma core. His intense reaction was the most powerful emotion he had ever experienced. Electric arcs of pleasure coursed over his skin and burrowed through his muscles, coiling deep in his bones. His hearts beat against his ribs, pounding on them as if they were trying to break through his chest to reach her. Lar shuddered when his spine plates snapped erect, sending a strong vibration that echoed off the walls and made them shimmer with iridescence. His cocks jerked, longing to be buried within her, to claim her as his and achieve unity through their unique soulmate bond.

The crashing wave continued to pound through his mind and body. He didn't dare envelop her in his arms. If he did, he would never let go.

So, he waited. Standing as still as he could until he could force his spine plates down against his back. He held them there with a diamond will. His muscles cramped painfully, but he ignored it. He urged his cocks to calm as he retracted his claws, and disregarded his frantic hearts.

Sophie slid down his chest till her feet touched the floor. Each millimeter of friction was an exquisite agony. A trail of fire remained in her wake, his chest filled with energy that he had no means of releasing. She reluctantly let go of him and stepped back, wrapping her arms around her middle and tightly hugging herself. Lar wasn't surprised at the shell-shocked expression on her face. He knew she had to feel their connection.

He needed to explain. But how could he? How could he tell her that a choice he had made as a child would prevent them from ever achieving the happiness they could share if they bonded. That he had never actually had the hope of finding someone to love, with so few Cygnian females left in the universe.

He had believed he would never find his soulmate. He had been wrong and the knowledge was about to crush him.

She stood before him, more beautiful than he had dreamed possible. So frail, and yet so fierce. She was an intoxicating mix of strength and fragility. Braver than he could ever have imagined. His aching hearts still managed to swell with pride that this was his soulmate. This glorious, radiant, beautiful sentient. He couldn't have her, but he could help her.

He cleared his throat, then said, "We can take my shard. It's a small fighting vessel."

"Right. Okay."

Her voice was faint, her eyes unfocused. Concern filled Lar as another thought occurred to him. According to Becca, Sophie and her dog had been nearly inseparable before Sophie's abduction. He had taken that place for Dash as much as he could while Sophie was captured. Since her rescue, he hadn't seen her so much as touch Dash.

"What about Dash?" he asked.

Sophie winced at the name and looked away. Lar stifled a gasp as an almost crippling wave of guilt surged out from her—guilt and fear. The emotions so strong they were tangible.

"She's been hanging out with Nuar and Lian a lot lately," Sophie said, her voice oddly flat. "I think she's kind of sweet on their St. Bernard, Ed. She'll be fine."

Dash might be fine, but Lar was beginning to wonder about Sophie. He had to figure out what was truly bothering her. Perhaps once they were away from the *Arrow*, she would open up to him.

"What will we tell the others?" Sophie asked, her eyebrows knitted together with worry.

He smiled, knowing he could at least ease this concern. "Would you like a view of your solar system?"

Her face brightened. "I'd love that!"

"Then let me show you. And if we happen to pass by Ceres while we're out…" He let his voice trail off and he shrugged.

She grinned as her emotions shifted toward relief and hope. For a moment, he thought she might hug him again. He wanted her to, though he wasn't sure he could resist the temptation to hold her back this time. He locked his muscles into place to help himself resist.

"Let's get going," she said.

He should be feeling relief, not disappointment. But as she turned and headed for the exit, his chest felt empty. His skin still tingled from where they had touched. He wanted more of that. He wanted more of her.

She turned at the door, her brows furrowed again. "Are you sure you're okay?"

He nodded and forced himself to smile. "Of course."

She lingered for a few moments, as if weighing his words. Then she nodded and walked down the hallway. Lar's legs felt oddly stiff as he followed her. He wasn't used to having to use so much will to hold himself still. He was a Cygnian warrior, meant for action and battle. His muscles loosened the more he walked, though the pressure in his chest remained. He doubted it would ever go away as long as they weren't bonded.

Being close to her is enough. It has to be.

As they headed to Lar's shard, Sophie began to speak. The timbre of her voice and cadence of her speech soothed the ache in his hearts.

"I've never seen Becca so in love," Sophie said. "Actually, now that I think about it, I've never seen her in love at all before."

"Such is the way with soulmates."

Sophie was quiet for a moment, then asked, "What's it like?"

Lar was giving more focus to keeping his legs moving, one step after another, than to his words. His mind spun as he tried to remember what he had said. His breath hitched when he did. This was his chance to help her understand. How could he explain in a way that would give her comfort?

The only way I can. With the truth.

"Soulmates feel drawn to each other, even before they meet," Lar said. "Once they are in each other's presence, the pull becomes like a force of nature. Like gravity." Their own link had helped Lar lead the others to Sophie when she'd been taken, though he hadn't told anyone how he'd managed it.

"Is it… physical?" Sophie asked. "Or just emotional."

Lar grew even more confident that she was feeling the same pull to him that he felt toward her. "Both," he said.

Sophie was quiet for a few moments once more. The

silence was filled with her curiosity and hope. He hated that he had to disappoint her.

"Becca told me you can find your soulmates on Earth now," she said.

This was precisely the opening he had hoped for. It did little to soothe his hearts. How did he explain that yes, they could find their soulmates on Earth, but not if they had given a vow to another, as he had to Kral?

"I have hope for the others," he said.

"But not you?"

His hearts gave a twinge, the pressure upon them intensifying. He rubbed the center of his chest absently, where Queen Ehmach had put the mark of the Maker on him during the ceremony that accompanied his vow to her son, Kral.

"The prism bond that I share with Kral and the other warriors aboard this ship is something like a soulmate connection, only not as strong," Lar said.

"So you're already soulmates?"

"Of a kind. The bonds are stronger between some of us than others. Kral and I met when we were children, reckless and full of swagger. We fought in a crystal forest and ended up nearly getting killed."

"Wow," Sophie said. "That sounds kind of...epic."

He chuckled. "It was. We saved each other's lives that day. Not much later, I swore an oath to him—that I would always hold him above all others."

"He didn't make the same oath back?"

"He couldn't. As the crown prince to our people, he knew that he had to put their needs first."

Sophie stopped suddenly. He felt anger lash out from her. Concern and confusion flooded him at the unexpected emotion.

"So, if he has to for his people, he'll break up with Becca?" Sophie asked.

Lar turned to face her. "No. The soulmate bond is more precious to us than any other connection. Now that they are bonded, he could no more turn away from Becca than he could tear his own soul from his body. They have achieved unity, and nothing can break that. Our people will understand."

"But wouldn't it apply to you, too?"

The wistfulness in her voice matched the longing flowing out from her. A longing he shared. His hearts ached, so close to matching her beat, yet kept from doing so.

"I made my oath to Kral a long time ago," Lar said. "It is the most sacred vow among my people and carries with it its own type of soul bond."

Sophie shook her head. "I still don't understand. I mean, if you were that young, they shouldn't have let you make such a binding oath."

"I was old enough to understand."

In a small voice that made his hearts clench, she said,

"Did you not want a family of your own?"

The ache became a sudden stabbing pain, those needles pushing farther into his hearts. An image came to his mind unbidden. An image of children with sapphire blue skin and chestnut hair running through a green field on Earth, Sophie's black-and-white dog chasing behind them. Their eyes would be the same rich brown of their mother's. They would have his strength and her laugh and joy would flow out from them, brightening the entire universe.

"Lar?" she prompted gently.

He swore he heard the sound of crystal breaking within her voice, but knew it must be only in his mind. He steeled his expression so as not to trouble her, but found the muscles of his neck so tight that he had to clear his throat before he could speak.

"I would love to have a family of my own," he said, his voice rough. "More than anything. But only ten percent of our population is female. Most of them were past the age of bonding or already bonded before I was born. When I made my vow, I had no hope that I would ever find a soulmate. I didn't know…" He hadn't known that one day he would be standing right next to her—so close he could reach out and touch her.

There might as well be an entire galaxy between us, he despaired.

"I gave my word," Lar said, his voice a quiet rasp. "That I would hold Kral above all others until the day I die. I can never claim a soulmate. I know in my hearts that if I did she would become the light of my universe and I would not be able to keep my vow. And if I broke my vow —"

"You wouldn't be you," she finished for him.

Her eyes shimmered. He could feel her sadness. It echoed through him. Hollowed him out. But there was more. Something that glimmered and took his breath away.

Acceptance.

She understood. He could hardly believe it. And yet, it made perfect sense for her to understand. They were soulmates, after all. Perfectly matched, though they would never know how it truly felt for them to meld their souls together.

"We should go." She sniffed once, then straightened her shoulders and turned down the hallway, maintaining a brisk pace.

"Sophie," Lar called after her.

She paused and turned. "Yeah?"

He smiled with a desolate hope that he could perhaps lighten their terrible situation. He pointed down the corridor in the other direction. "It's this way."

"Oh." She returned, pausing in front of him, her neck craned back so she could look him in the eyes.

"Thank you for explaining," she said. "And for helping me any—" She cut herself off and winced, a moment of despair striking him harder than any blow she had ever managed during their sparring sessions. She shook her head, and the emotion was replaced with the same determination she always faced him with in the training room. "And for helping me."

This time, it was he who finished her sentence, though he didn't dare say it aloud.

"And for helping me, anyway."

Even though she knew it would be difficult for him—for them both. Even though she knew he should stay away. He nodded, then gestured for her to precede him down the corridor that led to the lower shards.

Each warrior had a personal fighter that could detach from the *Arrow's* main body. Lar's shard made up the lower-right edge of the ship. It was just next to Kral's in the center.

An unfamiliar feeling swept through Lar as he thought of his place of honor next to Kral. Not resentment. He could never feel that for Kral. No, it was something else. Something he had never felt before. Not like this.

Regret.

Lar's legs were heavy as they made their way to his ship. Regret was not an emotion he was familiar with. The weight of it slowed his pace, making it easier for Sophie to keep up with his long stride. He was lost in his thoughts as he struck his wristbands together and hummed the note that opened the upper hatch to his small fighter, automatic reflex completing the sequence.

A flutter of surprise swept through him. Not his own, but Sophie's. Her eyes were wide as she stared into the shard. It was only when he followed her gaze that he realized his mistake.

"Wow," she said. "That's going to be a tight fit."

Chapter Three

Sophie's heart pounded as she watched Lar step into his personal fighter. Her arms were already tingling as she imagined herself in the small space with him. Light shimmered over the milky-white crystal walls. Picturing them both inside, she was surprised that she wasn't afraid she'd feel claustrophobic. Their journey was going to be... cozy.

He lowered himself until he was lying on his stomach within the shard, then stretched his long legs out behind him. It hadn't struck her before just how huge he was. The muscles of his back flexed beneath his shirt as he reached forward to grip the controls at the front of the vessel. The slightest raised line along his spine hinted at his spine plates.

She wanted to run her fingertips over them—over all of him. Heat built in her belly as she let her eyes do what her fingers couldn't. His ass was epic, the muscles of his legs strained against the denim of his jeans, and his biceps were so huge, the sleeves of his T-shirt stretched tight.

She was sure he was proportional. Times two. Images

flooded her mind of the two of them embracing in the shard, limbs tangled, his cock stretching her—

"Sophie," Lar said, frowning at her with eyes that burned like searchlights.

She shook herself, pushing away the wayward thoughts. How long had she been standing there, ogling him?

"Sorry," she muttered with a tinge of pink flushing her cheeks.

Rippling movement caught her eye. His spine plates were moving beneath his shirt. He turned back to the front of the vessel, his chest expanding and contracting with slow, even breaths. The movement of his spine plates stopped.

This was going to be torture. She wasn't making it easier for either of them by letting her imagination go crazy, but didn't know if she was strong enough to control it. Her legs dangled as she sat on the edge of the ship's upper hatch. She had space to lie next to him on either side, but not without touching him, even if she pressed herself up against the wall. The interior was tall enough that she could crawl around and even sit up once she was inside, if she was okay with climbing on top of Lar.

She was so okay with climbing on top of Lar. Or lying on top of him. Especially if he rolled onto his back and she —

"*Sophie.*"

It sounded like an admonition this time. Her stomach clenched. Could he read her mind? If so, the nonstop flow of her sexy thoughts had to be upsetting him. She wasn't sure how this soulmate thing worked. She just knew that he was hers and they would never be together.

Tears filled her eyes. Her heart felt like it had turned to lead. She had never truly understood the word 'heartache' before, but the dull pain that coiled within her chest made the word clear in a way she wished she had never experienced. The only up-side was that the erotic thoughts finally stopped.

She settled in next to him, keeping herself as close to the wall as possible. Her side still brushed against his, letting his warmth seep into her. She clung to it, even while hoping it wouldn't be too distracting for either of them. The top of the ship slid into place, sealing them in.

Dorn, the Cygnians' head of security, had explained to her that the Cygnians grew crystals in the shapes and forms of almost everything they needed, even their spaceships. Each warrior had a personal fighter, called a shard, which was grown from the same milky-white material as the rest of the *Arrow*. The main ship was gorgeous— a giant, luminous crystal, with the numerous shards connecting to it and forming additional complex planes and facets.

Cygnians primarily controlled their technology through their wristbands, the commands activated by a mixture of striking the bands together and humming certain control notes. A steady vibration came from Lar as he activated the shard's systems.

"Hey, I want to hear that," she said, leaning against him a little harder. "Hum loud enough for me to hear the notes."

She couldn't resist giving him another nudge. His scent filled the ship, pine-like and sharp in a strong, masculine way. She hoped being so close wasn't upsetting him. His soft laugh reassured her, as did the wave of amusement that flowed out from him. It warmed her heart. She loved that she knew how he felt without needing to see his expression.

"You want flying lessons now?" he asked.

Was that possible? Her heart quickened with excitement. Who wouldn't want to learn how to fly a spaceship? And the knowledge might help her rescue Hayley.

"That would be amazing," Sophie said.

Lar chuckled and shook his head. "Perhaps later."

She pouted, then remembered he couldn't see her face, so she sent a wave of teasing disappointment to him. It had just been instinct, but he stiffened and turned to her, his eyebrows raised and his lips parted.

Oh shit… He felt that.

Being soulmates was more powerful and complex than she realized. It was so natural to reach out to him in that way. Her throat tightened at the knowledge. They weren't even bonded, from what he had said. What would it be like if they actually connected as they were meant to?

"I... I'm sorry," she said.

For an instant, such anguish flowed through her that she couldn't breathe. She wasn't sure if it was his emotion or her own. Lar turned back to the front of the ship. He said nothing, a strange coldness coming off of him both physically and emotionally. She retreated closer to the outer wall of the ship.

The crystal panel in front of them shimmered. A moment later, a viewscreen appeared on it. Floodlights set into the ground just outside the hangar where the *Arrow* was berthed illuminated the grassy field that surrounded the starport that was disguised as a regular Earth airport just outside the small town of Harbor. Beyond, dark silhouettes of trees bent in an evening breeze while fireflies danced around their trunks.

"It's really pretty here," she said.

"Perhaps your family should consider relocating."

She glanced over at him.

"Harbor is the only town on Earth where everyone knows aliens exist—and understands the importance of keeping that a secret for now," Lar said. "You and your family would fit in well here."

She would have to think about that. They had relatives not far away. Her mom would love to be closer to their

Aunt Trudy. If Kral and Becca started having kids anytime soon, they could visit their second cousins much more easily. Unless, of course, their kids were blue. That might pose some awkward questions.

Sophie would love to have blue kids, if she had them with Lar. Her heart ached knowing she would never have a chance. She wanted kids. Tons of kids. But the idea of having them with anyone but Lar... She couldn't face it right now.

She shook herself. She shouldn't be thinking about this. Hayley was out there, she reminded herself for the hundredth time. Blocking all thoughts of anything else, she held her focus on that, and not the gorgeous alien beside her that lit her up brighter than anyone ever had before.

"Are you ready for this?" Lar asked, looking at her over his shoulder.

She nodded. He twisted the controls he held in each hand. The shard dropped from the *Arrow*, making a sound like wind chimes. Her stomach lurched as she watched the ground rush up at them, but then they stopped, hovering a few inches above it. Lar glanced over his shoulder at her and chuckled.

"Smooth," she said, grimacing at him in what she hoped was a playful manner.

"Just wait." With a genuine smile, he turned back to the view before them. White light flashed across the screen.

"What was that?"

"The cloaking field. We are following all the Coalition protocols while remaining on Earth, including their rule about only flying at night and keeping our cloaks active."

"Do we need to tell them where we're going?"

He shrugged. "Perhaps we are following *most* of their protocols."

A definite sense of playfulness emanated from him as he smiled at her over his shoulder. Her breath caught in her chest. Tingles spread all down her spine, then flowed over her back and down her arms and legs. His gaze softened, then warmed. The soft glow of his golden eyes intensified. Heat flooded her core. She leaned closer to him again.

Lines of strain appeared at the corners of his eyes. He turned back to the front of the ship, his smile more subdued. A moment later, the shard bolted out of the hangar.

Sophie squealed in surprise, gripping his shoulder. They raced across the field, then over a wide plain. Grass bent as they rocketed past. Trees and farmland were a blur on either side of them. The shard suddenly angled up— straight up—and the view filled with stars and a huge quarter moon above.

Sophie heard laughter. She realized it was her own. Her grip on Lar's shoulder tightened and she plastered her body to his side. When they passed the moon, he rolled the ship, almost as if he was showing off for her. She squealed again, the changes in their inertia affecting her like she was on a roller coaster, even if diminished by the ship's systems. Then they were heading into a field of black velvet studded with glimmering stars.

Her laughter faded as a sense of calm and wonder settled over her. She let herself remain where she was, snuggled against Lar's side. She even dared to rest her head on his shoulder. The most profound peace she had ever experienced flowed through her heart. She relaxed against Lar even more. The peace echoed from him, leaving her floating in a cloud of serenity.

This was enough. If this was the most they could hope for, she would make it be enough. For both of them.

This was the most perfect moment of Lar's life. Sophie rested next to him, her head propped against his shoulder. Warmth flowed through his body everywhere they touched. The rest of his skin was cold in comparison. His hearts beat in near synchronicity, matching hers. Her contentment washed through him, wiping away the despair that overcame his mind more and more often.

Around them, countless stars burned against the void, defying the darkness with their light. He could fly off toward one—he and Sophie—and find a planet to escape their obligations, to start a new life. His chest seized painfully at the thought, the bond-point with Kral searing him with a strange, cold energy.

Sophie stiffened, then shifted away. He wanted her close. By the goddesses, he wanted her close more than anything. But his vow…

"This is the worst design for a ship I've ever seen," Sophie said. There was purpose behind her words. A need that focused on him, but that he didn't understand. Perhaps she was trying to distract him from his morose thoughts?

"Shards are designed for efficiency in battle, not comfortable travel." His words came out with a breathless wheeze. His chest was tight. "My apologies," he managed.

"It's just… Lying down? You have to fly lying down? I would have such a crick in my neck after two minutes."

"Our anatomy is different. We can lock specific muscles into a position when needed, requiring little effort to stay that way."

"So, you can turn yourself into statues."

"I suppose."

A chill swept over him. He suppressed a shudder. That cold spot on his chest was still there, but it couldn't mean…

"Are you all right?" she asked.

He shook himself, then forced a smile onto his face. He would have tried to send a wave of reassurance to her, but his thoughts were too grim. "My apologies."

"What were you thinking about just now?"

"Death."

Her unease filled the shard. He chided himself for speaking so bluntly, yet he knew he would never deceive her.

"Why?" she asked. "The Tau Ceti are gone, right? I don't want you in danger."

Her concern for his safety chased some of the chill away from his bones. She was fierce, his Earthling.

"The Tau Ceti base has been wiped out," he said. "When Queen Ehmach sets her intention to destroy something, she destroys it."

"She must be fun at parties."

Lar chuckled. The idea of Ehmach at an Earth-style party was unfathomable. He doubted that such an event would end well, unless they enjoyed sparring or brawls.

"Why did the statue comment make you think of death?" Sophie asked.

Lar pondered how best to explain before he began. Perhaps if she knew more about their culture, it would help her understand their circumstances better.

"Many sentients will swear by a Maker," Lar said. "They are the entities who created us."

Sophie propped her head on her elbow, still leaning against the wall. "We have something similar on Earth, but there are lots of different belief systems."

"Cygnians also believe in an Unmaker. The Goddess of Death."

A strong pulse of unease struck him again. Sophie

shivered, as if she'd caught a chill herself. Lar glanced at the internal readings for the shard, but the temperature was normal.

"She is not to be feared," Lar said, turning his attention back to Sophie. "She comes when it is our time—the greatest of all Cygnian warriors. None can stand against her."

"I still don't get what that has to do with statues."

"When death nears, our bodies begin to crystallize. As the change comes upon us, we tell our loved ones, and they follow us in procession to the Chambers of the Dead. Once there, we stand in our assigned spot and give ourselves over to the Unmaker. Our bodies turn to crystal statues."

Sophie's chest stilled, as if she was holding her breath. The cadence of her heart paused then began to pound. His own followed as best they could.

"How long do Cygnians normally live?" she asked.

"Several hundred Earth years."

"And you are…?"

Lar chuckled. "Nowhere near that."

He had not considered the difference in their ages before. The advanced alien technology of Harbor would extend her lifespan for a long time. Centuries, perhaps. He hoped she would find someone who helped her fill those years with happiness. With children. That familiar despair rose in him, crashing through his senses. His hearts ached and the chill in the center of his chest spread, sinking into his bones.

"Show me how to fly this thing." Sophie rested a hand on the control bar closest to her.

If he were to guess, he would say she was trying to distract him again. A furrow deepened the skin between her eyebrows. He didn't need their bond to notice her concern.

He hummed a few notes, setting an autopilot for Ceres and enacting a few safety measures, limiting their speed and maneuverability. The inertial dampeners in shards weren't as powerful as those in most small vessels, and he didn't want Sophie harmed. When he was done, he rolled to his side. That odd stiffness in his joints was back.

"It's on autopilot for the moment," he said.

Sophie scooted closer. Her proximity warmed him. Everywhere his body faced her, his skin lit up, waves of tingling pleasure causing refractions to rise in his skin, as if seeking her. The light in the shard brightened. That shouldn't be possible unless they were achieving unity, and for that to happen… For that to happen, he would need to be driving his mating cock into her, over and over again.

Her ripe ass filled out her jeans perfectly. He could easily tear them from her body, lift her hips, and bury himself deep in her core. The shard was small, but they had room to work. The thought was enough to make his cocks begin to harden and his spine plates to rise. He pressed himself against the wall, forcing his spine plates to stay flat against his back. With a deep breath, he willed the blood away from his groin, focusing all of his attention on not reacting to her.

Sophie's breath quickened and her heart raced. He knew she could feel his need. Her desire for him hit him like a shock cannon. The scent of her arousal filled the ship. He wanted to reach for her, to pull her into his arms and claim her. If she asked, he would do so. His strength had fled him.

"Sophie…" The needle-like pain returned in his hearts, the stabbing sensations inching deeper and stealing his breath. The cold in the center of his chest seemed to feed them.

"The flying lesson." She swallowed hard, her attention fixed on the screen in front of her. "What's the note I need to hum to turn off the autopilot?"

Apparently, she was strong enough for both of them. The pain in his chest ebbed once more. Relief and disappointment warred within him. He focused on the first emotion, grateful that she was helping him to keep his vow, and hummed the note for her.

"The controls can move in any direction you need," he said, his voice rough. "The more forcefully you change them, the faster the ship alters course and speed. Go ahead and try. There's nothing out here for you to run into."

She nodded, then cautiously rotated her hands in the

same direction. The star field changed as they flew to the left. She did the same to the right, then up and down, each time moving the controls and the ship more quickly. For the next hour, she put the shard through its paces, getting a feel for it. The tension in the shard eased, her delight taking over.

"You're a natural," Lar said.

"Thanks." She smiled at him, warming his hearts once more. Then her smile faded and her eyes grew wide. Dread flowed out from her. "Maybe you should take over."

He looked at the viewscreen and saw that the black velvet of the void with its many stars had company. Lots of it. Asteroids.

Lar nodded. Sophie released the controls and scooted out of the way. They were close to Ceres. Her anxiety grew as he maneuvered the ship between the asteroids. Whatever was behind her fear, they were about to face it together.

He piloted them under the geological formation that hid the opening to the Tau Ceti base, then down into the dark pit. Sophie shifted closer to him. She fisted some of the fabric of the pale blue Earth style T-shirt he wore.

When the prism had arrived to rescue her, dozens of ships filled the main cavern. He was certain most of the Tau Ceti stationed at the base had escaped. Sophie had insisted on warning Tobek, the Tau Ceti soldier she had formed an alliance with during her short imprisonment.

Even so, there were several piles of twisted, blackened metal fused to the walls of the cavern. The entrance to the main base had been incinerated, along with most of the outer wall. He could see down the wide corridors that led deeper into the base. Queen Ehmach had most likely sent shards down each one, destroying everything and everyone they encountered.

Sophie let out a sound of anguish—a half-moan, half-sob. Her despair was sharper than the pains in his hearts, more immediate and laced with fear. Whatever she had been hoping to find when they arrived, this was not it.

Chapter Four

Tau Ceti Epsilon Base
Ceres Dwarf Planet
Sol Asteroid Belt:

Tobek's steps echoed through the darkened hallway of the deserted Tau Ceti Epsilon Sol base. Well, nearly deserted. Rixon and Jaxa walked ahead of him, the helmets activated in their brown and bronze-trimmed uniforms. They were the other two members of the triad assigned to this mission.

The magnetic fields they had each activated in the cybernetic implants in their legs slowed their gaits. Water dripped from a damaged pipeline in one of the adjacent rooms. Char and cinders floated in the air surrounding him. The Cygnians had been zealous in their destruction of the base, but not as thorough as they thought.

Rixon paused at the end of the hall and pulled off a glove. Ice crystals formed almost immediately on his pale skin, intensifying its greenish hue. The nanites in his system would have to work quickly to keep up with the impact of being exposed to a vacuum. He pressed his hand against a hidden access panel. Wires snaked out from under his skin, attaching to it. Mechanisms whirred to life behind the wall, hissing and grinding noises letting them know that the space beyond was being pressurized. The secret door slid away. Light spilled into the hallway and Tobek squinted against it, his helmet and cybernetic optics not filtering out enough.

"Fuck," Jaxa said, lifting his arms to shield his eyes. "Norem is the top Tau Ceti bioengineer. Why the bright lights when he knows our eyes are sensitive to it?"

Because he's a sadistic ass.

Tobek knew better than to voice his thought. It wasn't always easy, but it was safer. He waited impatiently for Rixon to finish his task.

"Stop complaining." Rixon pulled his hand back from the panel, his connector wires retracting into their housings and the open skin sealing in seconds. He stepped aside to let Jaxa through.

It didn't matter that there was plenty of space. Jaxa directed his path so that Tobek was in his way and slammed his shoulder into Tobek's as he passed—the organic one. Tobek's vision filled with static briefly and he grunted as pain lanced through his arm from the nearly healed wound where Dean had demonstrated his displeasure with how badly their last mission had gone.

Tobek's own nanites had barely kept him alive when

Dean had stabbed him. Tobek did everything he could to hide his shudder as he remembered the quicksilver in the Scorpiian's body burrowing and spreading through his flesh. Showing weakness to Jaxa and Rixon was always a bad idea.

Once all three were in the small chamber, the door behind them slid shut. The lights brightened, beaming down on them and heating their uniforms. Tobek closed his stinging eyes, waiting for the decon procedures to complete. After a few moments, the lights dimmed to a more tolerable level and the interior door slid open.

The triad activated the function of their uniforms that folded their helmets back into the collars of their suits. Tobek ran his hand through his short blondish-brown hair, then tried to follow Jaxa from the chamber, but Rixon stepped in front of him, glaring.

The intimidation tactic didn't work on Tobek. He wasn't afraid of pain, thanks to Norem's 'treatments and upgrades.' His only possession was the uniform he wore. He had nothing else to lose.

Nothing I haven't lost already.

"Are we just going to stare at each other all day, or are we going to get this done?" Tobek asked.

Rixon's lips twitched into a brief smirk. "We are going to finish this mission with zero mistakes. Norem needs us in and out as quickly as possible. It won't be long before the Vegans or their mewling Sadirians overrun this place."

Tobek forced his face to remain slack as he said, "Or Dean comes back to the Sol system and sees what's left of the base you were in charge of."

Rixon let out a laugh that was barely more than a breath. He leaned in close. "If Dean shows up, Norem won't be here to make sure you're spared." He pulled back, then said, "No mistakes," before following Jaxa from the chamber.

Sophie's anguish wound its way around Lar's hearts, tightening them further. His skin burned with the need to comfort her, to reassure her, to destroy the base all over again if that would make her feel safe. What he sensed from her was not fear for herself, though. She was searching for something—or someone.

He wondered if it might be the Tau Ceti cyborg who had helped her while she was a prisoner. They had not seemed overly close during the rescue, though Sophie expressed concern for his survival. She had said that she needed Tobek to survive the Cygnian attack, but not why. Was the possibility of his death enough to create such anguish in her soul?

The thought brought a crushing rage to Lar, his muscles bunching with the urge to fight. She was *his*. He couldn't claim her, but she was still his. She would never belong to a Tau Ceti. He would kill Tobek first. Kill all of them. Lar's hands twitched on the controls as he imagined squeezing the life out of the Tau Ceti scum.

"Lar…" Her pleading voice brought him back to his senses. "Please."

His body shuddered as he regained control. He shouldn't be thinking of such things. Not when she needed him. Not when they were so close. Her warmth still spread through his body where they touched. Her longing and concern. He would not distract her from whatever personal mission had brought her to Ceres.

"If you tell me what you're looking for, I could help you better," Lar said.

Again, he sensed her warring desires. She wanted to tell him—she desperately needed someone to share this burden with her—but she wouldn't let herself reach out. What could be holding her back?

A tremor threaded through her voice. "Can you take me to the place where I was kept?"

With the resultant damage from Queen Ehmach's warship, accessing the corridors with his shard would be easy. He turned back to the controls and piloted them through the remains of blasted-out corridors. Neither spoke as they drifted through the ruins of the base.

Charred bits of metal twisted out from the walls and hung from the ceiling in frozen rivulets. The bronze-colored substance had melted from the heat of the bombardment. No life signs pinged his ship, the place was eerily silent.

He had walked these halls with Kral, Bron, and Becca not two days ago. Tau Ceti soldiers had been everywhere. Had they escaped before Ehmach arrived, or had they disregarded Tobek's warning? Why was the cyborg so important to her? The questions spinning in Lar's mind were driving him mad. One loomed larger than all others —why would she not tell him what was going on?

If they were joined in unity, he would be so much better able to protect and support her. His strength would be hers, and vice versa. She would know that she was never alone, her soul at last whole. His vow weighed heavily on him.

They neared the area where Sophie had been held prisoner. Lar hummed the note that activated his ship's scanning function, which superimposed a layout of the base's original design over the view on his screen. The difference between the reality before them and the original structure was incredible. Ehmach had been thorough indeed.

The shard's display was oriented toward the pilot, which would distort Sophie's view from her place off to the side. Lar was certain she would want to see what he saw. Her inquisitive nature was just one facet of her soul that drew him in. As he both feared and longed for, she leaned in closer, her body pressed against his side as she tried to get a better view.

His cocks hardened beneath him. The muscles around his spine plates cramped as he kept them clamped against his back. Her soft, floral scent filled the shard, filled his senses. It would be so easy to pull her beneath him, tear off her clothes, and drive them both toward unity. He closed his eyes, pushing away the thoughts. His muscles tensed further as he willed his body to still. Sophie needed his help, not his desire.

Whatever compelled her to return to Ceres was strong enough that she seemed oblivious to his reaction. She leaned closer to the viewscreen, her breasts pressing against his back and her hand clutching his shoulder for purchase.

"There's nothing left," she said.

The anguish in Sophie's voice quenched the lust threatening to overpower him. Her body trembled next to his. He looked over his shoulder and his hearts seized at the sight of tears glimmering in her eyes. She blinked them away and shook her head, then sniffed.

"Um... the labs," she said, her voice raspy. "Please, can you take me to the labs?"

The look she cast at him was pleading. He would have done anything in his power for her in that moment. He would *always* do anything for her.

Pain radiated out from the center of his chest, stabbing at his hearts with that needle-like grip. His soul—the part that was his—felt as though it was tearing down the middle. He turned back to the viewscreen, forcing his expression to blank, hiding his pain. Her own must be blinding her to what he was going through.

So much need.

Unity would bring her comfort, but his soul was not his own to share with her. The pain in his chest was a constant reminder of his vow. Yet tendrils of warmth sank into him wherever they touched, fighting the cold that spread through him. Her need came with it, searing him. She needed him—needed their unity—and he had to deny her. But he could give her this.

"Of course," he said, his own voice thick and rough.

He spun the shard away from the prisoner area, the front of the crystal ship scraping against the wall and dislodging a chunk of charred metal. The labs had been deeper in the base—in the most protected part. He doubted it had survived the Cygnian assault any better than this place, though.

Sophie remained close as he navigated the corridors, running deep scans of the areas they traversed. She kept her focus fixed on the viewscreen. Lar's spine plates had stopped trying to rise. They seemed frozen against his back. It shouldn't surprise him, with how much effort he had used to keep them under control.

The scans revealed nothing aside from total devastation. There were no energy signatures or life signs of any kind. Ehmach and her forces had indeed been thorough.

The thought should have pleased him. Ehmach was not only his queen, but the leader of his house. She was renowned for her ruthlessness and efficiency in battle. Instead, he grew angry. Sophie needed something from this base. Something Ehmach might very well have destroyed.

"You're going to break those controls if you keep holding onto them so tight," Sophie cautioned in a gentle voice.

He glanced at his hands. Their normal cobalt hue had drained to a slate blue, a strange shimmer glistening on their surface. He tried to loosen his grip, but his fingers wouldn't respond. Sophie reached up and rested her other hand on his shoulder. Her touch eased the tension in him, made his hearts relax. Their asynchronous beats slowed and grew more steady, striving to match hers. Even without achieving unity, their bodies gravitated toward becoming one.

He needed to stop wallowing in self-pity. He needed to get over the idea of—

"What's that?" Sophie said.

His thoughts fractured as Sophie stiffened next to him, excitement coursing through her, her body plastered against his as she half-crawled onto his back, inching closer to the viewscreen. She slid the hand that had been resting on his shoulder over to his spine. His spine plates spasmed, still clenched to his back, as an excruciating pleasure wracked through him. His cocks jerked beneath him, pinned between his body and the ship. He let out a sound he didn't recognize—a groan of longing that reverberated through the crystal of the ship.

"Lar, are you all right?"

She pressed her body closer to his, her attention diverted from whatever had initially caught it. She dragged her hand down his spine in a long, firm stroke he was certain she meant to be comforting. How could she know his spine plates—when touched by his soulmate—were one of the most erotically charged parts of his body?

"Lar?"

Her emotions washed through him. Not sexual, but caring. Loving. She needed him to be okay. Her soul knew his importance to her.

Lar's spine plates broke free from his control. They snapped up, tearing through the fabric of his shirt, shaking with a vibration so strong, the crystal of his shard reverberated with it, iridescence racing across its surface. His muscles pulsed with the need to hold her close, to drag her beneath him and drive his mating cock into her over and over again, until they plunged into the ecstasy that was true unity. His hands jerked on the controls, accelerating the shard suddenly.

Sophie yelped, clutching him tighter as inertia pulled

her toward the back of the vessel. His shard struck the wall in front of them hard enough that their momentum made the back of the vessel swing up. It swung back down, striking the ground with a loud clang before the hover capability caught up with the ship's movements. Still gripping onto his back, Sophie's heart raced, her breathing heavy. He could feel her fear and confusion.

Most of all, he could feel her proximity.

"Sophie," he ground out.

He looked over at her, where she had slid up to be on eye level with him. She was unbearably beautiful. Her dark eyes were wide, her hair wild around her face. Her lips were parted as she took quick breaths.

"Please," he said.

Her heart was just beginning to calm when he uttered his plea. The panic fled her eyes and a new energy flooded them. Heat. Warmth. Desire.

He shook his head, wincing as the pressure built around his hearts once more. He couldn't breathe without her. Not when she was this close. She glanced down at her hands, one clutching his arm and the other so close to his spine plates he could hardly bear it. They vibrated, as if trying to move closer, longing for her touch. She jerked back, plastering herself to the wall of the vessel—as far away as she could get from him.

It would never be far enough.

Lar clenched his eyes shut, fighting to regain control.

"Activate... Activate the controls for atmospheric shielding."

She only paused for a moment before striking her wristbands together and humming the note that would cause them to generate shielding against harmful radiation and energy, as well as creating a thin cocoon of breathable atmosphere around herself. The moment it was active, he hummed the same note for himself, then another that opened the bottom ramp of the shard.

He wrenched his grip from the controls, then slid down the ramp, turning as he did so that he would land upright. The vessel hovered several feet above the ground. As soon as he touched down, he paced as far as the artificial gravity field around his shard allowed, unable to bear the energy coiled inside of him. He needed to distance himself from Sophie, but couldn't bring himself to leave her side. His spine plates were vibrating with a painful intensity. His hearts felt as though they were being simultaneously stabbed and crushed.

"Lar?"

Sophie's voice pulled him back from the edge of darkness. The need in it. The desperation. He turned toward her, tearing away the tattered remains of his shirt. Her eyes widened as she stared at his chest. More of that heat flowed through him. More desire. Hers.

"Sophie," he pleaded.

It didn't matter that his body was nigh-invulnerable. It

didn't matter that he had Cygnian strength. She was a temptation that he could not resist. He wasn't strong enough.

She was strong enough to resist for both of them. Her lips clamped shut and she stood straighter. What felt like an invisible wall slammed down between them. Her desire for him became muted, replaced by a driving need to accomplish... something. Whatever they had come here to do.

She let out a shaky breath. "Are you all right?"

He was not even in the same sector as "all right."

Before he could respond, a chunk of the wall dislodged itself, falling onto the shard and then bouncing to the floor. Ripples of iridescent light flowed over the milky crystal as it absorbed the energy of the impact. His ship had wedged itself into one of the base's walls, piercing the metal—a wall that his scans had not penetrated. He had assumed the other side was solid rock, but the shard would not have embedded itself as deeply if that were so.

Thank the goddesses that the wall hadn't been very far from where they were when he had accelerated. With greater distance to gather speed, Sophie might have been hurt.

He had to be better than this. Sophie needed him. Bonded or not, he had to help her. The thought gave him the strength to bring himself back under control. His spine plates lowered and his claws retracted. The pressure in his hearts lessened to a steady ache.

He closed his eyes and took a few deep, steadying breaths. "I'm fine. I apologize for frightening you."

She shook her head. "I understand, but…" The wall of focused intention that she was projecting amplified. She pointed toward the shard. "Can you get me through that wall? Without depressurizing the area on the other side?"

"My shard can cast an energy barrier that will contain whatever atmosphere the space might contain."

"And we'll be able to go through it? Without disrupting it?"

"Yes."

This time, she nodded. "Then do it. Please."

Sophie's brother, Buddy, had been the unwitting catalyst that brought Kral and Becca together. Buddy had become something of an honorary member of their prism, spending much time with them over the past few months. When he had spoken of Sophie, he portrayed his younger sister as noncommittal and—*what was the word he used?* —flakey. At the moment, Sophie was anything but. Lar saw the will of steel that seemed to run through the entire Myers family.

Buddy had also described Sophie as perpetually joyful. Lar had yet to see more than a glimpse of that aspect of her personality. Whatever she needed here, he hoped it would help her recover that part of herself.

Lar strode to his shard and climbed back aboard. He

made some adjustments to expand the containment field. It was much easier to focus without Sophie in the small space with him, but he missed having her close. Shaking the thought from his mind, he brought his focus back to the task at hand.

He backed the ship out of the hole it had made. A web of translucent white energy spanned the gap in the wall before him. Through his viewscreen, he saw Sophie head toward the opening. He quickly exited the shard, running to her side to prevent her from stepping through without him.

"I should go first," he said.

Her eyebrows rose and she opened her mouth, the argument she was preparing to make building within her so strongly he could sense it.

"I need to stabilize the field as we cross it," he said. "I can do that best from the other side."

That seemed to placate her. She crossed her arms and stared at him, reminding him of her older sister, Becca. These Earthlings might be frail of body compared to the Cygnians, but they had wills stronger than the gravity well of Cygnus X-3.

"I know you're trying to protect me," she said. "Just… be careful. I want to protect you, too."

Chapter Five

Sophie's heart pounded against her ribs with bruising intensity. Her back was still tingling, molten heat pulsing along her spine and flowing to her core. Becca was going to get her butt kicked. She should have warned Sophie about Cygnian spine plates being erogenous zones.

Even without knowing Sophie and Lar were soulmates, Becca knew that Sophie had trouble resisting tall, strong, gorgeous men. Who the heck wouldn't? And Sophie had always been a little… handsy.

A sudden chill extinguished the last of the heat flooding her body as she remembered that Becca might not be Becca. Sophie shuddered at the thought. She knew that Lar was Lar, especially feeling what was still emanating from him as he contemplated her.

He was too distracting. Her focus needed to be on Hayley. A couple of Sophie's ex-boyfriends had been into meditation. She had used one of the visualization techniques they taught her a few moments ago, imagining that a clear crystal surrounded her, shielding her from Lar's emotions and preventing him from feeling hers. She pictured the same thing again.

Lar's eyes widened and he took a step closer. It was hard to breathe, staring into his eyes and yet not *feeling* him. A moment of panic hit her, but she reminded herself that she could sense him again—know that it was him—whenever she needed. She put more concentration into the image of the crystal shield, amazed at how well it seemed to work.

Lar paused, then stepped through the hole the shard had made in the wall, crouching so that he could maneuver through it. The opening had looked huge at first, but seemed smaller next to him. The white light spanning it made a fizzling sound, but stayed intact as he passed through. He looked around on the other side, then turned back to the opening. Apparently, there weren't any Tau Ceti lurking over there.

The thought sent another shudder through her. She did not want to run into any of her captors. The thought made her mouth go dry. It seemed the chamber surrounding them was spinning as she remembered being trapped in the small cell, waiting, not knowing what would happen to her or what had happened to Hayley. She took several deep breaths and fought back the fear and focused on where she was.

The schematics overlaid on the shard's viewscreen hadn't shown this part of the base. Whatever was in here, it was shielded even from Cygnian scanners. It had to be important—and might hold clues to where the Tau Ceti had taken her friend.

Lar reached through the field, leaving his wristband within the translucent light filling the opening. Surprise lit her stomach with butterflies as he extended his other hand toward her. She had never held his hand. Would it be rough and calloused? Or smooth as crystal? She knew it would be strong and warm, like everything about him.

After what had happened between them in the shard, she didn't think he would be eager to let her touch him. Then again, after what happened, he might crave her touch as much as she craved touching him. She shouldn't give in to temptation. One of them had to be strong to help him keep his damned vow.

When she hesitated, he said, "I won't let anything happen to you."

The earnestness in his voice was more than she could resist. She reached through the field and grasped his hand. It was colder than she expected. Cold enough to send a shiver down her spine. He gripped her hand gently but firmly, pulling her toward the field while keeping his wristband in position. The light tingled across her skin like static electricity as she stepped through the energy field. He let his arm drop from the field, but kept his hold on her hand, standing close.

Her heart was fluttering in her chest, but it wasn't just from his proximity. Part of her dreaded what they were about to discover. Tobek had hinted at some of the things Norem, the Tau Ceti scientist in charge of the Ceres base, was doing in his laboratory. 'Enhancements' to soldiers like Tobek that anyone else would consider torture. Experiments on specimens gathered from Earth. Specimens like Hayley.

"You're sure we're alone?" she asked, a tremor in her voice.

"My scans have detected no life signs in this area," Lar said. "But then, we didn't detect this section of the base at all earlier. It must have more advanced shielding. We should be careful."

Sophie nodded. She didn't doubt the shielding was better here. How else could it have survived the bombardment? Stepping around Lar, she squeezed his hand tighter, unable to let go. She didn't want him to know how terrified she was. She tried to keep up her visualization of the crystal shield, but other nightmare images kept popping into her mind, especially when she had a better view of the room.

Light gleamed off a large metal table resting at a steep angle in front of them. The heavy base had multiple interlocking components that looked a little like the structure of a car jack. It wouldn't surprise her if the table could move around or become flat, like a regular Earth operating table. Why was it being kept upright?

Thick straps dangled from the sides. They looked

pliable, like leather, but had a metallic sheen. Norem had positioned the straps where someone's hands and feet would be, as well as near their chest, hips, neck, and forehead. A surge of pity hit her as she imagined Tobek strapped to the table.

It could just as easily have been her. She tried to block out the thought, but then her mind pictured Hayley there. Norem had held Hayley for *months* on another secret base. A base not even Tobek could find.

Sophie slapped her hand over her mouth to stifle her sob. Lar pulled her against his chest and wrapped his arms around her. The crystal shield she had imagined earlier was long gone. Her sadness flowed into him, her fear for Hayley and her grief for everything she and Lar could have had if things were different.

He held her tighter, comfort and affection surrounding her. It was like she was melting into him, except for a cold spot in the center of his chest. The rest of his body seemed to pull at her, as if it wanted her closer. Her skin tingled from it and her spine was lit up like a live wire. That one spot on his chest almost repelled her, though, like holding the same polarity of two magnets together.

She held onto him, not wanting to let go, pushing against that odd force. Her hands slid to his back, careful not to touch his spine plates. The surrounding muscles were as tense as iron, and a strong vibration pulsed through them. With the side of her face pressed against his chest, she heard his hearts beating and his quickening breath. Beneath it, a low crackling sound spread out from that cold spot on his chest.

She pulled back, intending to ask him what it meant, but when she saw his expression, all thought vanished. His eyes blazed gold, his lips were parted, and he was leaning toward her. He was going to kiss her.

There was a reason they weren't supposed to, but she couldn't remember what it was. All she knew was the heat building in her belly and the pleasure racing up and down her spine and spreading out over her entire body. All she felt was the desire that coursed through her. To be one with him. To kiss him back.

They were a breath away when a loud chime sounded from his wristbands. His eyes widened in surprise as his arms stiffened around her. They had both been so lost in that moment. Sophie awkwardly stepped out of his embrace. His eyebrows furrowed as he lowered his arms, staring at them as if confused.

"Are you okay?" she asked.

He shook his head, but said, "I'm fine."

She didn't believe him. He would never lie to her on purpose. She was sure of it. He was probably trying to convince himself as much as her, but he was not okay. Before she could push him on it, his wristband beeped again.

"What is that?"

"It's a proximity sensor," Lar said. "My scanners are detecting something nearby."

Her skin prickled and her chest tightened. "'Something?' That's not very specific."

"The readings are weak, but there is a life form reading. Possibly several."

Tobek had told her that Tau Ceti cyborgs were assigned to triads, groups of three soldiers. Three was several.

"Several, but you can't tell?" Her voice wavered.

"The signal is very weak."

"Weak…" Did that mean they were in distress? Or sick or hurt?

Those life signs could belong to other innocents that Norem had collected for his experiments. Tobek hadn't had time to tell Sophie everything, but from what she knew, Norem didn't care about hurting others to get what he wanted. She wasn't sure what his end goal was— neither was Tobek—but somehow, Hayley had gotten on Norem's radar in the worst possible way. Norem had removed her from the base almost immediately after her arrival. Had he taken her to some place even worse?

Sophie's stomach was churning. She had to do something. Anything. There was a door opposite them with a control panel next to it. They wouldn't learn more standing around in this room.

"Come on," she said. "We have to go."

Chapter Six

"We need to call the others."

Sophie had known this was coming. She had been dreading it. How long could she hold off the cavalry?

"There's no time," she said.

When Lar hesitated, she let her desperation come through both in her words and from her heart. If there were any Tau Ceti left in this part of the base, they might destroy any clues that remained about where Norem had taken Hayley while they waited for backup, and she couldn't shake the thought that those life signs belonged to someone who needed help.

"Please, help me open this door," she pleaded.

Lar sighed, then approached her with a halting step. At the door, he struck his wristbands together and held one up near the panel. Light bathed the metal as he held a sustained note, different parts of the band glowing brighter than others. The door slid open with a soft whoosh.

Sophie tried to rush into the hallway beyond the door, but Lar held out an arm, blocking her. His expression warned her back. She needed to stay calm, but panic was strangling her. The quick beats of her heart were deafening. Her mouth had gone dry.

"Can you tell what sort of life signs you're getting?" she asked. "Are they human?"

Lar's brows knit in surprise. "Human?"

Just the thought of more Earthlings being held captive here made the room spin again. She shook off the dizziness and ducked under his arm into the hallway beyond. It extended several feet in both directions. There was another door on the opposite wall. The hallway to her right ended in a huge archway lit with blinking lights set around a double-door with thick reinforcements fused to its surface.

"Sophie," Lar hissed. "It is too dangerous for us to proceed."

"Try to stop me, and then see what's dangerous."

She bolted to the door across from them and struck her wristbands together. While the vibration still resonated in her arms, she hummed the note Lar had earlier, holding them up to the access panel. Lights gleamed on the surface and the door slid open.

At first, she thought she was looking at another hallway, but when she stepped into the room, she realized it was just shaped oddly. There was a wall near the door in front of her, but the room opened up to her right. Straight ahead, she saw a large wire cage built against the wall. Bile rose in her throat. Tobek had warned her about this, but words weren't enough to shield her heart.

"What is that?" Lar joined her, staring across at the cage. She was dimly aware of the door sliding shut behind him.

She forced herself to swallow, her throat tight. "It's a kennel," she said.

It held her complete attention, her feet moving, dragging her closer. There was a water and food dish built into one side, raised up to make it easier for a large animal to use. The floor of it was covered in a forest green cushion that padded the bottom third of the kennel as well. It looked comfortable, but it was still a cage for an animal that belonged on Earth. An animal that Norem had 'enhanced.'

Her hand shook as she lifted it to the wire and plucked a tuft of white fur from the mesh. Its texture was fluffy, but with a bit of coarseness. It might be from a Maremma or a Great Pyrenees, given the size of the crate.

"Tobek told me about this." Sophie ran her fingertips over letters stenciled above the crate. MIN-D. "Mindy."

"I don't understand. Is this what you were looking for?"

"Only partly." She shook her head. "The Tau Ceti in charge of this base is called Norem. He was trying to genetically engineer intelligent dogs with special abilities. This is where he kept the most advanced one."

"A dog?" Lar's spine plates rose. They vibrated, the

sound reverberating off the walls. His voice rose to a roar. "A dog? By the Unmaker, I will make him pay if he harmed her."

"He didn't. Norem insisted that everyone on the base be kind to Mindy. He was trying to get her to form some kind of psychic attachment to them. He was trying to... To get them to bond."

Sophie needed to calm Lar down quickly. They hadn't yet found the source of those life signs and had no idea what to expect. Still, his reaction infused her with warmth. Lar and his fellow warriors adored dogs from what she'd seen. It was yet another reason she already loved them all. She already loved—

Her heart broke as she carefully studied Lar. So perfect, so beautiful. The man who held the other half of her soul, forever out of reach. His chest rose and fell with powerful breaths. He curved his hands into deadly crescents, claws extended from his fingertips, and his eyes gleamed with a fury that warmed her instead of burning. He was ready to do battle with anything to protect an animal that wasn't even there.

"No one hurt her," Sophie said, seeking to reassure them both. "I asked Tobek all kinds of questions. Norem introduced DNA-altering agents to Mindy's parents while he was posing as someone interested in buying a puppy from a breeder. I guess he actually wasn't posing, since he did get Mindy from them."

Sophie realized with a start that the rest of the litter was still on Earth, relocated to who knew where. Mindy might have been the smartest of the bunch, according to Tobek, but the others were enhanced as well. Intelligent, semi-psychic Great Pyrenees... Under different circumstances, that would be unbelievably cool. Now, it was another problem for another day. She had to stay focused.

"Where is she now?" Lar asked.

Tears filled Sophie's eyes. Tobek had told her that Mindy and Hayley had achieved the bond that Norem was seeking. He was keeping them together because of it. If they found Hayley, they would find Mindy, too. She was sure Hayley was protecting Mindy, but who was protecting Hayley? Sophie tucked the tuft of fur into her jeans pocket, then turned away from the kennel.

"Sophie?" Lar's voice was painfully gentle, though she sensed how angry he still was.

"I don't know. But that's why we're here."

"To find and rescue Mindy."

Sophie opened and closed her mouth repeatedly, unable to mislead him, yet not ready to tell him the truth. Not all of it, anyway. Tendrils of energy rushed up her spine, spreading out over her back and along her arms and legs. He was going to ask her to reach out to the others again, but she couldn't. Not until she had some way of proving that they were who they said they were.

She didn't let him ask. She hurried over to a large

wooden desk that dominated the center of the off-set room. Deep, intricate carvings covered its sides and surface, except for a smooth square set in the middle of its top. An equally elaborate chair sat behind it, with thick green fabric the same as that in Mindy's kennel.

Across from the desk, walls created the strange, narrow space that made the room shaped so oddly. It was like a room within the room, with a door leading to whatever was beyond the wall in front of the desk. She supposed even Tau Ceti needed a bathroom, though the layout was terrible for the Feng Shui of the place. A smooth, dark panel covered half the height of the wall from waist level to the ceiling. If it was a monitor, it was the biggest one she'd ever seen.

"I bet this is Norem's office," Sophie said, hope and excitement rising in her. If she was right, it might contain a clue to where Hayley was. "I'm guessing you guys don't use paper, but might he have information disks or something? Can you see if you can get any data from it?"

Lar cast a wary look at her, but activated his wristbands and stretched his palms above the smooth square on the surface of the desk. He hummed several notes, the sound reverberating with the desk as beams of light connected it with his wristbands. A holodisplay appeared above the desk, static-filled images were flickering in and out of view.

"Dorn should be doing this," Lar said. "Or Bron."

"They aren't here," Sophie said.

"And why is that?" Lar curled his hands into fists and the lights blinked out. He straightened, and she knew there would be no more deflecting. His determination flowed to her. "Why can we not tell the others? We can't handle this on our own. I can't unravel the secrets of this place. The danger isn't just to the two of to us, but to everyone in the Sol system."

"I..."

The panel set in the desk lit up on its own. In the walls all around them, metal scraped against metal and unseen mechanisms could be heard powering up. Dread seized her throat as she started to realize the extent of whatever they had triggered. Some of the clanking seemed far away.

The dark panel across from the desk glowed bright green from within the small interior room—light blazed from three enormous cylinders that ran from the floor to the ceiling. At first, bubbles obscured her view of whatever was within the liquid. When they began to dissipate, her heart froze in her chest. Two of the tanks held bodies.

"Goddesses," Lar whispered as he approached what was actually a window. "Those poor souls."

Tobek said that Norem had taken Hayley away months ago, but what if he had brought her back? What if she was one of those bodies?

Sophie ran to the door that led to the small chamber

and struck her wristbands together. What was the note she needed? She couldn't remember how to hack the lock. Instead, she hummed the note that summoned the blaster function.

Keeping the wristbands touching, she twisted her hands back and forth quickly, as if she was holding an orb within them. Energy crackled between her palms. She flexed her fingers, urging the sphere to grow more intense as she spread her hands apart, giving it room to expand, then unleashed it on the door.

"Sophie!" Lar called out his warning a second too late. He was already moving toward her.

She drew her arms toward her chest, then shoved her hands outward, propelling the energy sphere toward the door. At the same moment, Lar's arm wrapped around her waist, spinning her around so that he was between her and the blast. The shockwave lifted them both from their feet. Heat surrounded her, but none touched her.

Lar landed heavily on his knees, one hand bracing him up off the floor. Sophie dangled from his other arm. His fear and shock leached into her. The spot on the center of his chest had become a burning cold. She arched her back to get away from it.

"Never discharge that weapon in close proximity to your target," he said.

"I'm sorry."

His tone was colder than his chest. Tears filled her eyes

as she felt his anger radiating toward her.

"You're reckless! You could have been killed."

And Hayley could already be dead. She could be in one of those tanks.

"Nothing is worth this," Lar said.

Sophie snapped. She twisted in his arms, writhing violently as she tried to free herself from his grasp. Her tears dripped onto the floor beneath them. She kicked at his legs, struck his arms, clawed at his hand, knowing it was pointless. Her hands and feet ached as if she had been pummeling a stone statue. It was futile to try to escape him.

Except, as her limbs grew heavy from struggling, fresh pain seeped into her awareness. Lar's pain. With him pressed against her back, she felt it scalding him from that cold spot. His hearts jerked in his chest, each beat was sending sharp spikes of agony through him. She gasped, trying to catch her breath and make sense of what was flowing into her.

Lar stood, bringing her with him. He set her on her feet and turned her to face him. His eyes blazed gold. Lines of strain traced their edges.

"What's wrong with you?" she asked.

"Nothing is wrong with me. I'm merely trying to keep you from getting yourself killed."

"That's not what I mean. You're in pain."

His eyes widened, his anger dissipating. "I'm fine."

"No, you're not."

He lifted one shoulder in a half-hearted shrug. "It is only pain."

"But why are you in pain?"

His lips parted, but then he pinched them shut and looked away. Why wouldn't he explain?

Maybe because it's my fault.

The realization hit her so hard, it knocked the wind from her. Was this the price of not fulfilling their soulmate bond? The weight of their loss was crushing when she let herself think about it. For the most part, she was keeping those thoughts at bay. She had other compelling things going on that seemed more urgent. What if it was different for Cygnians?

She reached up to cradle his face with one hand. The pain she felt from him intensified. She wanted to ease it. She would do anything to make his pain go away.

"Please," he said, grasping her wrist and pulling her hand away. He closed his eyes and his breathing steadied. Once it had, he looked down at her again. The golden glow had dimmed. "We can't."

Again, she felt as though she'd been struck. She knew they couldn't be together. He'd been clear about that, though she was still unsure why. Was it their proximity that was setting him off? Would bonding help him or make things worse? She had so many questions, but none of them seemed helpful at that moment.

She pulled away from him, her heart aching. He was dealing with enough already.

She turned back toward the door she'd blown open, walking a good deal slower this time. Whoever was in those tanks, this would not be pleasant. Each step filled her with more dread. Her palms were slick and her breathing loud in her ears. The somersaults her stomach was doing nearly made her sick.

Left, right. One foot after another. She entered the room and approached the first tank, looking up into the poor person's face.

It was a man. Tubes filled with a kaleidoscope of colored fluids snaked in and out of his body, along with glowing wires. Some of his limbs had been replaced with shining chrome prosthetics, the metal meeting his skin in angry red lines.

His hair floated around his handsome face and his eyes were shut, which was a mercy. The places where his cybernetics fused with his skin looked agonizing. Sophie's heart ached for him and her stomach churned. He must have gone through so much to have his body altered to that degree. Her fear for Hayley and her hatred for Norem both escalated, burning like a cold fire in her chest.

She passed to the second tank. It held the same thing. A man's body, floating in the water. No air lines, no movement, but many 'alterations.'

A counter ran along the wall opposite the window,

high-tech cabinets beneath it and monitors set into the space above. There was nothing strewn about the floor or on the countertop. No half-eaten donut or still-warm coffee. It looked like Norem had closed up shop before leaving with Hayley and Mindy.

"This is macabre." Lar had joined her in the room and was circling the tanks. "What purpose could this possibly have?"

Sophie didn't know. She looked out through the window into the room. Norem's desk was right in front of it. He had a clear view of Mindy's kennel and the sick bastard would have sat there and watched these poor bodies in the tanks.

Wait, why would he keep a view of dead bodies? Tobek said Norem was trying to enhance his soldiers. He had only brought Mindy to the base and left the others in her litter behind. Norem didn't seem the type to keep around his failures.

She looked back at the tanks. The metal at their tops and bottoms flowed seamlessly into the ceiling and floor. The tanks were part of the Tau Ceti base. She couldn't imagine how much equipment must be built into the space above and below them to keep those fluids flowing and the lights on.

Keeping the lights on…

Why were the lights on in the base? Why was everything still powered up when the Tau Ceti themselves had abandoned the place? Unless they were planning to come back. Unless they needed something to survive that they had left behind.

"Those life signs," she said. "Are you still detecting them?"

Lar lifted his wristband and drew a finger along its surface. It let out a higher chime than the ones before. He met her gaze for a moment, then drew closer to one of tanks, raising his arm higher. The chime grew louder.

"They're alive." She lifted her hands and rested them on the glass, gazing up at the man in the first tank.

His eyes snapped open. His glowing, orange eyes.

Chapter Seven

Sophie's fear hit Lar just as he heard her scream. He ran to her side, arms raised to do battle, but saw no enemy in the room. Sophie stood frozen, her eyes locked on one of the glass cylinders.

"What is it?" he asked.

She pointed at the tank. Lar turned, his spine plates rising and vibrating along his back. The man inside the tank had opened his eyes. They glowed with a light that cast an orange glow in the surrounding liquid. The same orange as Kral's.

"Maker," Lar gasped.

He approached the tank cautiously, then placed his hand on the glass. The man within followed the movement with his gaze. He lifted his own hand, the wires and tubes attached to him slowing his movements and his eyes closing as if the effort cost him greatly. He rested his hand opposite Lar's and opened his eyes once more.

Energy coursed through Lar as their eyes met—strange, yet familiar. This was a Cygnian warrior, but something was terribly wrong. He was not any kind of Cygnian that

Lar had encountered.

Gills opened on the man's neck. Lar leapt back, pushing Sophie behind him. A Tau Ceti? But Lar sensed his energy. *Cygnian* energy.

"What is it?" she asked.

"I... I don't know."

The man's arm floated back down to his side and his eyes fluttered shut. Lar could still sense him, though it was muted. The man was confused and in pain. It was no wonder, with how his body had been mutilated. Both legs and his right arm had been removed and replaced with gleaming chrome limbs. Lar had faced Tau Ceti cyborgs before, but never ones who were this heavily modified. What was going on here?

"Is this what you came here for?" Lar's confusion made his tone harsher than he intended, and she flinched. "I'm sorry, but this..." He gestured to the tanks, for once at a complete loss on how to communicate his thoughts, his emotions.

Sophie didn't need his words. She must sense his turmoil.

"I didn't know this was here," she said. "Tobek mentioned being put in tanks, but he didn't remember what Norem did to them while they were inside." She looked back at the floating men. "We have to help them."

More than you know.

Perhaps these beings started out as Tau Ceti soldiers,

but they were Cygnians now. Lar could sense the DNA in them, a humming energy that vibrated through their bodies. It was weak—*they* were weak—but it was there. They needed help.

"We must call the others immediately," he said. "This has gone too far."

"You're right." She ran her fingers through her hair and grabbed two fistfuls, pulling on it. Her despair and fear crashed into him. "You're right."

"Why do you fear telling the others? They will do everything in their power to help you."

"I don't even know if they're who I think they are."

Her words made no sense. "Why would they not be?"

"Because my family is still being targeted," she said.

"Your family is being guarded."

Dorn had set up the security protocols himself. The Cygnian security officer was incredibly thorough. Lar's words did nothing to calm Sophie's fear. The emotions rolling off of her increased in strength. She was trapped. In danger. Her mind and heart believed this, as if it was still happening. It was the only explanation for what he sensed from her.

His hearts ached from the burden of despair he could observe, but not help with. The tightness in his chest grew, making it hard to breathe.

"Sophie, you are safe now," he said. "We rescued you."

"But you didn't rescue Hayley!"

She slapped her hand over her mouth, stifling a sob. Her eyes were wide, and her heart raced with a panic that nearly doubled him over. He gasped, pressing a hand to his chest as the crackling sound of shattering crystal pierced his ears. Shaking his head to clear it, he brought his focus back to her as she stepped closer.

"Lar—"

He held up a hand to warn her off. If she touched him now, he wasn't sure what would happen. Their bond pulled at him, straining the link to Kral granted to him by the Maker. How much longer could he endure the strain? It was as though his soul was being pulled apart.

"You're not okay," Sophie said. "Don't try to tell me you are."

He shook his head. "Explain. Quickly. Then we'll call the others."

She hesitated. He forced himself to straighten, willing her to sense that he would not back down on this. She was not the only stubborn one of their pair. He needed to understand what was going on before they did anything else.

"My best friend is named Hayley," Sophie said. "Becca and Amy and I, we all live with her in her house. We moved in with her after her grandma died since she was still in high school and Becca had just graduated and she needed an adult living with her. Our parents are her godparents."

He struggled to understand the cultural idiosyncrasies of what she was saying. "So, you're close."

"We're more than close." She sniffed and wiped at her eyes. "She's like... She's like my soul-sister. We've been best friends since her mom died when we were little kids. My mom was her mom's nurse and promised to look after her. Hayley lived with her grandparents, but then they died, too."

The ache in Lar's hearts grew as he thought of Hayley's losses. Sophie hadn't spoken of this friend before, but as she did, her love for Hayley flooded into him, as strong as any prism bond. Despair tinged the emotion, but the more she spoke, the more determination took hold in her heart.

"When Hayley's grandma died, she was so lost." Sophie lifted her arm and held up a sparkling bracelet covered in small, metallic shapes. "I bought us charm bracelets, and every year since, on our birthdays, we take turns picking out a set of matching charms. This year, I chose a two-piece 'BFF' charm."

He shoved aside his frustration at trying to follow what she was talking about. This was important, all of it.

"I don't know what any of this means," he said.

Sophie stepped closer, holding up a pair of charms between her fingers. It looked as though they were two halves of a single form, letters were engraved on the silver. 'BFFs 4-EVAR.' The edge of one was scraped, the metal bent.

"My translation session did not prepare me for these words," Lar said.

Sophie lowered her arms, cradling her wrist close to her chest and staring at the charms. "'BFFs' stands for 'Best Friends Forever.' And the '4-EVAR' is also... forever."

"So it says, 'Best Friends Forever... Forever'?"

Sophie let out a short laugh. "It was a joke. Hayley hates it when people get acronyms wrong by saying things like, 'ATM machine.'"

Lar stared at her. He didn't understand this either.

"'ATM' means 'Automatic Teller Machine,' so it's another thing where people use redundant words." Sophie's voice shook as she continued. "Hayley would have thought it was hilarious if she'd ever seen it."

"Can you start at the beginning for me?" he asked. "I'm trying to understand."

Sophie took a deep breath, then let it out through pursed lips. "Hayley and I have the same birthday," she said. "February 24. We had just turned sixteen when her grandma died. She didn't have any other blood relatives in her life, but my parents were her legal guardians. I got us these charm bracelets and swore that every year I'd add to it. I wanted her to know that I'd always be there for her."

Understanding brightened his mind. No wonder Sophie had been so accepting of Lar's vow to Kral. She had made a similar promise herself.

"Hayley said we should trade off years. Every other year, one of us chooses a new matching charm and gives it to the other for our birthday. Our bracelets always match." She lifted the pendants again, cradling them in her hand and piecing them together with her thumb. "I had these charms special ordered so that the split is absolutely unique. This *has* to be Hayley's charm."

She paused, her voice trembling when she continued. "I found it in my cell when I was the Tau Ceti's prisoner. Hayley had been there. She tried to escape the same way I did. We used a charm to try to pry open the access panel in the cell. When I tried to open the panel, this charm— Hayley's charm—fell out."

"Why didn't you tell us the Tau Ceti had taken her as well?"

Sophie's lips parted, and she took a step back, her fear spiking. There was more. Something even more horrible. But what could be worse than this?

"Sophie, you must tell me."

Her eyes grew haunted as she looked away. "I didn't tell you because she'd already been gone for a long time."

"What?"

"Hayley was in Paris on our birthday this year. She's a travel writer, and wanted to do a piece about 'Valentine's Day as a single woman in the most romantic city in the world.' She told me the charm had been lost in the overseas mail."

Sophie's lips tightened, and her hands curled to fists at her sides. White-hot fury rose within her, along with crushing guilt. Lar wanted to reach out to her, but was afraid anything he did might stop her from explaining. There was more he needed to understand. The burden he sensed in her was easing a bit. If listening to her story was the only way he could help her, he would do so.

"She told me she'd met a guy. 'Mr. Wright.'" Sophie let out a harsh laugh. "Hayley didn't trust him. She kept telling me something was off, but I pushed her. He sounded so great. He was rich and gorgeous and kept doing these incredibly romantic things. She overanalyzes everything. I thought she was just dragging her feet, so I pushed her to keep seeing him."

Sophie pinched her eyes shut. The guilt she felt was suffocating. He reached for her, the need to hold her too strong to resist. She turned away, pacing in the small space.

"Sophie…"

"Hayley did get the charm. The *real* Hayley did. The person who came back to us was not my best friend." She bit her lips so firmly, all the color drained from them. When she looked at him again, tears were streaming down her face. "It was a Scorpiian named Dean."

Chapter Eight

Lar's mind balked at first, reeling from this knowledge. Dean had spent time with Sophie posing as her closest friend? Lar's hands curled into fists, his claws extending and scraping across his palms. The vibration of his spine plates suffused his body.

He knew of this Scorpiian. Dean was the shapeshifting mercenary behind the kidnapping of Nuar's soulmate, Lian. He had sent one of his agents to abduct the Lyrian infant she was caring for, and the man had taken both of them. If it hadn't been for Nuar's soulmate bond with Lian, both would have been lost forever. Now that Lar had seen this *Norem's* laboratory, his hearts surged with rage at the thought of what might have befallen the pair if Kral and their prism had not intercepted them in time.

"The night that Amy was..." A shudder racked Sophie, and she shook her head sharply. He felt her heartbeat pick up as she fought off the rising panic within her. "The night the Tau Ceti took me, Dean showed up and I just let him in. He told me he was Hayley's ex, and that she was in trouble and I believed him. When Hayley returned from her trip suddenly, I figured things hadn't worked out between them, even though she wouldn't talk about it. I didn't think it was that big a deal."

"You couldn't have known how dangerous he was," Lar said. At the time, she hadn't even known that aliens existed.

"That's the point. I hung out with him for months while he was posing as Hayley. *Months.* And I never suspected it wasn't her."

Lar and the others had wondered why Dean tried to abduct their friend Buddy's sister, Becca. They assumed the shapeshifter had simply been lucky, targeting their Earthling friend's family after learning about his relationship with the prism. Scorpiians were masters of deception and uncovering secrets. If Dean had spent months with Buddy's sisters, he would have been perfectly positioned to learn about Becca's soulmate bond with Kral.

"When was the last time you saw Hayley?" Lar shook his head. "I mean, Dean."

"About a week ago. She—he—said an opportunity came up, and he needed to jump on it." Sophie scoffed. "He might have even been telling the truth. Instead of it being a travel writing thing, it was a chance to kidnap Becca. Thank God for Tobek. If he hadn't helped us, one of us would be dead."

Lar's spine plates vibrated harder. The sound

reverberated off the walls. The thought of any member of Buddy's family being hurt because of his friendship with the prism was horrible. If it had been Sophie, Lar would not have survived the loss. Her soul had been calling to his even before they met. He had felt the pull toward Earth from the moment they had heard the family sing over Buddy's communicator. All the warriors had felt it.

After her rescue, Sophie stubbornly refused to explain her need for the Tau Ceti soldier to survive the attack on the base. Becca suspected it was a human psychological phenomenon called Stockholm Syndrome, where they would actually identify with their captors. Lar wasn't willing to accept that as an explanation anymore.

"The Tau Ceti nearly killed Amy," he said. "And they took you. How can you be grateful to someone who took part in that?"

"Because Dean's original plan was much worse and Tobek stopped it. At least, he messed it up enough that Dean needed to keep us both alive."

"What was his plan?" Dread rose in him as he considered the possibilities.

"Tobek's triad was posing as a group of soldiers from the Coalition of Planets. Dean was able to get them real Coalition uniforms and everything since he used to work for the High Council."

"You mean he took bounties for them."

Sophie shook her head. "From what Tobek has

overheard, he worked with them a lot more closely than that."

The idea was chilling. Scorpiians were mercenary freelancers whose services went to the highest bidder. Their loyalty was only to their payments. The High Council had been utterly corrupt before they had been destroyed in the war. If they had a favorite Scorpiian, Lar couldn't contemplate the resources they might have given to their asset and how Dean would use them now that the Council was gone.

Lar's mind went back to how the Sadirian imposter who kidnapped Lian had spoken of the Council—as if they had somehow survived after their entire planet, Sadr-4, was destroyed along with every single colony in their home system during the first battle of the Coalition's war with the Tau Centauran Assembly.

A chill swept over Lar's skin. If the Council had survived, they would have reasserted themselves over the Coalition by now. They certainly wouldn't be having Dean and his agents assist the Assembly in their attacks. Lar brought his focus back to the enemy at hand. The Scorpiian was the proximate threat.

"This seems too easy," Lar said. "Dean wouldn't let information like this about himself be known."

"It wasn't Dean who let it slip, it was Norem. He talked around Tobek as if he wasn't there. Tobek pretends that he's stupid, but he's not."

Lar had trouble believing that Norem would allow Tobek to live if he thought the soldier that unintelligent. "The Tau Ceti are not merciful to unsuccessful specimens."

"Tobek is another one of Norem's more successful experiments. He thinks Norem is keeping him alive to use his DNA later."

That, Lar believed.

"The plan was for the triad to break into our house and abduct Becca." Sophie swallowed hard, a curious separation forming between her speech and her emotions. Her eyes became unfocused as she continued. "They were ordered to kill one of us and leave the other alive as a witness. Then they were going to… to kill Becca and leave her body somewhere more incriminating. On some Sadirian warship that's close to Earth."

"The *Reckoning.*" Lar's claws had retracted as they spoke, but now they extended from his fingers again. He wanted to break something, to rip the metal from the walls and rend it to pieces with his hands.

"That sounds right," Sophie said. "Dean is working with Norem to make sure the Cygnians don't enter the war on the side of the Coalition. If possible, they want you on their side, with the Tau Centauran Assembly."

If Dean's plan had been successful, it would have worked. With Kral's fury over losing his soulmate, he would have been able to convince his parents to cast aside their neutrality and enter the war on the side of the Assembly.

"Tobek said Norem used to be obsessed with Centauran technology and had Dean steal whatever he could for them. Now, he's focused on Cygnians and Earthlings and whatever kind of psychic bond he's trying to create."

Lar turned back to the men in the tanks. He sensed them, though their minds were dormant. Norem had achieved a Cygnian bond here. The same thing had happened with Kral's sister, Sorca. The Coalition had genetically engineered Sorca with both Sadirian and Cygnian DNA, but all of their people considered her a Cygnian.

Queen Ehmach and King Korvin were desperate to find a way for the Cygnians to survive. They had given their own DNA to top Coalition scientists to find a way for their people to reproduce. Lar had never thought about what happened to that DNA after the fall of the High Council and Sadr-4. Could Norem have obtained it?

If Queen Ehmach learned of these soldiers' existence, she would claim them as her people. So would Kral and every warrior in his prism, but that didn't guarantee the Cygnians would join the war on their side.

This didn't sit right with him. Something else was driving Norem's experiments. Why gather Earth life forms? How was Mindy involved? He doubted Sophie had the answer to those questions, but there was one she might be able to assist with.

"How did Tobek help you?"

"Becca and I look so much alike, people mistake us for each other all the time. Tobek convinced the others that I was Becca and that they needed to move in early to be sure to capture me. He figured he had a better chance of keeping us all alive that way and planned to help me escape while Norem and Dean were trying to figure out what went wrong. He thinks Dean showed up when he realized things were going south."

It was a clever plan—for a Tau Ceti—though a desperate one by any measure. Lar doubted the Tau Ceti's motives had been altruistic.

"But *why* did he help you?" Lar asked.

Sophie caught her lower lip between her teeth, biting it so hard, he feared she would draw blood. Her eyes filled with tears again. He longed to reach out to her, but kept himself still, not trusting himself to hold her when his desire was running so strong. He wouldn't be able to let her go.

"He made a deal with Hayley," Sophie said. "Tobek told me... There was an Earth woman that Norem been experimenting on last year. Tobek didn't come out and say it, but I think they fell in love. Whatever Norem was doing to her, she responded well, so he moved her to an even more secret base. Tobek can't find her. Hayley—"

Sophie's voice cracked. She coughed a few times, then

forced herself to continue, the strain clear in her features.

"There was something about Hayley that caught Norem's interest, too," Sophie said. "When Tobek told her we were in danger, Hayley said that she would get Norem to send her to his other base and would try to find Tobek's friend, but only if Tobek promised to keep us safe. Tobek is keeping his word. I'm sure Hayley is as well, wherever she is."

Lar felt as though his atmospheric generator had stopped working. The pressure from his hearts was so great, he thought they might burst. A Tau Ceti who had honor. He hadn't known such a thing was possible. And now, he owed this Tau Ceti a debt. They all did.

"We will help him and his friend," Lar said. "And we will get Hayley back."

"How?" Sophie said. "We don't even know where to look. I was hoping if we came back here, I would find some clue about where Norem's other base is."

"We will. The others will help."

Her panic spiked again, squeezing his hearts. There wasn't enough room in his chest for everything he was feeling.

"We can't tell anyone," she said. "Any of them could be Dean."

"Sophie," Lar rasped.

"He isn't like other Scorpiians. He's better at tricking people. I told you, I spent months with him when he was posing as Hayley. We snuggled on the couch watching movies and did our nails and laughed. We had late night talks about life and our history and..." She shook her head. "He knew things."

"What things?"

"*Everything*," Sophie said. "I don't know how he did it, but it's like he had copied her memories as well as her form."

A chill swept through him. Scorpiians were feared throughout the galaxy for good reason, but even they had their limits. They only learned through observing and gathering data. But the High Council had done a great deal of work learning how to make copies of their citizens' memories. They could even alter memories to suit their purposes, or take someone's memories and implant them in another body, as they had done to Kral's sister, Sorca, when they cloned her for their experiments.

What if the High Council could transfer someone's memories to a Scorpiian infiltrator? With their natural shapeshifting abilities, it would make them almost undetectable unless people were specifically looking for them and had access to the right scanners. Once again, Lar was grateful the High Council had been destroyed.

"I understand your fears," Lar said. "Believe me, I do. But my warrior brothers are who I know them to be."

"What about everyone else? Becca? Buddy? I don't even know if my *dog* is my dog anymore. The only person

I'm sure about… is you."

The brief pause before her confession affected him even more than her words. His hearts surged with warmth, fighting back the cold tightness that had been plaguing him. He should not touch her again. He *could not* touch her. If he did, he would be lost.

They were both trying to resist the temptation. Her own need for him wrapped around his soul and urged him closer. How could they not be tempted when the other half of their souls was right in front of them?

His vow would stand between them until the day he died. They would never know unity or the happiness of bonding with their soulmate. A wave of resentment coursed through him, unlike anything he'd ever felt. He could barely believe he was capable of so much regret and despair. It was like a poison, seeping into his muscles, spreading through his aching hearts from that cold, desolate spot in the center of his chest. His yearning for her was more than he could bear. So was her pain.

"You need not fear about your sister," Lar said. "Her bond with Kral isn't something a Scorpiian can fake. The same holds with Lian and Nuar."

Tears filled her eyes again. "What about Dash?"

He shook his head. "We can scan her for Scorpiian DNA. We will need to monitor all the animals after this."

"Lar…"

"We can't keep this from them. If there is a Scorpiian

who has targeted you specifically, they need to know. Dean can become anyone anytime. We all need to keep up our guards."

She looked down and nodded. The need to comfort her warred within him. His ribs ached from the pounding of his hearts and that cold space in the center of his chest had grown. His joints felt stiff and his muscles heavy. They needed to call the others, not just to tell them of the threat. Something else was going on—something much more personal to Lar. His body was changing in ways that he didn't understand.

And he did not know how to stop it.

Chapter Nine

The intensity of Sophie's relief made her light-headed. Lar knew everything that was going on and was going to help her. She wasn't alone in this anymore. Her chest felt oddly hollow and her knees wobbled as she followed him toward the door.

His gait was off, too. His limbs moved stiffly and his back was absolutely rigid, his spine plates were vibrating like crazy. She could feel it through the surrounding air.

"You never told me what's going on with you," she said.

"There is nothing to say."

She hurried to join him as he exited into the hallway, reaching for his arm. He didn't pull away. Somehow, that didn't reassure her. His arm was oddly cold. He looked down at her hand resting on his forearm, then arched an eyebrow with a reproving stare.

"Lar—"

His eyes widened as he looked past her. Unease rippled out from him. She turned to see what had caught his attention and found the reinforced door at the end of the hall open. A low humming sound emanated from somewhere inside the wide archway, along with electric crackles and pops. Light flickered across the floor and flashed from within the darkened room.

"Wait here," Lar said.

"Sure, that's going to happen."

He must not have picked up on her sarcasm. Either that, or the ominous thunder-room was too riveting for him to be distracted from it. She activated her wristbands and gave the command to bring up a personal shield on her left forearm. It wasn't huge, but Dorn had taught her how to use it to block blasts. She followed a few steps behind Lar as he headed into the room.

A large, circular dais filled most of the center of the space. Lightning arced from one side to the other, making what she would only describe as a sphere of crispy death. Balls of crackling plasma several feet across rolled within it. She and Lar stood as far away as they could while still being in the room, keeping the open door to their backs.

He activated his own wristbands, humming a note that made them glow and illuminate the chamber more clearly. When she looked around the room, she wished it had stayed dark. Her heart pounded as she turned in a slow circle, inching closer to him. The floor was flat, aside from the raised platform of insta-death, but the rest of the space was an enormous sphere. Thick spatters of green fluid had dried on the walls, ceiling, and even the floor in some spots. They all radiated out from the central dais.

"By the Maker," Lar breathed.

Sophie shook her head. "She has nothing to do with this room. This is all the Unmaker. This is death."

He glanced down at her and frowned. "Didn't I tell you to stay in the hall?"

"There is no way I'd ever let you go into a place like this alone."

"Sophie—"

"Just... please tell me that's not what I think it is," she said.

His expression was grimmer than she'd ever seen as he hummed the note for his scanners. A series of complex molecule chains hovered above his wristband, the holoprojection flashing the words 'Tau Ceti' in blue next to them. The scan flickered and the text turned red. '97% match. 80% match. 93% match.'

"Why not one-hundred percent?" Sophie asked. "What other stuff is in there?"

"I'm not sure. When the others arrive, Nuar and Bron can analyze it further."

"Lar, is it blood?" Her stomach was in knots.

"It is," he said.

Sophie's breakfast threatened to come back up. So many people must have died in here. "Is this a punishment room or something?"

"It seems too elaborate, even for the Tau Ceti."

"Can you tell if—" Her throat tightened. She didn't want to know the answer to her question, but she had to. "Is any of it human?"

The way his eyes pinched at the edges and his lips parted answered her as clearly as the sadness that flowed out from him. She nodded and looked back to the dais. Just because some of this was human, that didn't mean it belonged to Hayley. Still, the thought was enough to make icy panic race up and down her spine. Lar stepped closer, his gait oddly stiff. Her concern shifted to him.

"Are you alright?" she asked.

He didn't look as vibrant as usual. The glow in his eyes had dimmed and what light they put off reflected from his skin strangely.

"I'm fine," he said.

Sophie crossed her arms, cocked her hip, and glared at him. It worked for Becca.

"I need to do a deeper scan before we leave," he said. "To give the others a better idea of what they're dealing with."

Dang. Apparently, it didn't work so well for Sophie.

Lar struck his wristbands together and hummed a note. A different holodisplay appeared above his arms, showing a schematic of the dais before them. It quickly grew to encompass the entire room, showing a complex network of wires and glowing conduits that ran behind every inch of the spherical walls, ceiling, and under the floor.

"What is this thing?" Sophie said, stepping closer.

"I have no idea, but I'm recording all of my readings for Bron and Tarn. If they can't figure it out, no one can."

"Actually, if they can't figure it out, we'll find someone else to help us."

"Cygnians have always done things on their own."

She arched an eyebrow at him, her unease lifting a bit as he smirked at her.

"Until recently," he amended.

"We have to help the Tau Ceti in the tanks, too," she said. "Norem is victimizing them. Not all of their soldiers are going along with this whole war thing willingly. Some want a different life for themselves, but don't feel as if they have a choice."

After a long pause, Lar said, "The very idea of a Tau Ceti wishing for anything but violence and chaos is... novel."

"Well, get used to it, because if Tobek is any indication, they're out there. We need to find them and help them. But first, we need to help the ones in those tanks."

Lar nodded and deactivated the scan, the hologram above his wristbands vanishing. He winced as he lowered his arms.

"You are not fine," she said. "How can I help you?"

He shook his head, then opened his mouth. She was sure he was going to try to placate her again, but then a chill swept over her skin and the room seemed to spin around her. She reached out to Lar for support, but he stumbled into her. They ended up gripping each other's arms and leaning on each other to stay upright. Was the room affecting him, too?

"I need to return to my prism," Lar said.

Sophie nodded. "Then let's get you home."

Tobek stared at the man floating in the tank before him, trying to remember what had happened when he'd been hooked up to all those tubes and wires himself. Norem had changed him. He had changed them all.

"What is Norem doing to us?" Tobek murmured.

Jaxa was reading data on a nearby monitor. "He's making us stronger."

That was true, but Norem wasn't just increasing their strength, he was making them *different*. There had to be more to it than just making them better soldiers. Tobek lifted his hand and pressed it on the glass. Something about these soldiers called to him.

His hand tingled. Was it electrical feedback? No, the glass wouldn't conduct that. But there was a kind of energy passing through him. Inside the tank, the man opened his eyes. Orange light diffused in the liquid surrounding him. His eyes looked Cygnian.

What the hell is Norem doing here?

"Saying your goodbyes?" Jaxa said with a sneer.

"Perhaps." Tobek let his hand drop. The man inside's eyes fluttered shut. "I doubt we're going to come back here again. Are you about ready to release them?"

"Release them?" Jaxa scoffed. "From their existence, maybe."

Tobek's skin crawled, his heart racing. Jaxa couldn't be planning to kill these men.

Who was Tobek kidding? Jaxa could absolutely be planning to kill these men. He'd probably smile while doing it.

"We're on a retrieval mission," Tobek said.

"Retrieval and shutdown." Jaxa tapped a few buttons on the monitor before him. "We can't let the Vegans and the Coalition get their hands on these specimens."

"You're going to kill them?"

Jaxa turned to face him, letting out a disgusted snort. "You're so fucking weak, Tobek. I don't care that you've 'integrated your new DNA better than ninety-five percent of the test subjects.'" Jaxa made quotes with his fingers as he spoke in a mocking tone, an Earth expression he had undoubtedly picked up during his years as a scout. "You're a disgrace."

New DNA?

Tobek looked back at the tanks. He wished he could remember what had happened to him. What Norem had done. It was important. All he knew was that when he'd come out, he was bigger, stronger, and deadlier.

And that Lorelei was gone.

"We can't just kill them," Tobek said. The skin on the back of his neck burned as he thought of the human prisoner who had been so kind to him. He had sworn he would protect her. He had failed.

Jaxa wouldn't just kill these soldiers. Tobek couldn't believe it, just like he couldn't believe they had killed Lorelei. They had transferred her to another facility. That's what Norem did with valuable specimens. He just had to figure out where.

Jaxa stepped closer, his words chilling Tobek. "I absolutely can kill them. And I can make it take as much or as little time as I want. I can even decide if they're awake for it. So why don't you stop being such a whiny bitch and go disable the transit platform while Rixon retrieves the one thing we're here to get, and then meet us back in Norem's secret exit so we can get the fuck out of here."

Tobek couldn't bring himself to leave. He couldn't let Jaxa kill these men. He wouldn't fail them like he'd failed Lorelei.

Rixon walked in carrying a metal box in both hands. Deep etchings in complex geometric patterns covered its surface.

"I have the lockbox," Rixon said. "We need to get it to a stasis chamber, just in case it's rigged with any traps."

He scowled as he looked at the tanks. "Why aren't you done yet?"

"Norem wanted me to download the latest data before purging the system." Jaxa pulled a small bronze disk out of a port near the active monitor. As soon as he did, the monitor flickered, then went dark. "Which I've done. Now we just need to fry these guys while Tobek takes care of the transit platform."

"Sounds fun," Rixon said.

Jaxa shrugged. "Norem told us to be thorough. But Tobek is having *feelings* about our orders."

"What kind of feelings?" Rixon's voice was calm, but his expression was murderous as he looked at Tobek. If Rixon wasn't holding that possibly-trapped box, Tobek had no doubt that Rixon would be slamming him against a wall by now.

"They're soldiers," Tobek said. "Like us."

"You're right, they are soldiers." Rixon stepped closer. "And every one of us should be ready to die at any moment if our orders tell us to."

From what Tobek had observed, Rixon was a lot more comfortable sending other Tau Ceti soldiers to their deaths than facing his own. He looked over at Jaxa and said, "Get it done."

Jaxa grinned as he drew his weapon and turned toward the tanks.

"I need help shutting down the transit portal first,"

Tobek said. He lifted his arms and dropped them back to his sides. "I don't know how."

Jaxa sneered in disgust. "Useless," he said, bumping Tobek's injured shoulder again as he left the room.

Tobek stood still, waiting for the pain to recede. When he turned, Rixon was standing in the doorway, staring at him with his cold eyes.

"Stalling won't save them," Rixon said. "When we get back, either you pull the trigger on them, or I pull one on you."

Chapter Ten

This wasn't the room affecting them, it was something else. As Sophie tried to pull Lar's arm over her shoulder, she found that his elbow wouldn't bend. He was stuck in that position somehow. She reached across his body and struck her wristbands together while half-supporting him, then activated their strength enhancing function. His weight became easier to manage. She hummed the note to keep the wristbands ready to receive commands as well, not knowing what to expect. They turned toward the open door, Lar grunting as he forced his legs to move.

Tobek stood in front of her. His green eyes grew wide and his mouth dropped open as he stammered a few incoherent sounds. He glanced over his shoulder, then faced her again, his eyebrows drawing down over his eyes.

In a low voice, he said, "Make it look good."

"What?" Sophie's mind reeled. What was he doing here? What did he mean?

Tobek took a step back and yelled, "Intruders."

He drew a blaster from his side and fired. Panic surged through her, her mouth going dry and her heart racing. The fear dimmed slightly when she realized he was only vaguely pointing the weapon in their direction. The blast sailed past them, striking the wall. She prayed the panels could withstand it. All that wiring that Lar's scan had detected looked delicate, and the crackling-death lightning still streaked across the dais.

She quickly dragged Lar to the wall next to the door, dropping his arm from around her shoulders. He leaned against the wall as she moved away, his limbs making strange crackling sounds as he straightened himself. His pain rolled into her, but it was muted. Was he trying to protect her from his pain or was there something wrong with their connection?

Her heart beat even faster as Rixon and Jaxa rushed into the room. How was she supposed to take on Rixon and Jaxa without tipping them off to her relationship with Tobek? That must be what he'd meant by 'making it look good.' Rixon carried a bronze box that was about the size of a mailbox and covered with intricate etchings. He held it close to his body with both hands, as if protecting it.

Activating her wristband's shield, she stood between them and Lar. She hummed the note to summon an energy blast, but with the shield on her left arm she only had one free hand to work with. She aimed at Tobek—well, to the side of Tobek—and released the blast. A ball of blue-white energy flew out from her hand and hit him in the shoulder. The force knocked him off his feet and to the ground. He skidded for several feet before coming to a stop.

"Oh my God, I'm so sorry," she shouted.

"You're about to be." Jaxa raised his weapon and fired.

She screamed as she ducked behind her shield. The blast hit it, lighting up the circular energy field before dissipating. Her teeth rattled from the impact, pain dancing up her arm and knocking her back a few paces.

She lifted her other arm and sent out a blast of her own, aiming right for Jaxa. The shot went wide, striking the dais instead. An arc of lightning escaped the circle, licking the floor near Tobek. He rolled to the side and rose on all fours, shaking his head as if to clear it.

This is not going well.

Sophie glanced over at Lar. He leaned against the wall, his chest heaving with each breath. Panic shoved away all other considerations. Something was very, very wrong. She had to get him out of here.

Jaxa had dodged to the side when she fired. He brought up his weapon again, this time aiming it at Lar. She lunged forward, deflecting the blast at the last second. The green-gold energy ricocheted away… and hit the dais.

"Stop shooting the fucking transit platform," Rixon shrieked. "You'll get us all killed." He was hanging back, clutching the box tightly to his chest. Whatever was inside, he held onto it as if it was a matter of life or death. That was good for her, since it meant she only had to deal with Jaxa.

Jaxa tried to flank them again. He fired, but Sophie kept herself between him and Lar, absorbing the blast with her shield. It was only meant to protect one person, though. She didn't know how much longer she could keep this up. Her arm was numb and her shoulder was sending throbbing waves of pain through her chest and back.

"Tobek," Rixon yelled. "Engage them."

Tobek was back on his feet. Her shot had burned a hole through his uniform on his left shoulder, giving her a glimpse of shining chrome beneath. He glanced briefly at Rixon, then leapt up to the ceiling... and stayed there.

"What the..." Sophie stared as he stuck to the surface with one hand and both feet, his other hand free to aim his weapon. "Oh, come on."

He could stick to the ceiling? How was she supposed to protect them against that? He gave her a pointed look as he aimed his blaster and fired.

"Crap!" Sophie lifted her arm just in time to deflect it.

It was bad enough that she had to protect them from three adversaries on the same level—having one of them on the ceiling was beyond unfair. She wished she had spent more time on target practice with Dorn, especially since she had to shoot at Tobek again. She hummed the note to fire an energy blast, aiming kind of near him but not directly at him. It hit the ceiling right next to his hand. Yeah, her aim really needed some work.

Tobek put on a great show, flinching away from the

blast. He clumsily 'leapt' off the ceiling, but mostly just fell to the floor, landing with a metallic thunk.

Please let him be okay.

A flash of light in the corner of her eye let her know she had been distracted just a second too long. Jaxa had already fired at her again. Sophie brought up her shield, but knew it would be too late. She scrunched her eyes shut, waiting for the blast to hit. Instead, she heard a low grunt.

She looked up to see Lar standing between her and Jaxa, a bit of smoke smoldering from his shoulder. Deep lines were etched into the corners of his eyes. His pain flowed to her through their bond, though it was still muted. He slowly turned, pulling himself up to his formidable height. Jaxa cringed behind him.

Lar's spine plates stood on end, vibrating so quickly they were a blur down the center of his back. She felt their pulsing through the air. He was standing and he was moving, so that was good, but the blue of his shoulder had turned an icy white where the blaster had hit him.

Fury rose up in her unlike anything she'd ever experienced. It burned away her fear for them, her concern for Hayley, her need to keep Tobek's cover intact. These people had shot Amy, and now, they had shot Lar. She was going to make them pay.

"Shoot him again, idiot." Rixon moved closer to the dais, keeping Jaxa between himself and Sophie.

Her vision clouded with red. She flicked her arm, humming the notes to summon her energy sword and amped up the power levels. With a scream more primal than she knew she could manage, she charged Jaxa.

The stiffness plaguing Lar had intensified until he could hardly move his joints. His arms felt leaden and his legs were as heavy as if he stood in the gravity well near his homeworld. He had barely managed to intercept the Tau Ceti's blast before it struck Sophie. He might not be so lucky again.

His mate was even fiercer than he'd realized. She charged at the Tau Ceti who had shot him, yelling a battle cry. Her opponent leapt for the ceiling, but she anticipated his move, slashing high with her sword. The bright blade connected with his leg, sending currents of energy jolting through his body. He convulsed in the air for a few seconds before falling, landing hard on the metal floor.

"Oh my God," Sophie said. "Did I kill him?"

Fear and guilt broke through her fury, flowing into Lar through their bond. Relief quickly followed it when the one called Jaxa stirred. She didn't want to kill any of them, though they would gladly kill her. Her need to protect Lar was even stronger, though. He didn't want her to take a life, realizing how it would haunt her. She stood between him and the leader, glancing at Jaxa and balancing her weight on both legs so she could move wherever she needed to help him.

"Tobek," their leader yelled, his face paling as he carefully tucked the box he was carrying under one arm. "What are you doing? Get up and fight!"

The leader reached for his blaster with his now-free hand. Jaxa was already rising on wobbly legs. Tobek glanced back and forth between Lar and his leader, frowning deeply but keeping his weapon pointed toward the floor.

Normally, three Tau Ceti would be no match for Lar, even if they were cyborgs such as these. He did not feel normal. His eyes burned painfully. When he blinked to try to ease the pain, the room split into a fractured, multi-faceted view, almost as though he was looking through a kaleidoscope.

Unmaker...

This wasn't possible. He was too young. Yet, with growing certainty, he realized he was crystallizing.

He had never heard of a Cygnian his age crystallizing unless they had suffered a grievous injury. Lar was uninjured. Or was he?

He thought back to the stabbing pain in his hearts. To the way his body seemed to freeze when he held himself still every time he longed to reach for Sophie. He thought of the push and pull between the established bond of his vow, and the yearning of his soul to join with Sophie's.

The strain was killing him. Worse, it was making him incapable of fighting. He had to protect Sophie with what time he had. Considering how quickly the crystallization was progressing, Lar realized he didn't have much. There was none left for mercy. He charged toward Jaxa.

Lar stumbled, but his will pushed him forward. The Tau Ceti's eyes widened in shock and fear, but only for a moment before Lar was on him. He grabbed Jaxa's throat, digging in with his claws and twisting. The cyborg's spine was reinforced with metal, but Lar's adrenaline powered desperation gave him strength. The loud crack of Jaxa's neck breaking almost drowned out the sound of a weapon firing behind him.

Lar hefted Jaxa's body and threw it toward the sound of the weapon, utilizing his acute hearing more than his distorted vision. He prayed to the Maker that it was the leader firing and not Tobek. In his fractured sight, he saw Jaxa's dead weight hit the lead cyborg, propelling him back toward the dais.

Tobek reached for them. At first, Lar thought Tobek was going to try to pull them to safety. Instead, he grabbed the box from beneath the leader's arm, then kicked him in the abdomen, propelling him onto the platform along with Jaxa's body. Tobek wheeled around and threw himself at Sophie, pushing her back. Lar heard her scream, felt her terror, but he was rooted in place. His legs wouldn't obey him.

The hum of the platform intensified. Lights streamed down from the walls, painfully bright. In his bizarrely faceted view, Lar saw the two Tau Ceti shimmer, their bodies contorting in impossible ways as lightning tore through them. It was as if their very molecules were coming apart and then reforming. The leader's eyes were huge, his mouth was open in a silent scream.

And then they were gone.

Chapter Eleven

The hum of the platform returned to normal, the arcs of lightning quieting as if sated by their recent sacrificial offering. The balls of plasma that had rolled around on the dais sank into the bronze metal, leaving only sparking lines of electricity behind.

Lar watched on with eyes that would not close. He tried again to force his legs to move, but failed. His arms were immobile in a position slightly raised from his sides. He felt nothing except a cold that burrowed into his bones. Nothing except for Sophie.

Her anxiety streaked through him, coaxing his sluggish hearts to keep beating. He wanted so much to protect her. He wanted to stay.

"What the hell was that?" Sophie asked.

"I… I don't know," Tobek said.

"Lar, do you—" She gasped when she turned to look at him, her face paling. Her fear crashed into him with the force of a plasma blast. "Oh my God."

Lar tried to force himself to smile as she hurried to him, desperate to communicate with her one last time. All he could do was will her to sense what he projected, hoping to reassure her through their bond that everything would be okay. She would go on. They hadn't joined in unity, so her soul would remain separate. The one mercy in their situation was that his death would not take her with him.

"What's wrong with your eyes?" She cradled his face in her hands, trying to tilt his head toward her. When it didn't move, she smoothed her thumb over his cheek.

He couldn't feel it. He couldn't feel anything anymore. At least, not in his body. No matter how hard he tried to force his vocal cords to say something to comfort her, nothing happened. They had already crystallized.

"Lar, what is wrong with your eyes?" she repeated, her voice more demanding. "They aren't glowing."

"Is he okay?" Tobek came to stand behind her.

Sophie didn't respond, though her fear intensified. "We need to get him to Nuar," she said. "The medic back on his ship."

She hummed the note that would increase her strength, then ducked under Lar's arm, positioning it over her shoulder and hanging onto it. The chill in his chest receded somewhat, warmth seeping into his body where they touched and fighting off the numbness that was claiming him. A bit awkwardly, she dragged Lar toward the large open archway that led to the hall beyond.

"I didn't know humans were so strong," Tobek said.

Sophie grunted from the strain of half-carrying Lar.

"Just shut up and bring that box. If Rixon wanted it so bad, it has to be important."

Rixon must be the name of the leader of the triad. A wave of pity surged through Lar. What fate had he condemned the Tau Ceti to by knocking him onto the dais? Rixon had called it something else—a transit platform—but that didn't make sense. What kind of transit could be achieved here? What were they trying to transport and how did they expect to get it through the walls of the base and the rock of the dwarf planet?

Lar thought of the blood on the spherical walls of the chamber and an odd sort of shiver snaked through his stiffening body. They couldn't be trying to transport people. That wasn't possible. And yet, it was the only thing that made sense from what Lar had seen. What exactly was Norem trying to accomplish? The only thing Lar was certain of was that Norem's sadistic experiments had cost many Tau Ceti their lives.

Tobek approached them cautiously, his eyes narrowed and his body always facing them as he drew near. "Rixon thought it might be rigged to explode if tampered with," Tobek said.

"Well, it hasn't gone off yet," Sophie said. "We're not leaving it behind."

The sluggish beat of Lar's hearts picked up. If the box had explosives in it, Sophie needed to get away. Lar wanted to warn her, to force air from his mouth, but it was all he could do to keep his chest moving enough to bring air into his lungs.

Tobek tucked the box under his arm and stepped closer warily, as if he expected Lar to strike at any moment. Even if Lar could move, he would not attack the Tau Ceti. Tobek had proven himself an ally. He pulled Lar's other arm over his shoulder, and it cracked loudly, the crystal in Lar's muscles fracturing.

Tobek winced. "What was that?"

Sophie hesitated for a moment, before saying, "I don't know."

Lar was grateful for the numbness spreading through him. Having his limbs broken from their crystallized pose would have been agonizing otherwise. Tobek took more of Lar's weight as they made their way down the dull bronze hallway. The door to Norem's laboratory was open, light spilling into the dimmer corridor. Tobek paused in the doorway, his eyes wide as he stared at the table in the center of the room.

"The ship is through here," Sophie said, her fear adding a sharp edge to her voice.

"I…"

Tobek shook his head. A tremor passed through the Tau Ceti soldier. Another surge of pity flowed through Lar. He needed to find a way to tell the prism that Tobek was honorable. That he was an ally, perhaps a friend. His fear of the room was palpable, yet he wasn't retreating.

Sophie picked up on his anxiety as well. "I can only imagine what happened to you in there, but we need to get Lar to his ship and his ship is through this room. Please, help me," she pleaded.

Tobek took a deep breath, then blew it out and nodded. Together, they dragged Lar into the room where Norem had conducted his experiments. Tobek squinted as they crossed the threshold.

The lights nearly blinded Lar, shining like suns in his multifaceted view. He hadn't noticed their brightness earlier. Cygnians could tolerate much more exposure than most other sentients—especially Tau Ceti. The walls were polished bronze, amplifying the effect. The brightness had to have been never ending agony for the poor souls strapped to that table and forced to face the ceiling or walls.

Sophie's concern expanded, the energy seeping toward Tobek. "Do you have atmospheric shielding?" Sophie asked, urging them toward the field of sparkling white light covering the gap in the wall his shard had created. "I don't know how Lar's ship is sealing this room. When we go through it, the atmosphere might vent."

"My uniform will protect me," he said.

"There's a giant hole in your uniform." Her guilt flowed into Lar, along with embarrassment and concern.

It wasn't right that Lar couldn't comfort her, that he couldn't be the one to help her. Instead, he had to rely on this Tau Ceti soldier. This surprisingly honorable Tau Ceti soldier.

"It's over my cybernetic arm," Tobek said. "My nanites will seal the edges of the material to the metal. I should be fine for a little while, but we should seal this room to protect the others." He paused. "You are going to help the others, right? The soldiers in the tanks?"

"I swear I'll do everything I can for them. Just help me get Lar to the ship."

Tobek nodded, then stepped away from them. Lar's arm remained sticking out, frozen in place.

"That's... not good," Tobek said. As gingerly as he could, Tobek pressed Lar's arm back to his side, wincing as he heard his joints and bones crackle.

"Tobek..." Terror emanated from Sophie in waves. Her voice trembled with it.

"We're going to get him help," Tobek promised.

He ran to the door on the other side of the room and pressed his hand against the access control panel. Wires snaked out of Tobek's hand, interfacing with the panel. The door whooshed shut. After a few moments, the wires retracted and he ran back to join them.

Rage and hopelessness coursed through Lar. He should be the one helping Sophie, not the other way around. Instead, he was the source of her pain. Lar fought to master his thoughts. He didn't know how much of his emotions Sophie was picking up on. He tried to send her warmth and reassurance and something he wouldn't have dared before. Love.

Lar imagined Sophie grieving for him and then finding love with someone else. He wanted that for her, though his hearts ached at the thought. He wanted her to be happy. Perhaps she would start a family. All without him. All because of the vow he had made when he didn't know that his soulmate was out there waiting for him. If only he had held onto what had seemed a futile hope back then.

He pushed away the regrets and focused on the love he felt for her now, willing it to find her through their bond. His body warmed where they touched. He wanted to wrap himself around her and embrace the warmth, but he couldn't.

"I sealed off this room so that the rest of the section keeps its atmosphere," Tobek said. "The generators are online, but they can't keep up with a hole in the perimeter that's this big. It will suck all the atmosphere they generate right out."

"If the field collapses, what's in here will be sucked out anyway," Sophie said. "Are you sure you'll be okay?"

"I can survive a vacuum for several minutes, even without my uniform. Long enough to get you into the ship and on your way."

New panic thrummed through Sophie. "The shard," she said. "There isn't room for you."

"It's okay," he said.

"Tobek—" She laced his name with her despair.

The Tau Ceti cut her off. "I'll stay here and monitor things. I imagine I'll have company from the Department of Homeworld Security soon enough. Just please let them know I'm on your side so they don't blast me when they see me."

Sophie nodded, her eyes glimmering. Her unshed tears sparkled like stars in each facet of Lar's fractured view of her. More than that, he sensed her turmoil. She wanted to help Tobek, but she was so worried about Lar. He hated that he was causing her pain. Finding one's soulmate was supposed to make life easier and more joyful, not harder and filled with despair.

Tobek handed her the box, then wrapped his arms around Lar and lifted him. If Lar hadn't already been dying, the embarrassment of the moment might have done him in. Tobek carefully navigated both of them through the opening, bending down to make sure they could clear the awkward space. The field made a fizzling sound as they crossed it, but held. The white light snapped back into place the moment they were through.

Tobek halted abruptly on the other side, his grip tightening. What was it now? Another threat, but one he couldn't help with.

No. Lar had to keep Sophie safe. He had to hold on for just a little longer.

He flexed the muscles in his arms and legs, forcing the

crystalline structures in his tissues to fragment. Pain jolted through him as his nerves woke up again and an agonized groan escaped him. Tobek jerked in surprise, but steadied Lar until he found his feet.

The Cygnian warrior's hearts were beating sluggishly, their opposing cadence stuttering in his ears. Pushing away from Tobek, Lar turned to see his prism. All of them. Even Tarn had left engineering.

Blue warriors flooded Lar's fractured vision—along with Becca, who stood at Kral's side, her wristbands humming with energy. Her brown hair was pulled back in a ponytail and a furrow etched the gap between her eyebrows. The *Arrow* hovered behind them, light pouring from every facet of the crystalline ship and casting rainbows on the blackened walls of the base's exterior. Nuar and Dorn stood shoulder to shoulder beneath the open hatch in the bottom of the ship, both defending it and ready to assist the other warriors in their prism.

"Lar, what is going on?" Kral snarled, his clawed hands curling at his sides and his orange eyes gleaming. He shook his head. "We felt... something. I don't know what it was. Something is wrong with our link."

Lar hadn't sensed their approach. Even now, he couldn't sense any of them. He reached out to Kral through their bond. The cold in Lar's chest flared, chasing away what little breath he held in his exhausted lungs. He forced them to pull in another shallow breath, then another, the air sliding tight between his skin and the shielding that generated it.

Sophie stumbled through the opening, clutching the box to her chest. She shouldn't be holding it so closely— or at all. Lar tried to reach out and take it from her, but his arms had once more frozen at his sides.

"Oh, thank God," Sophie said.

Lar said his own thanks to the Maker. No matter what surprises the box or the base held, Sophie would be safe now. Their relief flowed back and forth between them, pushing away the chill in his chest a bit once more. She looked at him and smiled. Her hope flooded through him. He hated to disappoint her.

Becca started forward, but Kral gestured for her to stop, his focus locked on Tobek. She glared at Kral, but didn't come closer.

"This is Tobek," Sophie said. "Some of you already know him. He's helping us and we can trust him." Sophie let out a burst of breath, frustration rising in her as she took in the skeptical expressions of everyone surrounding her. "We have more important things to worry about than him being a Tau Ceti. Something is wrong with Lar, and we need to get him to the medical bay. And Tarn needs to take this box and figure out what's in it, but really carefully, because it might explode. And Bron needs to check out the disintegration platform inside the base."

"Disintegration platform?" Bron raised an eyebrow.

Tarn shrugged. "I'm more concerned about the box."

"Just don't touch the platform or let its lightning touch you." Sophie shuddered, a shared chill sweeping through them both. "There are some Tau Ceti soldiers that are going to need our help, too. They're in some kind of suspension tanks."

"Suspension tanks?" This time, it was Nuar who spoke.

"I don't know what they are," Sophie said, her voice growing shrill as desperation rose within her. "That's what they'd be in a sci-fi movie. That's everything I can think of that might be a threat. The guys in the tanks seem safe enough for now, but Lar needs your help. He's sick."

"Cygnians don't get sick," Bron said.

"Bullshit," Sophie snapped. "Stop thinking that you understand everything about the universe. Nobody does, and your arrogance is not helping anyone. Now, shut up and get Lar to the medical bay."

Lar's cheeks made cracking noises as he smiled. His mate had such fire. It pleased him that his features would hold this smile for all time. He still felt Sophie, at least. Even without achieving unity, he felt her at the end. He sent a caress that he hoped would reassure her, along with all the love in his hearts. It was all for her. All that he had left. All that he was.

His breath rushed out of him, relief flowing through his body at the knowledge that Sophie would be safe and that people who loved her would surround her and comfort her through whatever came next.

For Lar…

The Unmaker had come for him. It was time.

Chapter Twelve

Sophie's heart pounded against her chest hard enough to make her head spin as her sense of Lar vanished. She shoved Rixon's box into Tobek's chest as she ran toward her soulmate.

Lar stood still as a statue, the gentle smile she loved so much frozen on his face. His eyes stared out at his prism. The light emanating from the white crystal of the ship behind them reflected in their faceted surface, but the golden glow of his eyes had vanished, leaving flat yellow irises behind.

"Lar?" Her voice shook as she reached for him. His skin was harder than before. Cold and smooth. "Lar!"

She gripped his shoulders and shook him. His entire body tilted forward. She yelped and lurched in front of him, holding him up and saying a silent prayer of thanks that her wristbands still augmented her strength. Wrapping her arms around his waist, she helped him to straighten as the others ran closer. His body was completely stiff.

"Please." She pressed her forehead against his chest. "Please don't let this be what I think it is."

Feet scuffed on the blackened metal of the base behind

her. She turned to see Bron and Tarn each pulling on one of Tobek's arms, holding him in place. Through the hole she'd blasted in his uniform, she could see the metal segments of his shoulder stretched far enough apart to make her wince in sympathy. Tobek wasn't even trying to fight back. The strange box sat on the ground before him, forgotten for the moment.

"What did you do to him?" Bron said, his voice a menacing growl.

"What did you do?" Tarn shouted.

Someone rested their hand on Sophie's back. Probably Becca. Sophie felt the touch as if it wasn't her body, as if she was floating far above and watching everything unfold.

"Please," she whispered, turning back to Lar and pressing her face against his chest. "Please, I need you."

She tried to reach for him through their bond, but only found a cold void. An answering hollowness echoed through her body. Her heart was breaking, a heaviness far greater than anything she'd experienced was weighing her down.

"Maker." Kral's voice was a pained gasp. "This can't be."

"What is it?" Tarn asked, his voice near panic. "Some kind of stasis field?"

"That couldn't interrupt our bond," Bron said. "It's some sort of disruptor."

Behind her, Tobek grunted. There was more scuffling. When they figured out what was happening, they would kill him. They might not even mean to.

"Let him go," she said, her voice raspy. Sophie looked over at them and somehow found strength to push demand into her voice. "Let him go."

Bron and Tarn relaxed their holds a bit, but still kept their grip on Tobek's arms. Tobek stared at Sophie, his eyes filled with pity as he shook his head.

"I said *let him go*," Sophie ordered. "Tobek saved our lives. He didn't do this."

"You heard her," Becca said. "Let him go."

Bron and Tarn shared a look, then released Tobek and stepped back. They kept the Tau Ceti soldier in their views, standing a few feet behind him.

"If it wasn't him, then who did this to Lar?" Tarn asked.

Sophie's heart was being crushed. Her chest contracted painfully, squeezing all the air from her lungs. She would have fallen to her knees if she hadn't been holding onto Lar so tightly.

This wasn't the Tau Ceti. Lar had already been in pain when they first left Earth. Maybe even before. Whatever was causing this, it had started before they journeyed to Ceres. Being together, having her close, seemed to have escalated the effects more quickly. He had been fine when they met. She had sensed his strength, even from the beginning, through their bond.

The bond...

Could that be it? She thought back to every touch that lit them up, yet made him flinch, every heated gaze that ended in him wincing in pain. He said he and Kral had bonded, been linked on a soul level, since they were children. What would happen to Lar's soul when it met its other half and wanted to join with hers?

"I did this," she rasped. "It was me, and Kral, and your stupid queen, and your goddammed Maker."

"Sophie, sweetie." Becca reached out again, this time rubbing Sophie's back. "What happened to him? How do we help?"

"You don't," Sophie said. "He's crystallizing."

"Crystallizing?" Becca said. "What does that mean?"

"Unmaker." Tarn dropped to one knee, leaning heavily on it with his elbow, his head bowed. The other warriors did the same, except for Dorn, standing beneath the hatch, and Kral, who stared into Lar's eyes as if he could spark him back to life with his own glowing orange gaze.

If only that were true.

"I can't..." Kral said. "I can't sense him."

"What does it mean that he's crystallizing?" Becca bit out each word this time.

"When Cygnians die, our bodies crystallize," Kral said.

"Die?" Becca's eyebrows shot up her forehead. "No, Cygnians don't die. I mean, not when you're this young.

You're invulnerable."

"Not completely," Kral said in a low voice.

"But look at him." Becca gestured toward Lar. "He's not even injured. We just need to get him to the ship and have Nuar fix him up."

"There's nothing I can do for him," Nuar said.

"We *just* saw him moving," Becca said. "He turned around and looked at us a minute ago."

Sophie closed her eyes and tuned out the argument. She held Lar more tightly, pressing her cheek against his chest. This wasn't fair. They didn't have enough time. They'd followed the rules and hadn't even bonded completely. Unless that wasn't the rule? Maybe they should have hooked up. It might have helped things. But then again, it might have made things worse.

She didn't understand how Cygnians worked. Two days ago, she hadn't even known that aliens were real, let alone that one of them was her soulmate. She hadn't known what she was missing until Lar held it so close, yet completely out of reach. The other half of her soul.

Ba...dum.

She gasped at the sound beneath her ear, her eyes flying open, then held her breath, straining to listen. The others kept arguing, their voices and loud movements drowning out the silence she needed.

"Becca," she said, not daring to move her ear from its spot. She had to raise her voice to get her sister's attention.

"Becca!"

Becca leaned in close, pressing her chest against Sophie's back and hugging her. Her voice was achingly gentle as she said, "What is it? What do you need?"

"Make them be quiet," Sophie said. "Hurry."

Becca tensed for a moment, then squeezed Sophie's shoulder. She moved away and shouted, "Shut up!" at the top of her lungs.

Everyone stopped. Bron had been going after Tobek again, who was backing away with his hands up in the air. Tarn was still kneeling nearby. Kral and Nuar were standing close to each other, Kral was fisting Nuar's tunic and lifting him from the ground. Dorn still stood in the light flooding down from the open hatch of the ship.

In the silence that followed, all Sophie heard was the hum of the ship, the rasp of Nuar's breath, her own heartbeat racing in her ear. She closed her eyes and focused, calming herself, bringing all her attention to Lar.

The other half of her soul was right there. What if she could hold on to it? If Cygnian soul bonds were strong enough to kill him, could they be strong enough to save him as well?

Please. Stay with me. I'm not ready to let you go.

She closed her eyes again and imagined their souls reaching toward each other, their yearning energies melding everywhere their bodies touched. Her face and arms tingled, and her stomach warmed. Was it working or was it wishful thinking? She didn't care. Not believing it was working meant giving up, and she wouldn't do that. She wasn't ready. She would never be ready.

Willing her warmth into him, she took in a deep breath and let it out through pursed lips, then took in another breath and held it, listening harder than she ever had before. An answering warmth feathered across her mind and the darkness behind her eyelids flashed with golden light for the briefest of moments. She could sense him.

Ba...dum, ba...dum.

Her eyes snapped open. "His heart is beating." In a louder voice, she repeated, "His heart is still beating."

Nuar's lips pursed into a thin line. He shook his head. "That means nothing. The body shuts down slowly during crystallization. First the joints, then the muscles. Loved ones have even sensed their bonds for days after the process begins."

"So, you've studied this," Becca said. "There has to be something we can do."

Tarn rose. "There is nothing to do except honor him."

"How about we honor him by trying to save his ass?" she said.

Nuar shook his head. "Our bond is already gone. We can no longer sense him."

"But I can," Sophie said, desperate for them to believe her. Desperate to believe it herself.

Becca's brow furrowed as she turned back to her.

"How?"

"Because I'm his soulmate."

Becca's eyes widened, and she sucked in a breath. Sophie had always been a flake when it came to guys, but this was different. Lar was different. Sophie had to make Becca believe her. Before Becca could say more, Sophie turned to her, desperation lacing her voice.

"I can feel him, Becca," she said. "I heard his heart. I can feel his soul—*our* soul. He's still in there. Please help me. Help *us*. I can't lose him like this."

Becca's mouth turned down in a stern line. She turned to Nuar and said, "Get him to the medical bay."

Sophie could finally breathe again. Her skin prickled all over and her stomach leapt like it was full of a herd of buffalo. This was Becca, and she believed Sophie. There was nothing Becca couldn't accomplish when she put her mind to it. She had always been commanding. Sophie understood it so much better now, knowing that Becca held the other half of Kral's soul.

"But—" Nuar began.

"At-tat-tat," Becca snapped her fingers, silencing him. "Soulmate trumps prism. You didn't even freaking scan him."

"I don't have to scan him to know—"

She interrupted Nuar again. "That his heart is still beating? That his soul is still hanging around? That he actually *is* alive and you're just standing there like a dope instead of doing your goddammed job?"

Nuar's eyes widened, and his mouth dropped open.

"*Do your goddammed job,*" Becca commanded. She had never sounded so menacing—and Sophie had never been so glad for her sister's overbearing nature.

Nuar reached for Lar, though his attention stayed fixed on Becca, a healthy amount of awe on his face. Sophie squeezed under Lar's arm and lifted from one side as Nuar took the other. They started toward the ship, their steps echoing in the cavernous space.

"This isn't our way," Tarn said, moving to stand in front of them.

"Last I checked, I was Kral's soulmate," Becca said. "Which means someday I'm going to be your queen. If you think I'm going to put up with 'but this isn't what I'm used to' as an excuse for not doing as I say, you aren't nearly as smart as these guys say you are."

"No one has ever—"

"I'm sorry, what was that?" Becca stepped in close as she spoke, so close Tarn had to either back away or let her chest bump into him. His face turned almost purple as he stepped back and bowed his head.

Hope glimmered within Sophie. She nurtured it within herself and pushed it toward Lar. They would find a way to help him. They would bring him back from this.

"I thought so," she said. "The funeral is cancelled. Everybody on the ship."

The Cygnians fell in step behind Nuar, Kral walking at Becca's side. She looked back over her shoulder at Tobek, and said, "You, too, soldier. You're in my army now. You have a problem with that?"

Tobek didn't hesitate. "Not at all."

"Then grab that box and keep an eye on it," Becca said. "Bron, help Tobek up to the ship and do whatever you need to do to secure that thing. I don't want *any* funerals today."

Becca hurried forward after giving her orders, falling in step next to Sophie. "I could really get used to this whole, 'I'm going to be the Cygnian queen someday,'" she said.

Sophie knew Becca was trying to help her feel better. The only thing that could do that was seeing Lar safe. To hear his deep laugh and watch his eyes glow as he looked at her. His body warmed against her side. Was he just absorbing her heat, or was he coming out of this? She kept visualizing their souls touching, hers holding onto his, their energies clinging to each other. She wouldn't give up on him, ever.

Chapter Thirteen

As soon as they were all inside the ship, Dorn sealed the hatch. Sophie felt better surrounded by the gleaming white walls of the *Arrow*. The others hummed the notes to deactivate their atmospheric shielding, and she did the same. It might be faster to let one of the Cygnians carry Lar to the medical bay, but she needed to stay close to him. She was his tether. She knew it somehow. Nuar was carrying most of Lar's weight, but Sophie made sure she never lost contact with her soulmate.

Tobek was just ahead of her, his shoulders tense and his back rigid. Bron walked next to him, occasionally glancing at Tobek with a glare cold enough to send a chill down Sophie's spine. Tobek must be terrified, and not just for himself.

"We'll go back for the soldiers in the tanks," Sophie said, as much to reassure herself as Tobek. They couldn't let those men suffer whatever fate Norem had in mind for them. "As soon as we help Lar."

Tobek nodded at her over his shoulder, then turned his attention ahead again. Bron's eyebrows pinched together as he stared at Sophie for a moment. Some of the frost seemed to leave his glare.

They passed through the large, circular common room where most of the warriors passed their off-duty time or gathered for important group activities. Nuar's soulmate, Lian, was curled up on one of the cushioned crystalline benches built into the wall, reading a book. Her dark hair was pulled back in a ponytail, and she wore oversized gray sweats. When she saw everyone, she leapt to her feet.

"What's going on?" she asked. "Did someone hit Lar with a freeze ray?"

"He's crystallizing," Nuar said.

Lian cringed as she looked at Lar. "This... doesn't seem good."

"We're not giving up on him," Sophie said.

Lian followed along behind them. "What can I do?"

Warmth flowed through Sophie. She had spent little time with Lian while she was avoiding everyone, thinking they might be Dean. Lian's eagerness to help and the concern in her voice made Sophie instantly like her. Plus, she had a really great dog. As soon as Lar was better, they would have a play date in the green field outside the hangar in Harbor, where the *Arrow* was berthed. They would... They would play frisbee with Ed and Dash, and she and Lian and Nuar and Lar would have a picnic.

A sob rose within Sophie that she could barely contain, her desperate desire for that future wracking her body. Her back was numb all up and down her spine, coldness was seeping out over her skin. Her legs felt like they were encased in concrete as she kept dragging Lar down the hall toward the medical bay, and her arms ached with each movement. Was this what it was like to crystallize? How much worse must it be for Lar?

If he died, would she die, too?

For an unutterably bleak moment, she didn't care. She wanted to. But then, what would happen to Hayley? Or Sophie's sisters? They weren't even aware of the true threat yet. Sophie had to hold on—and so did Lar. She needed him.

Dorn slipped past them, pausing at the door to the medical bay. It opened for him, and he gestured for them to enter before him. Everyone hurried inside, except for Bron and Tobek, who continued down the hall with the lockbox. The medical bay wasn't small, but it felt crowded with six members of the prism inside, along with Sophie, Lian, and Becca. Though it was made of the same white crystal as the rest of the ship, the lights weren't as bright. A large bed protruded into the room from the wall on their right, soft lights above it illuminating Amy in a healing stasis field below.

"What do you expect us to do now?" Tarn said.

"How do you bring out the other medical beds?" Sophie asked.

"What other medical beds?" Nuar asked.

Her heart sank. "Please tell me you have more than one

examination table."

"There's only one." Nuar gestured toward the bed. "And Amy is on it."

This couldn't be happening. Amy was still healing. She needed that table. But Lar... Sophie's face felt like it was on fire. Her mind was spinning—or was it the room? It was getting harder to breathe.

"Why the hell does this ship only have one medical bed?" Becca asked. "That's insane."

Only one bed. Sophie forced a breath into her lungs, held it, then let it out slowly. This was just panic, not some kind of side-effect from what was happening to Lar. She could handle panic on her own. She would absolutely not distract Nuar just because she was freaking out.

"It might be unwise for Earthlings to only have one medical bed, but not for Cygnians," Nuar said. "We had never even used this one before Amy needed it. Cygnians don't get injured."

"Well, apparently, they get crystallized, whatever that is," Lian said.

In a low voice, Kral said, "It means that his body has turned to crystal—a process that normally takes days, if not weeks, and only begins when we reach the end of our lifespans."

"But..." Lian looked back and forth between Kral and Nuar. "But Lar isn't that old. I mean, none of you are that old, right?"

"I've never heard of it happening in someone so young," Nuar said. "Or this quickly."

"He should have had more time," Kral murmured, his voice raspy.

"He's not gone," Sophie insisted.

Nuar stepped away from them. Lar remained exactly where he was standing, his eyes staring out at the room. She kept her arms around his chest, willing more warmth into him, silently begging his hearts to keep beating. Her own heart flung itself against her ribs with each beat, as if it was trying to get to him.

Nuar lifted his wristbands and struck them together, then hummed the note to activate their scanning function. He slowly passed his arms along Lar's body. Light coalesced into Lar's shape above Nuar's left arm—a holodisplay with his findings. Nothing was highlighted. Nothing blinked or flashed. The hopelessness in the look on Nuar's face would haunt her.

"There is no biological activity," he said.

Her breath rushed out of her. It felt as though despair flowed in to take its place. She turned and embraced Lar fully, her cheek pressed to his chest. Closing her eyes, she listened, desperate to hear his hearts beating, but finding nothing. All she felt was cold crystal.

This was not Lar. He was warmth and laughter, chiding looks and heated stares. He was everything she'd been looking for. He was love.

As he was crystallizing, Sophie had felt the warmth of his love coming from him in waves that shook her to her core. She was sure he had wanted her to know how he felt —vow or no vow. They loved each other, and she was not about to let him go without a fight.

She shook her head, then turned to Becca. "Please, Becca. We have to do something."

Becca always knew what to do. She always made things better, even if Sophie was the one who had screwed up in the first place. If anyone could fix this, it would be Becca. She *had* to fix this. Sophie's chest ached from holding her breath, but she didn't think she'd be able to breathe again until she knew Becca had a plan.

Becca stood with her hands on her hips, her gaze locked with Sophie's. "How long can Cygnians not breathe or go without blood circulating and not have permanent damage to anything?"

Fresh panic flooded Sophie. She hadn't even considered that. Her focus had been more on maintaining her hold on Lar's soul and less on what was happening to his body. Lar didn't seem to be breathing. His hearts might have stopped. Did that mean he was close to reaching a point he couldn't come back from?

"What?" Nuar angled his head, staring at Becca as if she'd just grown antennae.

"If human hearts stop for too long, we get brain damage or organ damage," she said.

He arched an eyebrow. "Cygnians aren't like that. Once this process begins, our bodies freeze in place and crystallize."

"So we have some time to figure this out," Becca nodded toward Sophie.

She tightened her grip on Lar, staring up at him. He was still in there. Her spine had started tingling again, and holding him this close, she felt something deep within her still yearning toward him.

"You said Amy only has another day in the stasis chamber," Becca said.

"Yes." Nuar drew the word out nervously.

"What are you thinking?" Dorn asked. His spine plates slowly rose, their warning vibration echoing off the wall behind him and causing rainbow patterns to streak across its crystalline surface.

Becca walked over to Amy. Nuar had encased their sister in a glowing, gold crystal shell that had formed over the medical bed. Light thrummed through the chamber, concentrated primarily on the area where the Tau Ceti had shot her. Over the past two days, the wound on her shoulder and chest had changed from blackened and charred to an angry red welt. But that was just on the outside. Sophie didn't know how deep the healing went.

"This queen thing is not as cool as I thought," Becca said. She covered her eyes with her hand and took a deep breath, then blew it out and put her hand back on her hip.

"What would happen if we took Amy out now?"

Every Cygnian in the room gasped. The vibrations from Dorn's spine plates were joined by those of the others, the walls were thrumming with them and flashing with iridescence. Sophie's head was spinning. Amy had almost died. Becca wouldn't risk their little sister's life… would she?

"Amy isn't completely healed," Dorn said, stepping right up in Becca's face.

The thrum of his spine plates amped up, making the air around him feel alive. Sophie wanted to move to Becca's side, to back her up, but she couldn't let go of Lar. Something inside her told her to stay close to him, and definitely not to let go.

Becca didn't even flinch as the white-haired, hulking Cygnian invaded her space, towering over her. Her voice was low and calm, but heavy with snark, as she said, "I didn't ask if she was healed. I asked what would happen if we took her out of stasis."

"She would heal much more slowly," Nuar said.

"But she *would* heal," Becca said, turning to face Nuar without moving away from Dorn, even though his green eyes burned with rage as he glared at her. "Her life isn't in jeopardy anymore."

"No, but there will be scar tissue," Nuar said.

Becca shook her head, then stared down at Amy. Were they really thinking of doing this?

"Get her out," Becca said.

"Becca…" Sophie's stomach churned and the skin on her back prickled. She wanted to help Lar, but she couldn't bear the thought of risking Amy.

"Amy isn't in danger," Becca said. "Lar is."

"Lar is beyond our help," Tarn growled.

"Lar is beyond *your* help," Becca said. "Not mine. Get Lar on the medical bed. Now."

"You need to accept that he is gone," Tarn insisted, his own spine plates adding more humming with a rapid vibration. Their tips were sharper than those of the other Cygnians and glinted like blades in the dim light of the room.

Becca stalked up to him, getting as close to 'in-his-face' as she could, given that he was almost two feet taller than she was. Sophie had seen Becca like this before, and knew it was time to duck and take cover. Tarn had no idea what he was in for if he didn't back down. Becca sure as hell wasn't about to.

Sophie left Becca to handle it and kept willing warmth into Lar. She pictured their souls connecting yet again. It was harder this time, as if he was slipping away from her. She fought back the image, holding on even more tightly, pushing her own energy toward him and wrapping it around him.

Please hold on. Just a little longer. Becca has a plan. I know it.

"You need to do as I fucking say," Becca said, her voice dripping with threat.

Tarn's lip curled up in a sneer. "What do you think you're going to do that we can't?"

"*Not give up*," she said.

Tears flooded Sophie's eyes. In that moment, she was certain everything would be okay. As long as they didn't give up, Lar would make it back to them.

"We're bringing you back," she whispered. "Just hang on."

Chapter Fourteen

Tarn's eyes widened, and he opened and shut his mouth a few times. Finally, his shoulders sank, and he looked away, his spine plates lowering and slowing their vibration. Sophie almost felt bad for him as Becca kept glaring for a few long moments. Sophie had been on the receiving end of that look many times. When Tarn refused to look at Becca again, she turned and headed to the medical bed. Kral joined her.

"Are you sure?" he asked quietly. "There's still a risk."

"I know, but I have a plan for that, too." Becca turned to Dorn and said, "Get out that portable medical thing you used to help get Amy to the ship when we first found her."

Kral's eyebrows rose and the ghost of a smile dusted his lips. He nodded to Dorn, who nodded back. Dorn crossed the room out of Sophie's sight. Sophie wasn't sure what they were talking about, but then, she had been a prisoner of the Tau Ceti when they found Amy.

Nuar went to work immediately. He struck his wristbands together and passed them over the healing stasis shell from Amy's head to her feet. The crystal above her face glowed. Light ate away at it, traveling down over the shell and dissolving it like a burning piece of paper. He passed his arms over Amy again and, this time, a holoprojection appeared, showing a scan of her body down to her bones and veins. There were still some golden highlights around her chest and shoulder, but they seemed mostly superficial with little involvement with the muscle and joints.

A sense of awe moved through her as Sophie watched her sister's heart beat within her ribs, her blood flowing through her veins. Sophie's own heart was still pounding, but she was relieved that Amy seemed okay. Nuar apparently agreed. He nodded to Dorn, who gently lifted Amy from the bed. She looked so tiny next to the hulking warrior. So helpless. Dorn stared down at her as if she was the most precious thing in the universe.

Was that a connection Sophie was seeing? Could Dorn sense if Amy was his soulmate, even while she had been in stasis? Sophie would ask someone eventually. She still sent a wish for happiness and luck to the pair, if her suspicions were correct.

A slab of clear crystal floated next to the medical bed. Dorn laid Amy on it, then struck his wristbands together and hummed a series of notes that were new to Sophie. Her heart beat so hard it hurt her throat. Crystal grew up from the sides of the slab, encasing Amy again. The crystal on the portable bed was silver instead of gold, but it was still as if a weight slid from her shoulders, seeing her youngest sibling safely in a stasis field.

"It's not as good as the medical table, but it will keep her in stasis for now," Becca said. "We'll figure out what to do with her next."

Rom, the ship's pilot, stepped forward to help Sophie carry Lar to the now-empty medical bed. Rom's violet eyes glowed brightly and a muscle in his jaw twitched beneath his stubble. They maneuvered Lar onto the bed, Sophie keeping at least one hand on him the entire time. She couldn't let go.

Fear flooded through her as she realized that Lar's body didn't relax onto the surface of the bed. He stayed in the same position he had been in when he was standing. Like a statue.

"This is how he is meant to be," Tarn said, his tone a bit subdued.

"No," Sophie said, her eyes burning with tears. "He's meant to be with me."

The door to the medical bay opened and Bron returned, along with Tobek. Relief took the slightest edge off her nerves at seeing Tobek and knowing he was safe.

"Once we've crystallized, there's no coming back," Tarn said.

"But he *did* come back," Sophie said. "Repeatedly. He's already broken out of it a few times before. I didn't know what I was sensing, but now I'm sure of it. Tobek saw it, too."

Tobek's eyes widened when she brought everyone's attention to him, but then he shrugged. "I have no idea what you're talking about, but if Sophie says I saw something, I'm sure she's right."

A rather strangled laugh popped out of her, the sound a mixture of relief and despair. She had another ally in Tobek. Between him and Becca, Sophie had even more hope that they might pull off a miracle. She wiped away a tear with her arm. They were going to bring Lar back.

"The Unmaker has claimed him," Tarn said. "We shouldn't interfere."

"The Unmaker isn't here," Becca said. "And Sophie claimed him first."

Sophie shook her head, her stomach sinking. "Kral did. I think…" Her throat was tight with emotion. She had to swallow before she could continue. "I think that the competing bonds did this. His link to Kral was already there, but when Lar met me, his soul recognized me and wanted to join with mine."

Sophie ran her left hand over Lar's forehead, then brushed the backs of her fingers across his cheek. She planted her right hand on the center of his chest, just above that cold spot. His freezing skin made her hand go numb.

Wait, why was it still cold? She rested her left hand on his forehead. It wasn't cold or warm, really. What was going on?

"Do you get cold when you crystallize?" Sophie asked.

Nuar shrugged. "Our bodies are no longer warm."

"But are you cold?" she insisted. "Colder than the temperature around you?"

"No," Nuar said.

"Then something is definitely still going on with him." Her skin tingled and her heart raced. "Feel his chest around where my hand is."

Nuar glanced at Kral, who nodded, then stepped forward. He reached toward Lar's chest. Sophie yelped as a streak of electricity shot out of Lar's chest as soon as Nuar's fingers neared the spot. Both of them jerked away instinctively, Nuar cradling his hand. His eyes were wide, their red glow intensifying as he stared at Lar.

Sophie's left hand was still on Lar's forehead. She put her right hand on his shoulder and gripped it tight. That had been too close. She had to stay in contact.

"There is something going on here, and it is not crystallization," Sophic said.

"I…" Nuar shook his head. "I don't understand what's happening. I don't know what to do."

"You have that crystal disintegration thing you used on Amy's stasis chamber," Sophie said. "And all this technology. You can't tell me there's nothing here that can help him."

"No Cygnian has ever tried something like this," Nuar said. "I don't know where to begin."

Lian stepped forward and rested a hand on his elbow.

"You didn't know where to start when you helped me, but that turned out okay." His red eyes glowed brighter as he looked at her. "You've got this."

Sophie's esteem for Lian rose even higher. They would get through this and become friends. Someday, they'd have kids who would play together. Sophie tried to imagine it as clearly as she could, letting herself picture her greatest dream since Lar had come into her life.

They would have little blue children with dark, wild hair and yellow glowing eyes. She willed Lar to share her hope, to share her dream, believing it would happen on a soul deep level. He had to have something to fight for.

Nuar nodded as he turned back to the table, his gaze roving over Lar's still form. "We can't use the disintegration technology. That would cause tissue damage."

Sophie cringed at the thought, her mouth going dry and her stomach churning. They couldn't bring Lar back to a horrible or painful existence. She wouldn't do that to him.

"I heard crystal breaking when he moved back in the base, and he was okay for a while after," Sophie said. She struggled to find words to explain what she had observed. "It didn't... It didn't damage him. Is there a way we can break up the crystals within his tissue without hurting him?"

"What about sound waves?" Becca said.

Tarn snorted briefly. "Don't be ridiculous."

"How is that ridiculous?" Sophie said. She was getting sick of this guy. "Cygnians use vibration for all kinds of things. Even on Earth, we have medical techniques that use sonic technology to break up things that aren't supposed to be in our bodies."

"The idea has merit." Nuar looked over at Bron.

Bron rubbed a hand over his short beard, then nodded. "We need to reconfigure the emitters."

"How long will that take?" Sophie asked, her voice rising as hope and desperation warred within her.

"Not long," Nuar said.

He activated his wristbands and began humming a series of intricate notes. Bron joined in, their voices resonating together. Within moments, lights beamed down from the ceiling, illuminating Lar's body in various places. Everywhere they struck his skin, different colors radiated from him, refracting from the crystal in his tissue.

"Sophie, you need to let go of him." Becca reached for Sophie, but she shied away, keeping her hands on Lar's forehead and shoulder.

"I can't," Sophie said. "I don't know how I know, but if I let go of him…" She shivered as a jolt of fear coursed down her spine, radiating out across her back and down her arms and legs. She shook her head sharply. "I won't let him go."

"The light won't hurt her," Nuar said. "We're using a very low intensity—just enough to break up the newly grown crystalline structures, but not enough to cause damage to regular tissue."

Becca's lips dipped into a frown. She glanced at Sophie, but didn't try to pull her away again.

"Come on, come on," Sophie said, staring at Lar and willing this to work. She focused on their connection, praying he would sense her and fight to stay.

Becca stood at her side. The rest of the prism had gathered around Lar in a circle, watching silently, though the intensity of their concentration was palpable.

"I can't lose him, Becca," Sophie whispered, a tear spilling down her cheek. "I just can't."

"You're not going to." Becca's voice was like steel. She turned to Lar and said, "You hear me, Cygnian? I am your queen... someday. And I did not give you permission to die. So get your ass back in your body so you can bond with my sister properly." Becca let out a sigh and murmured, "I can't believe I just said that."

Sophie smiled over at her and let out a nervous laugh, then sniffed. She rested her forehead against Lar's. He was close. She was sure she could still sense him. She would know if he'd truly left.

Nuar and Bron continued their work. A larger holodisplay of Lar appeared above him, sections of his body highlighted with bright white lights that formed crystalline patterns. The formations slowly began to break up and clear away. Healing lights flashed over those places, like the ones Sophie had seen shining on Amy's wounds, only there were so many more. Lar's body began to relax, settling down into a more natural posture on the medical bed.

"It's working, right?" Sophie asked. "It looks like it's working."

"We're succeeding in breaking up the crystal in his tissue," Nuar said. "But there's still no neural activity and his body is... not functioning."

"So, make it function," Becca said. "Put him on life support. Get out the paddles. Do CPR."

"CPR." Nuar snorted and shook his head. Becca crossed her arms over her chest and glared at him, jutting her chin in his direction. "Oh, you're serious," he said. "CPR is real?"

Lian sighed loudly, standing next to him. "Yes, CPR is real. Didn't you read about it when you studied Earth medicine?"

"I did, but I thought it was a joke," Nuar said. "The data also said it's used with distressing regularity to..." His eyes widened, their red glow intensifying as his voice trailed off.

"Used to what?" Rom asked.

"To ward off death," Nuar said. "And to bring humans back to life."

Tarn scoffed. "The dead belong to the Unmaker. No one can bring them back."

"Oh yeah?" Becca said. "Just because Cygnians don't bother to even *try*, that doesn't mean it's impossible. In fact, we use our medical techniques to bring people back from the dead all the time on Earth. This is going to work."

Tarn's lips peeled back from his teeth in a snarl. "All you're succeeding in doing is desecrating his body with your bizarre 'Earth medical techniques.'"

"Shut up, Tarn," Rom said. "If there's any chance we can get Lar back, we need to take it."

"How do you do chest compressions on a Cygnian, though?" Lian asked. "They have two hearts, and even without crystallizing, these guys are solid."

"We need something else," Sophie said, looking around the room as if the answer would be written on the crystal walls. "We need... Tobek." She searched until she saw him in the background.

Tobek was lingering near the wall, his arms crossed over his chest and his brow furrowed. When she mentioned his name, his eyes widened in surprise. "Me? What can I do?"

"You're a cyborg, right?" Sophie said.

"Yeah." He drew the word out, as if hesitant to make the admission.

"You have electricity flowing through you," she said.

Tobek shook his head, but he approached them. "I do not like where this is going."

"We agree on that," Nuar said. "What's your plan?"

"You keep decrystalizing him," Sophie said, nodding to Nuar. "I'll keep tethering his soul." She looked over at Tobek and said, "And you're going to jumpstart his hearts."

Chapter Fifteen

His pain was gone. Lar hadn't realized how much the aching, the stiffness, the numbing cold and the stabbing pain had intensified over the past two days. He was neither warm nor cold. He was weightless, as if in the vacuum of space. Nothing touched his body except the gentle dusting of his braids as they brushed across his back.

Was this the void of the Unmaker?

He opened his eyes, expecting to see darkness, perhaps stars. Instead, shimmering colors surrounded him in an expanse of milky-white light. Iridescence flowed through the light in filmy waves, filling his vision with rainbows. He drifted, awe flowing through him as he watched the beautiful swirls of color all around. The color shifted toward more blues, cyan through cobalt dancing closer in his view.

Something tugged at his sides just above his hearts. He tried to ignore it, wanting to focus on the lights. Peace filled him as he drifted closer to the blues, soothing him further, but then the pull on his hearts intensified, more persistent and... familiar. Something was missing. Something was wrong. Anxiety intruded through the peace and he tensed. He wasn't supposed to be here.

Lar looked down and saw tethers attached to his body —red, orange, green, blue, indigo, and violet. All of them trailed from his body, leading somewhere behind him. The strongest cord of light connected to the center of his chest. The orange cord. Its intensity flashed and ebbed, odd currents of different orange hues were swirling within it.

He reached for it, but as he moved his arms, he saw two other tethers. Their beautiful silver was so similar to the surrounding lights he hadn't noticed them before. They attached to his hearts, wrapping around his body as if embracing him. When he brushed his fingertips across one of the silver strands of light, warmth crashed into him, flooding his body with such need that he gasped.

Gasping... He remembered this. He still breathed. His body was somewhere... else. Lar had to get back to it, but he couldn't remember why. Hoping for answers, he touched the strand again.

"Please. Stay with me. I'm not ready to let you go."

The woman's voice held such pain, he couldn't bear it. He gripped the tether more firmly, trying to remember, desperate to help her. This was important to him. More important than anything. The orange cord throbbed against his chest, sending a pulse of excruciating energy through him. He ignored it, focusing on the woman.

Pain filled his hearts again. Weight assailed him, slowing him until his drifting halted. The tethers stretched taut. He wanted to keep drifting, to sever the connections and float away from the source of pressure and pain. But if he did, he knew he would lose something important. What was it?

No, not what. *Who.*

"Sophie…"

The silver strands thrummed as he whispered her name, their light flooding into his hearts until each gave a painful beat. Lar didn't care about the pain. He would endure a thousand times more—a million. Sophie needed him. He could never leave her.

Lar gripped one of the silver strands more firmly and used it to turn himself around. The tethers all led back the way he'd come, but only the silver strands were pulled tight. They joined into a single cord near to him, waves of light pulsing along their length in a steady beat. Sophie's heartbeat. The tether tangled with the orange cord, the two colors wrapped around each other, becoming twisted knots.

"This is not how it should be."

Lar agreed. But… Wait, he didn't recognize that voice. He glanced around, looking for its source. Above him, bright motes of brilliant blue light clustered together. Was this another soul drifting in the Unmaker's void? Could it help him return to Sophie?

"I need to return to my body," Lar said. "Can you help me?"

"Why do you need to return?" The motes of light swirled as the words sounded in his mind.

Not knowing who else to address, he spoke to them. "My soulmate needs me."

"You haven't bonded. She will survive without you."

"A hollow existence. I will not leave her."

Even without achieving unity, they could spend their lives together, support each other better than any other. He wanted to be there for her when she needed him.

"Will you bond with her?"

"I… I can't." Lar glanced down at the orange tether, its light livid and crackling with errant energy. "We can't join in unity. I made a vow."

"Others would have broken their vow. Or been released from it."

If only it were that simple. Lar would have approached Kral immediately if there was any hope of being released. He knew Kral would understand and would want Lar and Sophie to reach their greatest happiness and fulfillment.

"I am certain Kral would release me if he could, but it's not possible. The High Priestess of Cygnus-Prime herself linked our souls. The Maker has given her that power."

The blue motes scattered as laughter rang out in his mind. Was there anyone else in this expanse who could talk to him? Anyone who would help?

"Please," Lar begged. "She needs me."

He waited for what seemed an eternity, but the lights

didn't return. The pulse from the silver strand he held began to fade. He looked at the tethers. Their colors were dimming, becoming more transparent. All but the silver and the orange. He reached for the orange line, but when he touched it, it sizzled, sending pain searing along his nerves.

The orange cord was more solid than the silver. Whether it was the years of being bonded that Lar and Kral had shared or something the priestess had done, the orange tether was stronger. Lar released the silver strand and grabbed onto the orange line with both hands. He ignored the pain that curled up his arms like lightning serpents, stinging every nerve, and pulled himself along the cord. Hand over hand, one grueling pull after another, he made his way back toward his body. Back to Sophie and his prism.

His arms became heavier with every bit of progress he made, his joints were stiffening and his muscles ached. He was crawling toward the pain of his body, and he didn't care. All he cared about was being there for the people that he loved. He could do this. He *would* do this for them. For her.

"What are you returning to?" The blue motes of energy were back, swirling around him in a vortex of tiny spheres. *"Only pain awaits. Your soulmate will join you here soon. You will both be whole."*

"Why would she join me soon?" he asked. Pressure

seized his chest near his hearts. He wanted to be with Sophie, but not at the cost of her life. He had to protect her.

"Soulmates are meant to be together." The motes of light drifted closer, feathering across his shoulder as if urging him to stop. *"She will sense you are here and gravitate toward you. Her life would have been longer if you'd bonded. But then, so would yours."*

"We couldn't. The sacred vow had already tied my soul to Kral's." Lar gripped the orange tether tighter, pulling himself closer to his body. "Or hadn't you noticed?"

Sophie should have a century of life and love and happiness to look forward to. More, if she used the Vegans' healing technology. He grunted as a powerful wave of pain wracked through him, but kept moving forward. He would not let her life be cut short. They would find a way to be together, even though the orange tether burned like a freezing brand within his chest and in his hands.

"You are different," the voice said.

"Different from what?" His patience for this strange sentience was ebbing.

"Than those who came before."

Swathes of blue wove into the rainbows racing nearby. Thousands of them. Millions. More than there were stars in the depths of space. Shimmering beacons of blue filled the backdrop of light surrounding him. The swathes solidified into the form of Cygnians. His skin prickled with unease as he saw the oddly smooth faces of the featureless beings closest to him.

"What is this?" he murmured.

The motes of blue light swirled among the Cygnians souls surrounding him. His unease grew. Would they try to stop him? And whose was the voice that spoke to him? It held power, pressing against him, coaxing him to let himself drift farther into the void. Only one possibility presented itself to him, but he couldn't face it. The very idea was overwhelming, yet he had to know.

"Show yourself," he demanded.

The motes floated before him, pulsing in an irregular beat. They drew together tightly, forming a ball of energy that hurt his eyes to look upon. The energy pulsed again, then burst out in a blinding flash. Lar blinked against the brightness, angling his head away even as he tightened his grip on the orange tether he was certain led back to his physical form. The light behind his eyelids faded somewhat, and he dared to open his eyes.

Blue radiance shimmered in front of him. The light coalesced into a Cygnian warrior—a female more beautiful than any he'd ever seen on Cygnus-Prime. Her armor was part of her body—her entire form was translucent blue crystal. Patterns of glowing silver light ran through her like veins, pulsing at vital spots throughout her form. Sapphire hair floated around her face and tall, spiked antlers sprouted from her temples, like those of the beryl beasts on his homeworld. A slender tail curled and flexed behind her. She had no irises, but the orbs within her head glowed and shimmered with all the colors in creation. She lifted her arms—four of them—hovering close.

"Unmaker." The word was a breath and a name. Her name. The truth of it reverberated in his soul, filling him with awe.

She smiled. *"Who were you in this life?"*

"I am still Lar," he said. "I *am* Lar."

No matter who she was, he wasn't ready for anyone to refer to his life as something that had passed. He tightened his grip on the orange tether. Sparks flew from it near his hands. He grunted and shook his head, focusing on the cord, reaching farther along it and pulling himself closer to his body.

"Your bonds make little sense to me," she said, her gaze resting on the orange strand. *"This was not meant to cause pain. Something has gone wrong."*

She reached out with one of her arms and plucked at the orange thread connected to Lar's body. He hissed in a breath as another painful shock rippled through him. But he was breathing. It was a blessing to experience this pain, because it meant that somewhere—closer than before—his body waited for him to return. He just needed to reach it, to return to Sophie and his prism.

"Why were you bonded to another in this way if your soulmate still lived?" she asked.

"I don't understand."

"The bond of brother or sisterhood is a means to help my Cygnian children hold on to life for a little longer after their soulmates have returned to me. It is only to be used in dire circumstances."

Lar knew nothing of this. Had the High Priestess known when she linked his soul to Kral's?

The Unmaker turned a bit, gesturing to the surrounding Cygnian souls. *"So many remain. Too many. I have nowhere to send them, so they stay here with me. It is not right."*

"Not right for the dead to remain with their goddess? You are the Unmaker, after all."

Everything he knew of their spiritual teachings said that Cygnians went to the Unmaker when they died. The Maker created them, and the Unmaker claimed them upon death. And now, the Unmaker was right in front of him. Another wave of awe—and fear—coursed through him. If she claimed him, how could he return to Sophie?

The goddess turned to him and laughed. *"I am both your Unmaker* and *Maker. When I sense that a new Cygnian has been born, I send a soul back to the physical plane. The energy required to return splits the soul in half. A second Cygnian would always be born in time to receive the other part of the soul, and then they would find each other. What I sense when I reach for you now confuses me."*

The Maker and Unmaker were the same? He believed her, though he doubted anyone would believe him if he told them about this experience once he returned to his body. And he *would* return. Perhaps if she understood more of his situation, she might help him.

"Most of our children are male," Lar said. "The few females that are left are already bonded or beyond the age of bearing children."

The Unmaker's eyes widened, fragments of rainbows shimmering near them. *"But, my Cygnians... You will end. You* must *have children."*

Her words seemed to echo in his chest, hollowing him out. An image of beautiful children running through a grassy field flooded his mind. They had their mother's flowing chestnut hair and his yellow eyes and their pale blue skin gleamed in Earth's sun.

Longing crashed into him with enough force to loosen his grip briefly. He slid back along the tether for a few moments before clutching it firmly again, sharp pain stabbing his hands. The physical pain was so much easier to handle.

"We want children," Lar said, his voice raspy. "We're trying to change our DNA so that we can have them with members of other species."

"What?" Her rage swept over his skin, white-hot and

painful. *"You would dare—"*

"Survive?" He let his own anger and frustration seep into his voice. "We need children. You said so yourself. This is the only way for the Cygnians to go on."

"I have worked too hard for this to be my last gambit. They will not throw me out of it."

Her words confused him. "Out of what?" he asked.

Ignoring his question, she gripped the orange tether with one of her hands, placing two others on his shoulders. The strand connecting Lar to Kral flashed a brilliant blue as she tore it from his chest. Lar doubled over, every part of him throbbing with a pain so intense it clouded the edges of his vision. His consciousness ebbed, and he clung to it with all his strength. He didn't know what would happen to him in this place otherwise. His grip on the tether slipped again, but this time, the Unmaker was there, holding him steady.

She placed her hand on the center of his chest and warmth suffused him. A flickering light appeared—the orange tether was back, but now it looked exactly like the other energetic bonds connecting him to the rest of the prism.

The link the Priestesses had created was gone. He was still connected to Kral, but as he was intended to be. And now, Lar was free to bond with Sophie, if only he could make it back to her. All that stood between him and Sophie was death herself.

"Now, you will help me," the Unmaker said.

Chapter Sixteen

Lar looked down at his chest, trying to understand what the Unmaker had done. A flickering strand of orange light was still connected to him, stretching out in the same direction as the others, but it was no longer more vibrant nor roiling with erratic energy. It looked just like the others.

The tension that had flooded him since he'd met Sophie vanished. All he felt was... her. Their connection. Their love. The weight that burdened him as powerfully as standing in a gravity well vanished. As the Unmaker held onto the cord, Lar heard Kral's voice, though it sounded strange and echoing.

"I can no longer sense him," Kral said. *"Sophie, you need to let him go."*

"Sophie..." Lar breathed her name and felt air flow into his lungs. She was touching him, holding onto him. He focused on the sensation of her hands, warm on his face and chest, and drifted toward her. "Don't let me go."

"Your soulmate is not a Cygnian?" The Unmaker shook her head, motes of blue light sparkling around her hair as she drifted along with him. *"How?"*

"I thought it was your doing."

"I wondered where your other halves would go when your souls split upon return," she said. *"Your souls seek a way to propagate so that the Cygnians will go on and grow stronger. I did not know they could travel to other worlds—other sentients. It is an interesting development, but one that makes no sense."*

The Unmaker stared into his eyes as if she could see the answers she sought in their golden depths. She looked down at the silver cords that flowed into his hearts, encircling him and joining to become one strong cable linking him to Sophie.

Lar followed the Unmaker's gaze. The silver energy flowed into him now that the orange tether had been altered, filling him with a light that grew brighter with each passing instant. The Unmaker reached out and grasped the silver cord.

Energy flooded through him. His vision fragmented once more. Half of the facets remained as images of the Unmaker and her realm. The others showed him a room with milky-white crystal walls. It must be the *Arrow*, though he didn't think he'd ever seen quite this view of it before. The room was dimly lit, and he was staring up at the ceiling. Was he on the table in the medical bay? But if so, what had happened to Amy? She was still healing, the last he knew.

The pull from the cords became stronger. Not just

Sophie's, but each of the lines tethering him to his prism. He could sense the other Cygnian warriors encircling his body, focusing on him intently. Someone else was nearby. Someone new, whose energy was Cygnian, yet not Cygnian.

"I can't lose him, Becca." Sophie's whispered plea pierced Lar's soul. He gasped, clutching his chest as her pain filled him.

"You're not going to." Becca's voice was close. The orange tether in the center of Lar's chest thrummed with her power. *"You hear me, Cygnian? I am your queen... someday. And I did not give you permission to die. So get your ass back in your body so you can bond with my sister properly."*

He would have laughed if he could. He wanted so desperately to obey her command. The orange tether grew taut, pulling him closer. He sensed Kral and Becca's souls warming him, giving him strength. The Unmaker reached for the orange cord, but Lar snatched her wrist before she could grab it. The act pulled his awareness back to the void. She arched a brow and turned to him.

"This 'Becca,'" the Unmaker said. *"She has power."*

"She is Kral's bonded soulmate. One day, she will be our queen, and I will gladly follow her."

"You follow me," the Unmaker said, narrowing her eyes. *"You do as I command."*

"I do what you made me to do."

"And that is?"

"To find Sophie. To love her. And to fight any who would stand between us."

The Unmaker smirked. Something about the look sent a shiver of unease down his spine.

"Becca would be a good leader for our people. She is fierce."

"I am aware."

"You are *aware,"* she said. *"And only half of you is here. I can use that."*

Before he could ask what she meant, the Unmaker reached out and placed her hand on his forehead. His vision went white, all sense of time and movement gone, along with his sense of the others and their connection, of Sophie's touch.

Lar saw his life whirl through his mind from the moment of his birth. It sped forward to a view of the crystal forest where Lar had first met Kral. As children, they fought and crashed into the trees hard enough to knock their branches loose, causing deadly shards of crystal to shower them, rainbows of light swirling around with such violence and power that they blinded Lar for a moment.

Kral shoved Lar out of the way of a fragment that would have killed him, its sharp edge slicing open the still-vulnerable skin of Kral's youthful arm. Lar grabbed the fragment from the ground, then used it as a sword to deflect the other splinters as they fell, keeping them both safe until the debris stopped raining down on them. He still bore scars on his hand from the crystal's sharp edge—and still carried the sword Queen Ehmach had ordered crafted from it into battle.

The vision sped forward to the High Priestess holding her arms above Lar and Kral's heads as Ehmach and dozens of priestesses looked on. Kral rested his hand on Lar's chest, where the orange tether connected, his expression uncertain. Lar reached up and pressed Kral's hand more firmly against his chest, smiling and nodding in encouragement.

"I pledge myself to you—my prince, my kin, my warrior-brother." Lar's voice echoed strangely in the vision and his memory. *"I will place you above all others until the day I die."*

Lar had been so happy to bond with Kral. He had thought it would be the closest thing to a family he would ever experience. The vision rushed forward through time. Lar witnessed each moment when their prism expanded, how they had met and bonded, their family of warriors growing.

He found himself once more standing on board the Coalition's warship *Reckoning*, listening to Buddy's communicator as the Earthling frantically tried to broker some sort of peace between the Coalition and the Cygnians. He shared his mother and sisters singing a four-part harmony. It was the first time Kral heard Becca's voice and the first time Lar heard Sophie's. Lar had never been the same after that.

The vision changed to Earth. He saw the planet against the vastness of space—a beautiful, rich blue sphere, swathed with white swirls above blue oceans with green and brown landmasses. It looked so delicate, hanging in space with no crystal shell protecting it. So vulnerable. Yet it had taught Lar never to be deceived by appearances again. True strength was not always so obvious.

Sophie appeared before him, standing in a field of vibrant green grass bent by a gentle wind, a soft smile on her lips. The trees behind her seemed to sway under their own power, dancing to an unheard song. Animals of all kinds scurried among their branches and leaves. Flowers bloomed at her feet and birds were scattered across the beautiful blue sky.

This was not a memory. Not his, anyway. He wasn't sure what it was. All he knew was that it filled his heart with peace—and it was infuriating the Unmaker.

"That cheating thief,*"* she yelled. The antlers that were part of her head or her armor glowed deep within their crystalline structure. Lar squinted against her light. *"He's changed the rules of the game, again. Very well. I'm not out of it yet. Especially now that I have you."*

She turned back to Lar, her eyes blazing with scintillating colors. He wanted to ask what she meant, but before he could, she grabbed the silver cord connecting him to Sophie. Energy flooded his body, filling every cell, every atom of his being. He was bursting with light, the pressure so intense, he was certain he'd explode any moment.

"You will help me remake the Cygnian people, and then bring the other half of your soul to me so that I can study you and this Earthling properly," the Unmaker said.

She was going to use him to kill Sophie? His spine plates rose in the spirit realm, crackling with an unfamiliar energy.

"I will not allow it," he said.

"You do not have a choice."

He saw the room aboard the *Arrow* where Sophie, Tobek, and the prism stood with his body, but this time, his vision wasn't fractured. He felt Sophie's hands upon him, sensed the bonds linking him to the warriors in the room, as well as Kral and Nuar's soulmates. There was even a weak bond linking him to Tobek. But, most of all, he felt Sophie. Her touch ignited a fire along his nerves, sending silver light coursing through him so bright, it drowned out everything else for a moment.

"Again," Sophie yelled. "Tobek."

His vision whited out as electricity jolted through him, his chest convulsing from the crackling energy. His hearts gave a painful synchronous lurch. What was Tobek doing to him? The shock threw Lar's attention back to the void.

The Unmaker dropped the silver strand, sparks flying from her hand. She jerked away, shaking it, though she quickly schooled her expression to conceal her surprise.

"What are those fools doing to you?"

Lar didn't know, but he was still aware of what was happening in the room where his body lay.

"Sophie, you have to stop," Becca said. "The shielding isn't strong enough to protect you from all the voltage."

"It's insulating me." Sophie's breath whispered over Lar's skin. Was she risking herself to help him?

"I think it's working," she said. "Tobek, again."

"Sophie." Strain laced Becca's voice as they struggled.

"Let go of me, unless you want to be shocked, too," Sophie said.

A chorus of voices joined hers. Lar couldn't tell exactly who spoke.

"Do you feel…"

"…anyone else see…"

"…glowing…"

"What's happening…"

"…get a reading…"

"Tobek, stop." Then Becca shouted, "Let go of him. Sophie, let go."

"No," Sophie yelled.

He heard Kral's unmistakable roar. "Becca!"

Energy coursed out through all the cords connecting them. Lar was still in both worlds—the Unmaker's void and the physical realm. Panic stole his breath as Sophie screamed, her voice joined by Becca's. Was the Unmaker hurting them, or was it whatever they were doing to his body?

He brought his attention back to the void and saw the Unmaker staring at the cords connecting him to Sophie and his prism, manipulating them with her many arms. They glowed with an intense blue light the flowed into the cords. She was doing *something*, and it was hurting everyone that Lar loved. She was using *him* to do it. Sophie let out a pained grunt, but she still held tight to his physical form.

"I... will not... let you," he ground out.

He pushed all of his strength into moving his spiritual form in this realm, lifting his legs and lashing out at the Unmaker with a powerful kick and praying it would affect her. The blow caught her in the stomach. Her eyes widened and her jaw dropped. Her grip on the silver cord released.

"I will not let you take me from her," Lar roared.

He struck again, this time with his hands, aiming for the center of her torso, just beneath her rib cage. She released the remaining cords from her grip and flew away from him, her hair flying about her face as if in a maelstrom. Her antlers glowed brighter, crackling light arcing between them. Lar grabbed the cord that connected him to Sophie and closed his eyes, feeling the pull of all the cords from his prism as well.

"Bring me back to you, Sophie," Lar said. "Show me the way."

From what seemed impossibly far and right next to him at once, Sophie spoke, her voice breathless and pained. "One more time. Please, Tobek."

"Sophie, no!" Becca screamed.

The bright light filled with blue Cygnian souls surrounding Lar's awareness swirled into a vortex, pulling him forward. He held onto the silver cord with all his might, willing himself toward Sophie. Lar felt electricity course through his body, arcing between his hearts. Tobek's hands were firm against his chest, just above them. Sophie gripped Lar's shoulder while her other hand pressed against his cheek. Her eyes were screwed shut and her features contorted with agony.

She let out a breath and rested her forehead against his. "Come back to me," she pleaded.

Lar forced himself to speak, the last vestiges of crystal breaking away in his vocal cords. "I'm here."

Chapter Seventeen

Sophie's ears rang from the incredible jolt that had jumped from Lar to everyone in the room. It hadn't been the same as the electricity Tobek used to shock Lar's hearts. Her shielding had only let enough of Tobek's voltage through to make her hands sting with the worst pins-and-needles of her life.

The bright blue lightning that arced between them all was something else—something that had filled every cell in her body with an energy that lit her up past the brim. She'd never felt more alive. Her spine was electrified, the skin on her back was crawling with power. Was it some kind of side-effect of holding onto Lar while Tobek shocked him?

She thought she had heard Lar's voice just afterward. Was she imagining things? Fear and hope coiled through her. Her heart raced and her mouth went dry. She was afraid to look up at Lar—afraid he really would be gone. But what if he wasn't? He shifted beneath her, his arms wrapping around her as he sat up. Her eyes filled with tears that quickly overflowed down her cheeks. She squeezed her eyes shut tighter. She barely dared to breathe.

"Please be real. Please be real," she chanted to herself. She had wanted this so desperately, she couldn't believe he was back.

"Sophie," he said in his gentle voice.

He shifted her away, but only far enough for him to swing his legs over the side of the table. He drew her closer as he stood. She wrapped her arms around his chest, wanting to feel him and help if he needed to be steadied. He didn't waver at all.

How was this real? He couldn't go from being... from being how he was a moment before to standing next to her as if nothing had happened.

She pressed her hands firmly against his sides, just above his hearts. A strong beat pounded against her palms —rapid, like hers, though one was a tiny bit off from the other. He pulled her against his bare chest and held her, stroking her hair as she cried.

"By the Maker," Kral said behind her.

"I can't believe that worked." Nuar's voice was full of awe.

"I can't believe he survived it," Tobek said. There was a heavy pause before he added, "Like you were thinking any differently."

A laugh burst through Sophie's tears, and she squeezed Lar harder. She still couldn't believe this was real. All the skin along her spine prickled up into goosebumps so intense, it wouldn't have surprised her to see little spine plates of her own forming above it.

Lar pulled her closer, his cheek resting on the top of her head. His chest vibrated as if he was letting out a low, steady hum, and her fingers tingled as they neared his spine. She was careful not to touch his spine plates after what had happened in the shard. Her heart sank at the memory. She had saved him, but had anything really changed?

"I can't believe that humans do this regularly," Bron said.

Becca laughed. "We're tougher than we look."

"If there's anything we've learned from Earthlings, it is to *never* underestimate them." Kral's voice was closer. He rested his hand on Sophie's shoulder. "Thank you for not giving up on him." In a stronger voice, he said, "Welcome back."

Kral wrapped his arms around them both. One by one, the rest of the prism came and rested their hands on Sophie and Lar's shoulders.

"I don't understand," Tarn said. "The Unmaker claimed him."

"Sophie's claim was greater," Kral said. "Their bond is unbreakable."

What about Lar's bond to Kral? Sophie squeezed harder, digging her fingers into Lar's back. She still didn't dare open her eyes, afraid that she was dreaming. Nearly losing him was like having her heart torn out. She buried her head against his chest, and held on as tightly as she could.

Warmth flowed through her as he gripped the back of her head with one hand, the other resting at the base of her spine. She gasped as the contact sent a bolt of desire through her, stronger than anything she'd yet experienced.

The vibration within Lar's chest grew, and an answering wave of desire crashed into her, unlike the ones from before. This was unbridled and raw. It lit up her nerves with the strength of an entire power plant, as intense as staring into the sun.

"This shouldn't be possible," Tarn said, oblivious to what was passing between Sophie and Lar.

"It's what we call a miracle." Becca's voice actually trembled a bit as she spoke.

"'Miracle,'" Bron said. "There's no translation for that word in our language."

Becca laughed lightly. "It's when what we want more than anything happens, even though it's impossible."

"Hmm," Bron said. "I like it."

"We need to run more scans," Nuar said, standing close.

"You need to leave." Lar's voice was a rumbling growl. "All of you."

"But there's so much we can learn from—" Nuar began.

Lar cut him off. "Kral, I have fulfilled my vow to you. I

put you above all others until the day I died. That day has passed. I am now just a member of your prism."

Sophie's heart seemed to stop, time suspended around them. Lar had fulfilled his vow? Did that mean they were free from it? Her connection with Lar *was* different. More... fluid. She hadn't realized how jagged the energy between them had been before. All she felt was warmth and hope and... love. They could love each other now.

"You all need to leave," Lar repeated. "Immediately."

His hand resting on her back pulled her closer. Heat erupted in her core. His fingers curled in her hair, his claws gently raking her scalp. Energy coursed down her spine more intensely than the shocks she'd endured as they worked to bring him back—only this time, it lit up every nerve in her body with pleasure instead of pain. He'd torn his shirt off earlier and was already half-naked. The thought sent more sparks of lightning arcing through her nerves as she became acutely aware of his warm skin beneath her cheek and hands.

"I am so happy for you, brother," Kral said. Sophie could hear the smile in his voice.

"Sophie?" Becca sounded more uncertain.

"Leave," Sophie said. "I'll be fine."

Better than fine. She would bond with her soulmate, just... not in front of everyone.

"But—" Scuffling sounds interrupted Becca's protest. "Kral, put me down. That's my sister."

"Lar will keep her safe," Kral said. "Everyone out. Now."

Sophie listened to the shuffling of their steps and waited for the door to swish closed. She let out a breath as it did. Her heart raced as she realized that for the first time, it was truly just her and Lar.

"Sophie," he said. "Look at me."

She shook her head against his chest. "I'm scared."

"Sophie, please." He fisted his hand in her hair again. "Please look at me."

It would be so easy for him to pull her head away from his chest, to *make* her look at him, but he held her so gently. His longing coursed through her, mingling with her own, intensifying it until she couldn't tell whose desire was whose. Nothing stood in the way of them being together as soulmates, the way they were always intended to be. Her heart pounded against her ribs, her fingers flexed against his back. She turned her head and looked up at him.

Golden light poured out of his eyes, gleaming silver sparks streaking through that hadn't been there before. His eyes shone so brightly, it amazed her she didn't have to look away. Now that she was staring at him, she never wanted to stop. Arcs of lightning seemed to still shoot up and down her spine, radiating over her back and along her arms and legs. Heat pooled in her belly as a low, rumbling vibration flowed into her from him.

"Are you really here?" she asked.

"I am, thanks to you." He leaned down and pressed his forehead to hers. In a whisper, he said, "You never let go. I felt you. You held on to me, and that is how I was able to return."

She pinched her lips between her teeth and bit down hard, fighting the tears that welled up in her eyes again. The time for sadness was over. They had a future now. A real chance at happiness together.

"I need you to kiss me," Sophie said.

Lar's eyes flared brighter. "I can deny you nothing."

He tightened his grip on her hair, angling her head to the side, and crushed his lips to hers. The hand on her back shifted lower, clutching at the fabric of her shirt. The pleasure she'd felt before couldn't compare to what flooded her body as he deepened the kiss, his tongue tangling with hers as they explored each other. Heat and sparks cascaded along her nerve endings, lighting up every cell. She needed more. They needed to be closer.

She slid her arms to his neck and leapt up, wrapping her legs around his waist. Lar gripped her thighs, pulling her tight against his erections. He walked them to the nearest wall and pinned her there with his chest. Fabric ripped and cool air brushed her heated skin as she realized he had torn her jeans to shreds. She'd forgotten for a moment that Cygnians had claws.

He tilted his hips, his dicks rocking against her and

holding her up as he reached behind his back and pulled off her shoes and socks, intent on getting her naked. Only the thin fabric of her panties remained between her and the thick lengths of his shafts. His lower dick pressed against her core while the other rubbed against her clit as he ground against her.

I wish I had claws, too.

"What is it you want?" he broke off their kiss and murmured in her ear. Goosebumps raced along her neck.

She almost laughed. "Can you read my mind now?"

He smiled against her skin, then nipped it with his sharp teeth. "I sense your need."

"I want…" she gasped when he pressed himself harder against her. "I want to feel more of you."

With a low, rumbling growl, he lifted her shirt, keeping her pinned with his hips. She raised her arms to get the damn thing off as quickly as possible, squirming to get out of it. The movement created even more delicious friction against her clit and core.

"Sophie," he groaned, gripping her hips with both hands.

She reached between them and undid the clasp of his jeans. One of his dicks had already pushed past the waistband of his boxer-briefs, the dark blue tip glistening. She pressed her hand against the rock-hard muscles of his abdomen, then slid it down as far as she could to the base of his shafts. She gripped the one closest to his stomach, her fingers not able to reach around its girth. Lar groaned, pumping his hips against her hand.

"Let me taste you," Sophie said.

He looked almost dazed as she straightened her legs and slid to the ground. She kept going, dragging his jeans and boxer-briefs down a bit with her as she did. A shock wave of arousal rocketed through her as she saw him bared, her body growing slick at the thought of him sliding in and out of her until he spilled himself deep into her sex —and then did it again with his second dick. She couldn't wait to have him in her any way she could.

She gripped both of his shafts, stroking them and pressing the upper one against his stomach. Lifting herself up on her knees, she wrapped her lips around his lower dick, licking the velvet skin of his crown.

Lar groaned and leaned his elbows against the wall. She heard his claws scraping the crystal of the room. His pleasure flooded into her, stoking her own arousal with waves of sensation and heat. He thrust against her as she tightened her grips and stroked both of his shafts, alternating her attention between them with her mouth. His dicks throbbed beneath her touch, warning her she needed to slow down, but she couldn't. She was just as ravenous for him as he was for her. She had never wanted anyone like this before. It was an all-consuming fire that coursed through her, filling her with desperate need.

"Sophie…" Lar groaned. "Please."

It was so different hearing him say those words now that they could actually do something about it. She released him as he backed away and pulled her to her feet. He tore off her bra and panties with two swipes, his claws barely grazing her flesh with tantalizing strokes. The moment her skin was bared, he was on her. He grabbed her ass with both hands, kneading her flesh, and brought his mouth to her breasts, sucking one tight peak and then the other.

The fire within her from his earlier touch was a matchstick compared to the inferno he stoked with his mouth and hands. He trailed his ravenous kisses down her stomach, then shifted an arm to lift one of her legs and drape it over his shoulder. The midnight-blue of his fully erect spine plates glowed with streaks of silver. They looked different somehow, as if they had become translucent. Sparks of electricity snapped between them, crackling through the air. Was that normal? Maybe she should—

All thought shattered as he buried his mouth between her legs. He pulled her clit between his lips and pinched it tight. Pleasure wracked her body, building while he continued to plunder her core. She braced herself against his shoulders as he brought his hand up to stroke the slick folds of her flesh, parting them with two fingers that he slid deep into her.

"I need you ready for me," he breathed against her sex,

before once more capturing her clit, flicking his tongue against it.

Her core clutched around him, squeezing tight. The edges of her vision dimmed as electric lines of pleasure pulsed along her nerves. He moved his fingers within her, stroking her feminine folds and sending wave after wave of sensation echoing through her body.

"I'm ready," she said. "Please, I'm ready."

Lar's rumbling laugh vibrated through her, sending another spike of pleasure through her overstimulated nerves. He paused briefly to say, "Not yet."

He kept working her with his mouth, his fingers pumping within her, pushing her closer to the brink. She wanted so much more from him, but would take whatever she could get. He spread his fingers inside of her, stretching her core, and she came apart. She screamed his name, writhing against him as he relentlessly pursued her pleasure, demanding more than she had ever known her body could give. He only slowed when she sagged against the wall, gasping.

With a low growl, he rose, gripping both of her thighs again and pulling her legs around his waist. The fog of her orgasm scattered at the thought of him finally burying himself deep within her. She tightened her arms around his neck to hold herself up, pulling him closer with her legs. His upper dick was trapped between them, putting the most amazing pressure on her clit. The other was pressed against her core, only barely parting her entrance, yet still spreading waves of tingling electricity through her body. He was so close. She writhed on him, trying to pull him ever deeper, nearly desperate to bring him inside of her. She was going to go crazy if he didn't make love to her soon.

He raised a hand to brush her hair from her face, then said, "You are mine, Sophie. And I am yours."

Warmth flowed into her soul, flooding it with all of his love for her. Neither of them had to hold back anymore. She let her love for him rise within her and imagined it pouring into him. His eyes gleamed brighter. She stroked his cheek, then leaned in and kissed him.

"I love you," she said.

The glow in his eyes filled with silver sparks. She heard crackling from his back and knew that there must be more lightning snapping between his spine plates. Nothing would ever stand between them again.

The energy that had been racing up and down her own spine intensified as he said, "And I love you."

He drove himself deep, stretching her core and filling her body with fireworks. She gasped as her body lit up as if every cell had become its own sun. Without pause, Lar started moving within her, pulling out to nearly the tip, then thrusting himself in deep. His other dick matched each stroke, lined up with her slit and rubbing against her clit. Electric arcs of heat and pleasure raced up and down her spine. Her entire body hummed with it.

His thrusts grew faster, pushing her closer to the edge again. She closed her eyes, but lights still flickered behind her eyelids—arcs of lightning racing back and forth. Pleasure racked her body as he pumped into her mercilessly, all that energy coursing into her, filling every cell in her body with light. The pull of his flesh against hers, the intense pressure of him stretching her, his powerful hands gripping her ass and squeezing tight, his own pleasure reflected through her—it was too much. She screamed his name as her vision blanked out with brilliant light, her body pulsing around him as she burst into a million pieces. An answering pulse met hers as he found his own release, letting out a roar that shook the crystal wall behind her.

Her muscles were liquid. Every part of her had melted with warmth and contentment. She would surely just melt against him, happy to stay in his arms forever. She opened her eyes to see actual sparks of electricity coming off of his back. His eyes were orbs of crackling silver and gold. He slid from her body, and a moment later, he was at her entrance again, his other dick parting her, spreading her even wider. Without hesitating, he thrust himself in as deeply as he could.

Chapter Eighteen

Soulmate. The word kept repeating in Lar's mind as he lost himself in Sophie and the pleasure they shared. That, and 'mine.' They belonged to each other and no one would ever part them again.

He thrust into her, over and over, her sheath tight and slick. Each stroke sent tendrils of bliss burrowing through his body, breaking up the last vestiges of crystalline stiffness in him. His muscles were electrified. His primary dick pulsed, wanting to fill her with his seed. Even though he knew unity awaited for them both, he wasn't ready for their first mating to be over. He savored each shiver of Sophie's pleasure, each sigh, each gasp and each scream of ecstasy that escaped her.

She held him so tightly against her body with her arms and legs, with her core squeezing his dick, pulling on his skin and sending even greater pleasure along his nerves. The vibration of his spine plates resonated through him, flowing into Sophie. Her fingers dug into his back as another climax tore through her, yet she didn't relax after. She kept riding him, urging him on, her back arching, hips moving to meet his. She would take everything he had to give her. He wanted to prolong the ecstasy for them both, but he couldn't stop himself from thrusting faster and harder. Her core pulsed around him, coaxing him to give in.

Pushing away the promise of bliss, he reached up to cup one of her breasts, squeezing the soft mound and pinching her nipple between his fingers. Her gasp spurred him on. His first climax had only made him want her more. His skin rippled with energy, his body primed to give and receive pleasure. Already, his secondary dick was hardening again, and if it was...

He brought his hands back to the soft fullness of her ass, holding her in place as he once more began pummeling into her. Torrents of sensation raced along his spine plates, somehow even passing between their peaks. He had experienced nothing like it. The scent of ozone permeated the air. Sophie tightened her legs, her heels digging into his back. Her fingers clenched his shoulders as she threw her head back in yet another climax. This time, as her sex pulsed around him, he didn't hold back.

He pumped into her harder, faster, her core holding him tight, urging him to find his own ecstasy. His skin, his bones, his muscle—all of him was lit with a pleasure that crackled through him. His hearts were racing, their beats finally merging to match hers. His seed rose within him and then burst forth, filling her in wave after wave. She screamed his name, thrashing against him as he poured everything that he was into her, pulling everything she was into himself. Energy coursed through his spine plates, filling his vision with light.

He stilled within her, both of them breathing heavily, their chests pressed together. The steady vibration of his spine plates passed through him into her, a soothing hum after the intensity of their union. Her sheath squeezed him again, and he groaned as the pleasure of it sent waves of a more diffuse bliss through his body. She collapsed against him, almost as if sleeping. Light caught his attention. He turned his head to see rainbows dancing around them, floating in the air. They had achieved true unity.

"Sophie," he murmured, pulling back so he could stare into her eyes. He wanted to see the wonder he knew would be there when she saw the lights surrounding them.

"We made rainbows," Sophie said, a huge smile gracing her face as she looked out at the room.

"We certainly did." He turned back to her, as her delight coursed through him, feeling her—all of her—as their souls merged into one.

The light reflected in her eyes oddly for a moment. He almost thought he saw a spark of something in their rich brown depths. She blinked, and it was gone. It must have been a remnant of the intensity of their union.

It had been intense. Perhaps too intense. The need to join with her—the same need he sensed in her—had pushed them both. He let himself slip from her body, but then brought his secondary dick back to her entrance, slowly sliding into her again. She gasped, her eyes widening, then she laughed. The way her body shook with the joyous sound sent the most amazing shivers of pleasure through him.

"You have got to be kidding me," she said.

"I most certainly am not." Lar pulled himself nearly from her, then thrust himself back in. He kept his strokes gentle, languid. He had found the other half of his soul, and he would never let her go again.

She sighed and rested her head on his shoulder. "We could do this forever."

"We could," he murmured, then kissed her neck.

A mischievous spark sprang up in her. What was she planning? The next moment, she ran her hand along his spine plates. The gentle connection they'd been sharing immediately amped to more of the arcs of lightning flashing along his nerves. Sophie latched onto his neck with her mouth, sucking his skin and running her tongue over it in circles. As she did, she pressed on his shoulders, giving herself the leverage she needed to lift herself and slide up his dick, rotating her hips as she did so. The spiraling friction brought an additional source of pleasure. His fingers curled against her flesh as the stimulus coursed through him.

"What are you doing?" Lar gasped.

"Making sure you know I can give as well as I get."

She kissed him, a deep and possessive kiss. The vibration of his spine plates increased. He matched her passion with his own, though he let her take the lead this time. As she pulled herself up, she twisted her hips, increasing the friction along his shaft. His dick pulsed in approval. Then she let herself fall back down, impaling herself on his length. He thrust against her, matching her movements as she quickened her pace. His primary dick hardened again. She hissed in pleasure as it slid along her clit while she moved.

"We really *could* do this forever," he said.

She grinned. "I want to see if I can get you to make more rainbows."

"Always."

She laughed until he caught her warm lips with his. He focused on all the passion and tenderness and care filling his hearts, then willed those emotions to flow out into her. He wanted her to know how much he loved her, how happy she had made him, how proud he was that she was his—his fierce warrior. Tears shimmered in her eyes when she pulled back.

"Thank you for sharing that with me," she said.

"I will always share everything with you. Everything I have. Everything I am." He pressed his forehead to hers. "We are one."

This time, she kissed him, wrapping her arms around his neck and holding him close. Their bodies rocked against each other, bringing them to that ecstatic union again and again. He lost count of how many times they made love until finally they realized the rest of the prism was waiting for them and they needed to pause. Sophie held Lar's hand tightly as they stepped away from the wall. Her skin was glistening with sweat and her cheeks were flushed. She looked up at him and smiled.

"That's one heck of a workout." She took a few steps and her brow furrowed. "That's weird. I'm not sore at all."

"Sore?"

"After having sex for... however long that was, I'm surprised I can walk in a straight line."

He arched his eyebrows. "I didn't mean to make you uncomfortable."

"That's just it. You didn't."

He sensed her confusion, though all he felt himself was relief. Earthlings were fragile compared to Cygnians. Perhaps he should have controlled himself more. He had completely forgotten about the shielding that Nuar and Kral had mentioned using while making love with their soulmates, to be sure they remained safe.

"Are you certain that you're all right?" Lar asked.

Sophie laughed, then released his hand and spun in a circle. An odd light on her back caught his attention, his stomach fluttering with unease.

"I'm better than all right," she said, turning back to him and throwing her arms around his neck. "I feel amazing."

He arched over her, holding her close so that he could see her spine better. A dotted line of glowing blue light ran down its length, the glow most intense on the tips of her vertebrae. His hearts picked up their beats.

"But *you* do not feel amazing." Sophie pulled away slightly, touching her fingertips to her chest just above her own heart. Her brow furrowed as she stared up at him. "You're scared." She twisted in his arms, trying to see what he was looking at. "What is it?"

"We need Nuar."

"We need clothes." She stepped away from him, shaking her head at the shreds of fabric surrounding them. "Dang. Where's that shirt?"

Lar struck his wristbands together, then hummed the note that would open a communication line with Nuar. "Nuar, I need you in the medical bay immediately."

Lar had no sooner finished speaking when the door opened and Nuar rushed in. Lian, Bron, Kral, and Becca followed him. Lar's spine plates snapped up as Sophie's distress heightened, threaded through with embarrassment. He heard a strange buzzing sound, unlike their usual vibration when he was agitated.

"Hey, excuse us," she yelled, jumping behind him.

Careful of his spine plates, she reached around his waist and zipped and fastened his pants. He had pulled them up after their last mating.

"We sensed your distress," Nuar said. "What's wrong?"

"What's wrong is that I'm buck-ass naked," Sophie yelled.

Lar was much more concerned about the line of lights running down Sophie's spine. He thought back to the sparks he had seen in her eyes earlier. Perhaps it hadn't been a trick of the light after all.

"I can help with that." Lian hurried to one of the storage compartments built into the wall and opened it, retrieving a shimmering hematite-colored blanket. She handed it to Sophie, and said, "I helped Nuar organize this place. It used to be a total mess."

"It was not a total mess," Nuar said. "It was just... unused."

Lian rolled her eyes, then stepped back as Sophie wrapped the blanket around herself.

"Thanks," Sophie said.

Lar sensed Sophie's desire for privacy—and her nervousness that Lar was so upset. He tried to calm himself, but it was difficult. He needed to know that she was okay. Once she'd secured the blanket, he stepped aside and gently grasped her shoulders.

"Could you turn around, please?" he asked.

"You are being entirely too polite," Sophie said as she turned. "It's freaking me out."

When her back came into view of the others, they all gasped. Even Kral's eyes widened, his jaw dropping open.

"What the fuck is that?" Becca demanded, stepping

toward Lar and pointing forcefully at Sophie's back.

"I don't know," Lar said. "That's why I called for help."

"Would someone please tell me what the heck you're talking about?" Sophie again tried to crane her neck over her shoulder. Her concern grew. "I can't see anything."

"You have the coolest streak of blue light all down your spine," Lian said. "Your vertebrae are totally glowing." She turned to Nuar and added, "How come she gets to be a human flashlight and I don't?"

"Perhaps it's a side-effect of bringing him back from the Unmaker and then bonding?" Bron stepped closer and activated his wristbands' scanning function.

Nuar did the same. Lar pulled Sophie closer against his chest, wrapping his arms around her while doing his best to stay out of the way of Nuar and Bron's scans. He tried to send reassurance to Sophie through their bond, but it was difficult when he himself was so afraid. His skin prickled with it and his chest tightened. His claws surged from his fingertips as every instinct he had screamed at him to protect his soulmate.

"This is awkward," Sophie said, watching as the warriors circled them.

"Nuar." Bron's voice sounded like a dirge. A pang of anxiety from his prism-mate struck Lar as Bron stepped behind him. Though the prism bond wasn't as strong as his connection to his soulmate, the emotion still came through clearly.

"Cygnus-X, what is that?" Nuar said.

Becca hurried to join them, Kral and Lian following.

"If it's bad enough to make you use a Sadirian swear word, I want to—" Becca's eyes widened as she came into view of Lar's back. Now it was he who tried to curve his neck to see his own back.

"By the Maker," Bron murmured.

"Okay, Sophie's spine lights are pretty cool, but I want a set of *those*," Lian said. "They're like... freaking Godzilla's spines when he's about to blow shit up."

"Godzilla?" Lar said.

"He's the King of Monsters," Sophie said, her own anxiety growing. "We can binge watch all of his movies as soon as someone tells me what the heck is going on. Aren't your spine plates supposed to light up? I thought it was a soulmate thing."

"It most definitely is not." Nuar passed his arm along Sophie's spine to get more readings.

"Neither Nuar's nor my spine plates changed in this way when we took our soulmates," Kral said.

"Yeah, and Lian and I didn't get the glowing line down our backs, either." Becca's expression was calculating as she stared at both Lar and Sophie, but he could feel an echo of her unease through his link with Kral.

"Scan the material." Bron leaned closer, staring at Lar's spine plates. "I want to double-check my findings."

"They almost look as though they're made of crystal," Nuar said. "But what's that light crackling within them."

Nuar reached toward Lar's back, then hissed in pain as a sharp crack sounded. The smell of ozone grew stronger.

"I'm going to go out on a limb and say it's electricity," Lian said.

Nuar glared at her. "I noticed."

"Perhaps it's a result of how we brought him back?" Bron said. "Sophie made Tobek shock him at least twenty times."

"Twenty?" Lar arched an eyebrow and looked down at his mate.

Sophie shrugged. "You took your sweet time coming back to me."

"I will not keep you waiting again," he said. "But I wasn't idle while I was away."

He remembered what the Unmaker—no, the Maker—had said. She could use him to change the Cygnian people. With her power, she had manipulated the bonds connecting him to his prism and their soulmates and done something to them through those links. The Maker's energy had even struck Tobek.

"What do you mean?" Sophie asked.

Lar shook his head. "This affects us all. We should go to the common room, where everyone can listen."

"Okay," Sophie said. "But if I'm going to be in a room full of people, I need some pants."

Chapter Nineteen

What a difference a pair of pants makes.

Sophie felt so much better now that she was wearing clothes, even if they belonged to Becca. They needed to stop by the house and gather more of their things. If they did return to Earth soon, Sophie could see Dash again. She was eager to check with Bron about how to scan for Scorpiians. The moment she saw Dean, he'd be in for a world of hurt. A sinister glee threaded through her as she realized she could ask Dorn for more target practice as well.

"What are you thinking about?" Lar arched an eyebrow at her as they headed toward the common room. He must be picking up on her emotions.

"Wouldn't you like to know?" she teased.

His brow furrowed. "I would. That's why I asked."

Sophie laughed, then grabbed his arm and hugged it as they continued down the hallway. Low voices rumbled ahead of them. She wouldn't let anything diminish her good mood. Not the weird lightning spine plates she suddenly had or Lar's electric-crystal spine plates or the huge list of Very Important Things she needed to get done, and certainly not an asshat-Scorpiian running around trying to make her life miserable.

Okay, that last one brought her down a bit, but only as she thought of Hayley. Sophie had helped Lar find his way back to her. She would do the same for Hayley—especially now that she had help. Feeling more confident than she ever had, she strode into the common room at Lar's side.

Huge blue warriors filled the space. Becca and Lian stood beside their soulmates, and Tobek was standing near the table that stuck out from the wall in the circular room. Bron hovered nearby, eyeing Tobek suspiciously. Odd that it wasn't their security officer, Dorn, keeping an eye on the Tau Ceti cyborg.

Warmth spread through her as she realized Dorn was busy standing in front of the hallway to the *Arrow's* guest quarters. She was sure Amy was in one of those rooms, and the way Dorn kept glancing over his shoulder made Sophie more certain than ever that her little sister was in for a soulmate-sized surprise when she was finally ready to come out of stasis.

Everyone stopped speaking and turned to them when they entered. Her heart beat faster as she wondered how they would react to all that had happened. Rom was leaning against the wall of the passageway that led to the cockpit. Tarn stood near Bron and Tobek, though Lar and Sophie held his attention from the way he stared at them.

Nuar and Lian hung back a bit, but Kral and Becca were front-and-center, Kral's arms crossed over his massive chest and Becca's hands planted on her hips. A wave of unease passed through Sophie at the sight of Becca's glare. Too many times, that particular pose and look had meant that Sophie was in trouble.

"Took you long enough," Becca said.

Sophie's cheeks heated. "We had to get dressed."

Becca glanced at Lar's exposed torso and bare feet.

"Okay, *I* had to get dressed," Sophie said.

Becca crossed her arms over her chest and stuck out her chin, her eyes narrowed in a clear message. She wasn't buying it, with good reason. Sophie's cheeks prickled and the constant tingles down her spine ramped up to shivers. This was going to take some getting used to.

She had managed a peek at her new lighting spine plates while she was dressing. Her vertebrae glowed with blue light that was brightest on their tips, giving her spine a sort of serrated look. They had zapped Nuar when he tried to touch them, just like when he'd reached out to Lar's spine plates. Sophie didn't feel any pain from the change. She was energized and... empowered. It was the only word that described what she was experiencing.

Lar had also touched Sophie's spine plates, back in the medical bay after Becca had brought Sophie clothes and left for her to get dressed. They hadn't zapped him, though his own spine plates had snapped up, super-charged with his own electricity. The glow of hers had intensified, along with... other feelings. They had been delayed in heading to the common room after that little discovery.

Sophie mirrored Becca's posture and said, "Don't we have more important things to talk about?"

When Becca grimaced, Sophie knew she'd won. She tried to hide the excitement that zinged through her at finally scoring a point against her big sister. As they continued their sibling staring contest, Rom was the first one to jump into the conversation.

"So, after Sophie brought Lar back, his spine plates remained crystallized, but they're infused with electricity?" Rom asked.

"As near as we can tell," Bron said.

"I suppose that sort of makes a kind of sense, given that Tobek was shocking the crap out of him," Rom said.

Bron angled his head at Rom, his face pulled in a disgusted grimace. Tobek simply shrugged.

"It's an Earth expression," Rom explained.

"What do the lights along Sophie's spine indicate?" Dorn asked.

Sophie was curious about that as well. Lar tensed, his unease flowing into her. She took his hand in hers, interlacing their fingers. She smiled up at him and sent as much reassurance as she could muster through their bond. He returned her smile and nodded.

"I have a theory about that," Lar said. "But it may be

hard for you to believe."

"You just came back from the dead." Nuar lifted his arms, then let them drop to his sides. "I'm willing to entertain all kinds of theories at this point."

"When I died, I crossed into the void of the Unmaker," Lar said. "I was conscious. I remember everything."

The room went so still, Sophie wondered if anyone was even breathing. Well, except for the three Earthlings and Tobek. Tarn stepped forward, his face smooth with awe.

"You saw the souls of those who have passed?" Tarn asked.

Lar nodded, but the hesitancy that percolated through him made Sophie wonder just what else her soulmate had experienced.

"I saw Cygnian souls, but I couldn't identify them," Lar said. "They are whole on the other side. Their features are not recognizable after merging."

A shiver wove its way down her spine. There was a creep-factor here that Lar was trying to conceal. She did her best to help not draw attention to it, mostly by not rubbing the goosebumps on her arms.

"The only person I recognized was…" Lar looked down at Sophie, his unease growing. She nodded and squeezed his hand. He sighed, then turned back to the others. "Was the Unmaker herself."

Rom moved away from the wall, his mouth dropping open. Bron's eyes went wide. Tarn shook his head rapidly, murmuring something she couldn't hear. Kral dropped his arms to his sides and stepped toward them. Everyone spoke, their words overlapping to the point that Sophie couldn't make out a thing. All she knew was that every Cygnian in the room was suddenly on high alert.

"Pipe down!" Becca yelled, holding her arms up and stepping in front of Lar and Sophie. Everyone quieted as she met each warrior's gaze. Kral's small smile held a world of meaning. Sophie didn't think she'd ever seen someone look at Becca with more pride.

"If you want answers, you need to listen, not speak." Becca turned back to Lar and nodded. "Go ahead."

"The Unmaker spoke to me," Lar said. "She told me things… Things I must consult with our priestesses about. Our dwindling numbers displease her and it surprised her that we are discovering our soulmates among Earthlings. She wants to find a way for us to reproduce."

"Birth is the province of the Maker, not the Unmaker," Tarn said.

Lar opened his mouth, then shut it again. He shook his head. This was the part he was afraid to say—not that he'd spoken to their goddess. Sophie stepped closer to him and rested her hand on his arm, still keeping a firm grip on his other hand. She sent as much encouragement to him as she could through their bond.

"She told me that she is both the Unmaker and the Maker," Lar said. "They are one and the same."

Tarn's features twisted in fury. He snarled, baring his sharp teeth. "Whoever you saw in this void, it was a liar."

"She was not," Lar said, his voice calm.

"How do you know?" This time, the question came from Rom.

"I know," Lar said.

"That's not good enough." Tarn slashed his arm through the air, as if cutting off the idea. "It could have been a trickster spirit. A hallucination. A side-effect of the bizarre Earth technology—"

"Enough!" Kral roared.

Tarn snapped his mouth shut and stepped back. Kral stalked toward him, his face scant inches from Tarn's. Sophie held her breath, not knowing what would happen next. The Cygnians were warriors and things became physical between them all the time, but a fight about this... It would be more than just tussling.

"Your mother is one of our priestesses," Kral said, his voice softening somewhat. "Your faith is strong. Don't tell me it's also blind."

Tarn looked away, a muscle in his jaw working. Sophie could imagine his confusion and why he'd want to hold on to what he had been taught—especially if his mother had been the one teaching him. No wonder he had been so opposed to what they'd done to save Lar.

"The Unmaker told me things that I must share with our priestesses," Lar said. "She spoke of some sort of game that involves other entities. Entities I surmised are like her." He shook his head, the awe and confusion flowing into her from him telling her even he struggled to believe what he was saying.

"What you all need to know is that she said she could use me to help the Cygnian people go on," Lar continued. "I think my link to Sophie gave her access to this plane." He looked down at Sophie, his brow furrowed and a heavy guilt was surging through him. "I don't understand what she did, but the energy discharge was not an accident nor a side-effect of Tobek shocking my hearts. It was the Unmaker—the Maker—doing something to you. To all of you." Lar glanced around the room as he said the last. "I think we have *all* been changed. Not just myself and Sophie."

Sophie rubbed her chest as her nerves twinged from remembering the arcs of blue lightning that had shot out of Lar's body, connecting with everyone in the room as Tobek administered one of the jolts that restarted Lar's hearts. It was like every cell in her body was being fried, but afterwards, she was fine. Better than fine. She had Lar back.

"I don't care what the Unmaker did to me," Sophie said. "She gave you back. That's all that matters."

"About that…" Lar said.

Sophie arched an eyebrow. Another surge of guilt flooded through her from Lar.

"She didn't intend for me to return," Lar said. "I sort of... attacked her."

"You attacked the Unmaker?" Tarn said, his eyes wide.

"I thought she was hurting you all through our bond, and... She was keeping Sophie from me." Lar puffed up his chest, making himself even bigger. His claws extended, their tips barely scraping across the skin of her hand. "I could not allow it."

"And neither could I." Sophie cast her sternest glower at Tarn. While Lar was fighting off the Unmaker, Sophie had been dealing with Tarn. Rom and Dorn had held Tarn back at several points to keep him from attacking Tobek—maybe even Sophie, too. The anger she had felt stirred to life again, her spine prickling with sharp surges of energy. If Tarn dared to say anything bad about Lar returning, Sophie would rip him a new one.

Sophie glared at Tarn and said, "If you don't blink soon, your eyes are going to fall out of your head."

Tarn didn't seem moved by her warning. At least he looked more awed than angry now. She was still nervous. How would he react to knowing that the Unmaker had been against Lar's return?

"The Maker created us to be warriors," he said. "The greatest warrior of all is the Unmaker—death. Yet you defeated her. Your bond, your love is that strong." He shook his head, then pressed his fists against his hearts and straightened, his focus settling on Sophie. "I apologize. I was wrong to try to dissuade you when you wanted to bring Lar back. Thank you for returning him to us."

"I…" Sophie stammered a bit, overwhelmed at his unexpected support. Her voice was raspy and her throat tight as she managed, "You're welcome."

Tarn smiled at her and nodded. Sophie let out a breath that seemed to take a hundred pounds off her shoulders. She wanted to get along with everyone in Lar's prism. A wave of love flowed through her as she realized they were all part of the same family now. The way Tarn had reacted when they tried to save Lar… She had been worried that they would never move past it. She reached out and grasped Tarn's arm briefly, giving it a squeeze as she smiled back.

"I'm glad we have that sorted," Becca said. She turned to Kral. "You've been pretty quiet through this. Now would be a good time to rally the troops. What do you think of all this?"

"What do I think?" Kral smirked, then walked up to her and pulled her close to his side with one arm.

Leaning down, he kissed her. Becca stiffened at first—she wasn't much for public displays of affection—but then she melted against him, her arms twining around his neck. Sophie had never seen her sister kiss anyone before, and she would never let Becca live it down.

Sophie giggled and started to sing the playground kissing song. She made it as far as the tree when Becca broke off the kiss and glared at her.

"You and your boyfriend may have taken on Death and won, but don't think for a minute that I can't still kick your ass," Becca said.

Sophie pulled her lips between her teeth and bit them, stifling her laughter. She didn't doubt Becca's word for a moment, but what little sister could resist teasing their sibling like that?

Becca turned back to Kral and said, "So, what *do* you think of all this?"

He smiled. "I think Lar is right and that the Maker did something to us through our link, but that it's a blessing. Lar has come back to us and the Maker has gifted us with something more. The changes to Sophie and Lar are a sign of that. I can feel it in my hearts."

Becca returned his smile, though it took a moment for it to break through. "Me, too."

"Time will reveal the Unmaker's gifts," Lar said. "For now, there is business to attend to."

Sophie's elation plummeted faster than she thought possible. Her heart rate picked up and the room even spun a bit as all the things she'd been holding at bay while she focused on Lar suddenly rushed back into her awareness full-force.

Hayley was still missing. Dean might be impersonating loved ones close to their family. Now she had Tobek and the two Tau Ceti soldiers in the tanks to worry about, as well as the weird box that Rixon had been so protective of. Plus, there was the 'transit platform,' whatever that meant.

Lar smiled down at her, and this time he was the one squeezing her hand and sending her reassurance. Warmth suffused her, and some of her earlier confidence returned. She looked around at the warriors surrounding her—Cygnian, Tau Ceti, and Earthlings—and she knew in her heart that everything would be okay.

Chapter Twenty

Even bolstered by everyone's support, Sophie's heart rate raced as she thought about everything they needed to accomplish. How long would those soldiers survive in Norem's tanks? What was he doing to them, and would it hurt them to stay where they were while Sophie focused on other things?

She had been one of Norem's prisoners. Her skin crawled and a sick nausea flooded her at the thought of leaving them in there a moment longer than necessary. But they seemed relatively safe. She didn't want to focus on them first unnecessarily and put everyone else in more danger.

Rixon had been so afraid of the box that they'd brought onto the ship. How dangerous was it? And was he really gone? They needed to bring in the Vegans to figure out that transit platform. With the *Arrow* at Ceres, everything on the base was being guarded, but what if Norem had other surprises for them? They might get hurt exploring the base. But if she and Lar hadn't returned, Norem would have his hands on that box. Leaving could make things even worse.

She shook her head, as if that would shake loose the thoughts bouncing through her mind, and tried to focus. If Norem—or Dean—wanted something, Sophie would do her best to keep it from them. Her spine prickled at the thought, energy surging through her vertebrae. Her stomach twisted as she realized that was another thing she should probably look into. She wasn't sure if there were any doctors or scientists that were *capable* of figuring out what had happened to her, even among the super-advanced aliens in her life. A freaking goddess had been involved.

"I don't know where to start." Sophie's mind was spinning in circles. There was too much to deal with, and it all seemed so important.

"How about we start with Hayley," Becca said.

Sophie's breath rushed out in a gasp that left her as dizzy as if the wind had been knocked from her. "How... How do you know about Hayley?"

"Tobek told us." Becca walked up to Sophie and pulled her into the kind of hug only a big sister could give.

She wrapped her arms around Sophie and squeezed her tightly, pressing her cheek against the side of Sophie's head. For the briefest moment, Sophie's hope returned. This was her big sister—Sophie had always idolized her. Becca would make everything alright.

But then Becca said, "I'm so sorry."

Sophie's stomach flooded with icy dread. She buried her face in Becca's shoulder and clutched her shirt, trying so hard not to cry. Sophie was probably reading too much into those words, but to her, 'sorry' was something you said to comfort people after a loss. 'Sorry' was for when things were over. The universe was vast. Was Sophie fooling herself in thinking they would find Hayley in it?

Lar rested his hand on Sophie's back. His touch was even more comforting than Becca's embrace. Sophie would take all the support she could get. The others drew closer, as if sensing her need. They might *actually* sense it, like she sensed them. It was amazing to be standing in the center of so much love and concern.

Warmth and affection swirled around and through her, each with its own distinctive energy. She sensed every single warrior through her bond with Lar—even Lian and her tentative wish to help comfort Sophie, though they'd just met. Finally, Sophie knew who she was dealing with. She didn't have to worry about Dean fooling her when it came to the prism and their soulmates.

She focused on Becca, and the surrounding warmth surged like she was standing right next to a furnace. Becca's love and determination and fierce protectiveness took Sophie's breath away. She knew her sister loved her, but experiencing it through the bonds with their soulmates was unlike anything she'd felt before. She hugged Becca harder, soaking up as much of her confidence as she could.

"We're going to bring her home," Becca said. "I promise." She rubbed Sophie's back and added in a near-whisper, "I can't believe you were trying to do all this alone."

The words broke through Sophie's restraint. She wasn't alone anymore. A shuddering sob wracked through her body, relief and despair warring in her soul as she thought of everything she'd been through and what her best friend might *still* be going through right now. Becca kept holding Sophie, not saying anything, but she felt the warmth of her sister's love, support, and resolve. She did her best to send her own gratitude and hope back.

As Sophie finally stood straight again, she wiped at her cheeks and said, "Dang, this Cygnian bonding stuff is pretty cool."

"Yeah, it is." Becca cast a quick smile at Kral, the love between them brightening Sophie's heart.

Whatever else they were dealing with, knowing she would experience that with Lar gave her the courage to face it. They would have a lifetime with each other now—plenty of time to learn more about each other, to go on adventures and explore the universe. They would figure out how to have children and raise them to be fun-loving warriors, like their mom and dad. The entire prism would find their soulmates and bring up their families together. But first, they had to find Hayley and help take down Norem and Dean.

The Scorpiian was Sophie's primary concern. He was still skulking around Earth. An angry shiver ran down her spine. She stepped away from Becca, closer to Lar. He took her hand and interlaced their fingers.

"Did Tobek tell you about Dean?" Sophie asked.

Every Cygnian warrior sneered and growled. The room filled with the *shhk* of their spine plates snapping up. The combined vibration caused a warning chime to echo around them. Nuar hugged Lian close against his side, a sharp wave of fear and guilt coming off of him so strongly, Sophie sensed it clearly through their shared bonds. Rom and Dorn stepped closer to Lian as well, their stances ready for battle as they all but blocked her from everyone's view.

"I'm going to take that as a 'yes,'" Sophie said.

"We have dealt with Dean before." Kral said Dean's name as if it were bitter poison, curling his lips and baring his sharp teeth.

"Getting claustrophobic here." Lian elbowed Nuar and then pushed at Rom. They grudgingly gave her space. "Come on, guys. Sheesh, everything turned blue there for a minute."

"I'm guessing there's a story behind this?" Sophie said.

Lian shrugged, then straightened her shirt. She cast a warning glare at Nuar when he leaned closer again, then shook her head.

"Dean sent one of his minions to kidnap Ellie, a Lyrian nestling who lives in Harbor," Lian said. "Lyrians are these huge white-furred aliens with four arms and bad attitudes." She grinned as she said the last, a wave of affection rippling out from her. It quickly chilled. Her low voice was even raspier than usual when she continued. "Since Lyrians are total badasses, the guy waited till I was alone babysitting Ellie. He took me, too. Norem wanted Ellie for something. I don't... I can't think about it."

Lian shook her head sharply, then stared at the ceiling and blinked a few times. Sophie's chest tightened in sympathy, her heart pounding against her ribs. Lian blew out a breath, then said, "These guys came to our rescue, thanks to my soulmate bond with Nuar." She shifted her weight from one leg to the other uneasily and hugged herself. "We should start an 'I was abducted by a Scorpiian douchebag's minion and almost handed over to a sadistic Tau Ceti scientist' club. Membership will be booming."

And Hayley was the charter member.

Except Hayley actually *had* been turned over to Norem, even if she had orchestrated it herself to help Tobek—and Sophie's family. The energy prickling along Sophie's spine spiked, her skin erupting in goosebumps. Lian was trying to mask it, but she was still terrified by what had happened. There was a hefty amount of guilt and helplessness there, as well. Sophie felt the same about Hayley and Amy. She should have realized Hayley was gone sooner. *She* should have been the one the Tau Ceti shot, not her baby sister.

Baby...

Something Lian had said popped back into Sophie's mind.

"Wait, is a nestling like… a baby?" Sophie asked.

Lian nodded, her eyes glittering in the light. Her guilt surged, and everyone in the room winced. Nuar wrapped his arm around her, and this time, she leaned into him. Rom reached out and rested his hand on her shoulder. A muscle twitched so hard in Dorn's jaw, it looked like he was about to crack his teeth.

"It wasn't your fault," Nuar said, the words coming with practiced ease. "He was going to take her the first chance he had. That you were there when it happened is what saved her."

"I know," Lian said. "Now shut up. You're going to make me cry, and I hate crying, especially in front of new people."

Sophie's spine heated, energy crackling along her skin. She sensed the underlying guilt and anger Lian still carried, no matter what she said. All Sophie felt was rage. It was like a living thing growing inside of her. Jaxa may have shot Amy, but Dean was holding his leash. Whoever had kidnapped Lian and a *baby*, had been acting under Dean's orders.

"He's a fucking coward," Sophie nearly yelled. She ignored the startled looks from everyone. More heat spread over her cheeks and down her neck and back as she went on. "Dean hides behind other people. Minions, stolen forms. Tricks and deceit. We will find him and we will take him down."

"Sophie," Lar said, squeezing her hand and sending waves of cooling calm toward her.

He was urging caution. But why? Did he think Sophie couldn't handle going after Dean? That just made her angrier. Dean had left a path of destruction and despair behind him. Sophie could almost smell the smoldering ruins of the things he touched, sharp and acrid in the air, like smoke and fire. Her stomach filled with acid and her heart pounded as her muscles tensed. He had to be stopped before he could hurt more people.

"We're going to find him," she said. "And when we do…"

She wasn't sure what she would do, but she and Lar had just taken on the Cygnians' Goddess of Death and come out stronger. Victorious. The word sent a shiver of pleasure down her spine. They were the victors, and they would be again. Dean had no idea what was coming for him. Sophie… Even *she* didn't know what she was anymore. The Maker had changed her. She was Cygnian now, at least partially. When the time came, she would act like it.

The memory of Lar lurching forward with his last uncrystallized step to grab Jaxa by his neck and snapping it flashed through her mind. She'd been too freaked out to register that she had just watched Lar kill someone. Even though he had acted to save her, a chill ran down her spine —one that burned white hot. Now that she could actually process what he'd done, she didn't have the sick feeling she would have expected—only a cold sense of purpose. What had Lar's encounter with the Unmaker really done to her?

"When we find him, I'm going to kill him," she said. The energy along her spine intensified. Her muscles coiled for battle.

"Sophie—" Becca began.

"I mean it," Sophie said.

She had never wanted another living being to end before. If she had the chance, she would do whatever she had to do to keep her loved ones safe. Power coursed up and down her back, spreading through her shoulders and arms. Her fingertips tingled and the smoldering odor intensified, intermingled with a more familiar scent, like when she left her hair in a curling iron too long.

"Sophie!" Lar grabbed the collar of her shirt and tore it off, throwing it to the ground and stomping on it.

"What the hell, Lar?" she yelled, covering her breasts with her arms. She spun around both to shield herself from view and to glare at him. Was everyone in the prism going to see her naked, eventually? Her cheeks glowed at the thought.

"Jesus Christ, Sophie," Becca said. "What is that?"

Sophie's stomach dropped. What did she have to deal

with now? She glanced at her sister, who was staring wide-eyed and open-mouthed at Sophie's back. They all were.

"What is what?" Sophie asked, yet again trying to see her own spine. "Dammit, I need to do more yoga or something."

Bron struck his wristbands together and strode forward quickly, waving his arm up and down along her spine to scan it. Nuar joined him. Lar pulled Sophie against his chest as the others examined her back, his hands on her biceps instead of wrapping around her. She might not be able to see her back, but she *could* see Bron and Nuar's faces and the bright light gleaming on their features. Becca came closer as well, though Kral grabbed her arm to hold her back. Becca's face was awash in blue light.

"Pure energy," Bron said.

"And the cellular structure near it is in flux." Nuar shook his head. "I've never seen anything like it."

"What is going on?" Sophie demanded, twisting around as much as she could, trying to see her back. "I can't see."

Becca bent down to pick up the shirt Lar had dropped. She held up the remains. Sophie's heart stuttered and her mouth went dry. The shirt had been practically burned in half in a line right above her spine. The fabric was scorched on either side of the split.

"Oh my God," Sophie said. "Did I do that?"

Only when Becca's scowl amped up a thousand-fold did she remember she had borrowed what she was wearing from Becca. Sophie didn't know what was happening to her or how the Maker had changed her, but that look in Becca's eyes was one she was intimately familiar with. It comforted Sophie, even though she knew she was in big trouble.

"That was my favorite shirt," Becca said, scowling.

Chapter Twenty-One

The line of crackling energy pulsing along Sophie's vertebrae mesmerized Lar. It rose and fell in continual crests, like spine plates made of beautiful blue lightning. Why was he not more concerned? This was his soulmate —an Earthling—and the change to her body was nothing short of radical. But because she was his soulmate, he could feel her. Her confidence buzzed through him, and he stood straighter. Her drive readied him for battle.

"That is so freaking cool," Lian said. She turned to Nuar and swatted his chest. "Why don't I have spine plates like that?"

Lar suppressed a chuckle. From what he knew of Lian, he suspected she was trying to reassure Sophie in her own way. Nuar's eyes were wide, staring at Sophie's back. His mouth opened and shut as he stammered incoherently.

"I have spine plates?" Sophie asked, twisting her head around with renewed enthusiasm.

"Show her," Lar said, nodding toward Nuar.

Nuar activated the holoprojection function of his wristbands. He held his arm out to where Sophie could see the projection. A perfect image of her back hovered above it, showing the beautiful waves of her spine plates.

"Wow." Sophie's voice was suffused with awe. "That *is* cool."

"It's a gift from the Goddess," Tarn said. "You defeated her together. She's marked you both."

"Well, that is some bad-ass marking," Lian said.

"What are your thoughts?" Kral turned his attention to Bron.

Bron shrugged. "I think Tarn is correct."

"You think your Unmaker did this?" Becca asked.

"If Cygnian souls have indeed found homes in some humans, then you would fall within her domain," Lar said. "And she told me she is both Unmaker and Maker. The Maker has power over our forms while we live."

Becca arched an eyebrow, but remained silent.

"That funky lightning hit all of us," Lian said. "If Becca and I didn't change, does that mean we don't... have Cygnian souls or something?" She shook her head. "I can't believe I just said that."

Nuar dismissed the holoprojection so he could pull Lian into his embrace. She scowled at him, but burrowed closer into his arms as he said, "Sophie was more intimately connected to the Maker's power, since Lar is her soulmate and he's the one who had crossed into the void of the Unmaker. We'll monitor you and Becca for changes."

"Keep detailed records of everything," Kral said.

"We'll need to share them with our scientists and perhaps even the Vegans as we sort through this."

"Don't forget to check out Tobek," Sophie said. "The lightning hit him, too."

The Tau Ceti soldier had been lingering outside of the group, arms crossed over his chest and lips pulled in a deep frown. His eyes widened in surprise as everyone turned to him.

"It did," Bron said. "But why? Our Maker only has power over Cygnians."

Tobek shrugged. "I have no idea."

"Monitor him as well," Kral commanded. "We need to understand this better. I don't want any more surprises."

"The Maker will reveal her plans in time." Tarn reached out and rested his hand on Tobek's shoulder.

"Great," Tobek said. He stared at Tarn's hand, then up at his face, one eyebrow arched.

Lar could imagine the confusion and need for caution Tobek must feel. After seeing for himself how much Tobek risked helping Sophie, Lar was determined to also help the Tau Ceti. The prism was already accepting him. Lar would make sure that continued.

"Everything we have witnessed is…" Bron turned to Becca. "What was that word you used?"

It only took her a moment to guess what he meant.

"A miracle," she said. "We've all witnessed a miracle. Several of them, it seems."

"We must tell Ehmach." Tarn's eyes lit with excitement. "Surely now, she'll admit that our soulmates are on Earth."

Lar was certain all of their soulmates were on Earth. Who knew how many more Cygnians might discover their other halves among humans? His hearts warmed at the prospect. They hadn't just found their soulmates on Earth —they had found hope. Hope for themselves and for their entire people.

Kral nodded. "Lar, are you able to open a channel."

"I am," Lar said.

A surge of anxiety crashed into him from Sophie. His spine plates rose, crackling with their own new energy. What could cause her to oppose contacting their queen? Was there an additional threat on top of everything else?

"Um, excuse me, but I'm not exactly dressed to meet anyone," Sophie said.

Lar's shoulders dropped, and he let out a breath. He laughed as his relief shuddered through him and his spine plates relaxed against his back. At least this problem was easily fixed. Or it would be, if he had a shirt to give her.

Tarn stepped toward Sophie, pulling his sleeveless tunic over his head. The eggshell-white leathers had openings down the front and back, with strips of material holding them together and leaving space for their spine plates.

"Here, take this," Tarn said.

She arched an eyebrow at him, but took the tunic, still keeping one arm over her breasts and her body turned toward Lar. He kept himself close, shielding her from view as best he could. The leathers were tougher than the shirt she had burned through. Hopefully, they could handle the energy of her spine plates should they rise again. He angled his head over her shoulder to check on her spine. The power coursing along it had settled to a glow beneath her skin that rippled and pulsed.

"Bron programmed our replicators to alter the material and make it soft enough for humans," Tarn added.

"What was it like before?" Sophie asked, rubbing her thumb across the tunic.

"Your brother complained that our leathers felt like sandpaper when he first spent time with us," Bron said. "Since we've been living among humans, we altered their composition so that any humans we might brush against wouldn't be uncomfortable."

"That's nice of you." Sophie held the tunic closer to her body, the laces hanging loose. "But this won't cover what I need to have covered. Plus, it'll be huge on me."

"We can adjust it," Lar said.

She kept a skeptical brow raised, but lifted her arms so he could slip the tunic over her head. It settled over her form, hanging almost like a blanket. Lar tightened the laces on the front of the tunic so that only the smallest strip of her skin was visible running down from Sophie's collarbones to the waistband of her jeans. Once she was covered, he spun her around and pulled the laces on the back tighter as well, though he left a gap for her own unique spine plates.

"There," he said. "Better?"

Sophie looked down at the leathers that fell past her knees. "I'll say. This so beats Becca's shirt."

"I guess I don't have to worry about you stealing my clothes anymore." Becca crossed her arms and glared at Sophie, then turned to the others. "Too bad for you guys. She'll be raiding your closets now."

"It'd be better if it was a little shorter." Sophie spun in a circle, still staring at the white leather. "Still, this could easily become a trend."

A heady joy washed through him at the sight of her in Cygnian leathers. Her tan skin gleamed next to the pale fabric, and the tunic let him see the smooth lines of muscle on her arms. She pulled her hair from beneath the material, and as Lar watched it brush across her back, his fingers flexed, wanting to bury themselves in it. His shoulders and arms tingled with the urge to grab her and hold her close, then run his hands along her spine and discover if he could summon her lightning in other ways.

He didn't need to control himself anymore. He stepped closer, turning her to face him. His cocks began to harden as he leaned down to kiss her. The only thing that stopped him was her hand against his bare chest. Her cheeks were flushed and her lips parted. Sparks of light gleamed within the brown depths of her eyes, and a faint hint of ozone filled the air.

"Lar." Sophie's voice carried a low, seductive rasp. "I *just* got dressed. And we're in a room full of people."

"They can leave," he said.

"Thank the fucking stars." Tobek immediately headed down a hallway, disappearing from view.

Sophie giggled as she cast a quick glance after Tobek, but then returned her attention to Lar, her hand trailing down along his skin and leaving a blaze of pleasure in its wake. Her desire for Lar burned within him, feeding his need for her.

"Hey," Becca said. "Hey! Cut that out. Oh, God, I'll need to shower for days after that." She shuddered and shook her head.

Sophie laughed more strongly, then pushed away from Lar. He followed, but she held up both hands and said, "Not right now. We have the queen to call, so make yourself… presentable." She slowly looked down his body, freezing on his cocks.

"Come on, seriously?" Becca rolled her eyes, then grabbed Sophie by the shoulders and turned her around. "Fun fact. You know how everyone in the prism connected, and we, as their soulmates, are also roped into that? Well, guess what? It doesn't screen out… *this*, and I, as your sister, am supremely grossed out right now, so stop it."

"Oh," Sophie said, a wave of embarrassment dousing her arousal. "Oh crap. Sorry."

"Becca's just complaining because she hasn't had to learn how to block it out, yet." Rom smirked at her. "Ever since Nuar and Lian hooked up, we've all had plenty of practice."

"It's good to know that's possible," Becca said. "But for now, please keep your hands and thoughts to yourself."

"Yes, ma'am." Sophie brought her hand to her forehead in an odd gesture, straightening her stance.

"I'll open a channel to Cygnus-prime," Lar said, smiling at the siblings.

He struck his wristbands together, then hummed the note to bring up the holocontrols of his communications console. In a few moments, he'd established the connection. The prism and their soulmates took up positions around the edges of the room, Nuar pulling Lian to his side as Kral and Becca stood at the forefront of the group.

The holodisplay began projecting, flooding the common chamber with light. Ehmach and Korvin stepped into view, appearing to emerge from nowhere. Kral looked like Korvin with his orange eyes, full beard, and wild, sapphire hair. Korvin's skin was paler, though, closer to cerulean. Ehmach had the same cobalt skin as most in her and Lar's house. She kept her dark navy braids shorter than Lar's, a jagged crystal helm reminiscent of their Maker's antlers holding them away from her face. Ehmach's eyes gleamed gold, their light blazing brightly as she glared at Kral and the rest of the prism.

Lar knew they were holograms, but the images were so real, it was almost impossible to tell the difference. He felt Sophie's heart race—his own hearts matching its beat. She shifted closer to him and reached out, interlacing their fingers. It was no wonder she was afraid. Ehmach's crystal armor did more than reveal her strength and stature. It was designed to intimidate, with sharp edges and complex planes that made her look even taller and stronger than she was.

Lar looked down at Sophie and projected the calm and peace he felt, smiling softly. Ehmach and Korvin would understand. They would support the prism in their search for soulmates. Lar was sure of it. Sophie's heartbeat calmed as his emotions flowed into her. He had no more fear. No pain. No worry. He had Sophie, and as long as they were together, they could accomplish anything. They had defeated death. He knew this conversation would not be easy—not with Ehmach's expectations of him. But now, she had no hold on him.

"Kral," Korvin said. "You were supposed to leave the Sol system."

"My soulmate is here," Kral said. "Her world is here. I will not leave."

Ehmach's lips pulled back in a sneer. "I have given you a command. Your ship is part of our fleet."

"My ship is our home," Kral said. "Would you take that from us, mother? As well as any chance we have for love and hope?"

She shook her head. "Not this again."

"Yes this." Kral looked over at Becca. "Always."

Ehmach turned to Lar. "You were to lead him away from this madness."

Lar took a deep breath, broadening his chest and standing straighter. "It would be madness to try."

She turned her attention to where Lar and Sophie's hands were joined. Ehmach narrowed her eyes, her spine plates snapping up in the gaps grown into her crystal armor.

"Nuar and Kral have fallen to whatever power these Earthlings wield, but you are bound," Ehmach said. "Your vow protects you from being swayed by any other. Your devotion is to Kral."

"It was," Lar said. "But now my soul is at last whole."

Her eyes widened. "You cannot have broken your vow," she nearly yelled. "It isn't possible."

"I did not break it." Lar shook his head. "I put Kral above all others until the day I died. That day was today. Sophie brought me back—through our soulmate bond."

"It's true," Tarn said, stepping forward. "We all witnessed it."

"Trickery—" Ehmach said.

Lar's hearts sank. He had feared Ehmach would react badly to his vow being fulfilled, though a wave of disappointment coursed through him, regardless. They needed to help her accept the truth, and he was supposed to be the chief communications officer. How could he convince her when he didn't understand why she resisted so strongly? His people's survival depended on Ehmach recognizing that their soulmates were on Earth.

"Enough." Kral's shouted word echoed through the room. "I don't know why you refuse to believe that Earth is home to our soulmates when you're fine with the idea of us mating with Sadirians, but it doesn't matter. The Maker herself has spoken."

"The Maker?" Ehmach sneered and shook her head. "These Earthlings are clouding your mind. The Maker does not speak to us."

"Only because none of us have been able to reach her before," Kral said. "But Lar has."

"My soul traveled to the void of the Unmaker when I died," Lar said. "I spoke with her. She told me she and the Maker are one. Through me, she discovered that Cygnian souls are being born in Earthlings. Our other halves are here."

Ehmach let out a disgusted snort. "None of this is possible."

"He crystallized." Nuar stepped forward, striking his

wristbands together and humming the note that linked up the holoprojection data stream with the ship's records. Lar checked the communication line and saw that he was transmitting all the data they'd collected so far about what had happened to him and Sophie to Korvin's personal computer.

"Becca and Sophie reminded me of several Earth medical techniques I studied before coming to their planet that we've never tried on Cygnus-Prime," Nuar said. "We reversed the crystallization process and Lar was able to return to us, thanks to his connection with Sophie."

"Something happened when we were reviving him," Bron said. "To him and Sophie both. Something our scans can't explain."

"It was the Maker," Tarn said. "Or the Unmaker. Both."

"Beloved…" Korvin spoke with care as he looked at something they couldn't see. "Perhaps we should hear them out."

"Foolishness," Ehmach said.

Lar hoped Korvin was reading the data they'd sent. Ehmach was not being as reasonable as Lar had expected. He knew their queen had a temper and could be stubborn, but never dreamed she would let that get in the way of supporting her people. As his own anxiety grew, Sophie's transformed into anger.

"Why is it so hard for you to believe?" Sophie asked.

"That he died and returned?" Ehmach shook her head

sharply. "In all of Cygnian history, no one has ever defeated death."

"Well, none of them had me as a soulmate," Sophie said. "And nobody gets between me and my man. Mate. Whatever."

Lar did his best to hide his grin, not wanting to antagonize their queen. Sophie released Lar's hand and crossed her arms over her chest, glaring at the queen and cocking her head in a gesture that reminded him strongly of Becca. Ehmach stalked toward Sophie, towering over the Earthling. Pride rose up in him as Sophie held her ground. Though he knew Ehmach was a hologram, the projection was so realistic, it would have been impossible to tell the queen wasn't in the room with them unless they already knew she was a projection. The technology was new to Sophie, but she remained unfazed.

"You Earthlings are leading our warriors from their path," Ehmach said. "There will be consequences for your actions."

"So far, the consequences of my actions are that Lar is alive and with me," Sophie said. "And I'm fine with that."

Ehmach narrowed her eyes. "The Cygnians have not yet decided who to side with in this war."

Ice seemed to flood Lar's veins. Ehmach did not make threats she did not intend to keep. Surely, she wasn't implying that she would support the Tau Centauran Assembly. Angry voices rose around him as the warriors made clear their thoughts of her threat. Sophie's mouth dropped open and a wave of light pulsed down her back.

"If you join the Assembly, you will force us to fight our own people," Kral said.

Korvin stepped forward. "You would side with the Coalition?"

"We would side with Earth," Kral said. "All of us."

For a moment, pain flickered through Ehmach's eyes such that Lar had never seen before. She steeled her expression, then said, "My own son. A traitor to his people."

"We are not traitors." Tarn stepped forward forcefully. "We are following the will of the Maker."

"This has nothing to do with the Maker and everything to do with Earth's trickery," Korvin said. "They're even worse than the Sadirians. They can face their fate together."

Kral puffed out his chest, his hands fisted at his sides. "We will stand with our soulmates. We will defend them and their homeworld—as will the Vegans. Please, there are so few of us left. Don't do this."

Lar had to help Kral convince his mother to avoid this dangerous path. His chest tightened and his spine plates rose, their vibration joining with that of the other warriors. The thought of doing battle against other Cygnians brought a sick feeling to his stomach.

"Cygnians have moved beyond going to war with each

other," Lar said. "Do not take us back to those bloody times."

"Earth started this conflict," Ehmach said. "By warping your minds. We must cleanse you of their influence."

Sophie stepped forward, inches away from Ehmach's projection, hands fisted at her sides and stance ready for battle. Crackles of energy arced up from Sophie's back, sharp spines of blue energy humming with a high-pitched vibration. More light spread in glowing lines beneath her tunic and raced down her arms, where they wound around each finger and erupted in claws made of light.

"Don't you dare threaten my homeworld," Sophie said, her voice filled with more menace than Lar would ever have imagined her capable of. "And *never* threaten to come between me and Lar again."

Ehmach was still standing right in front of Sophie, looming over her. Sophie lashed out, as if to grab Ehmach. She must have forgotten that the queen and king weren't actually in the room. Except, when Sophie's hand closed on Ehmach's throat, the queen's eyes widened in shock. Her mouth dropped open in a silent scream as arcs of electricity jolted through her form, wrapping around her body and making her limbs twitch and spasm.

"Ehmach!" Korvin ran to Ehmach's side, grabbing her arm. The moment he connected, the blue lightning coursing through Ehmach flooded into him, causing him to convulse.

"Sophie," Kral shouted. "Release them!"

Lar's hearts pounded as fear swept through him, his muscles tensing. He grabbed Sophie's shoulders, prepared to be shocked as well. The energy flowed into him, lighting him up and crackling through his spine plates. It didn't hurt at all, but energized him instead, made him feel *alive*. He pulled Sophie away, breaking her connection with Ehmach and Korvin. The queen was left bent double, one hand on her throat and the other on her leg. Korvin's hands rested on his mate's arm and back as they both panted and stared at Sophie. Their holoprojections flickered a few times before stabilizing.

"And you had us believing that Earth was a low-tech planet." Korvin's voice was tight with pain. "How dare you use such a weapon against us. This will not go—"

Lar had had enough. "This will go nowhere," he roared. "It is you whose minds are warped and blinded to the truth. My gift from our goddess is my life," Lar said. "This is what she gifted Sophie."

He turned Sophie at an angle so they could see the crackling blue spine plates rippling and vibrating down her back.

"This is the truth," Kral said, pointing at Sophie. "Sophie is Lar's soulmate. The other half of his soul is within her—a Cygnian soul—and their bond was powerful enough for them to defeat the Unmaker. Do not be so foolish as to think that you can stand against her will."

"If you side with the Assembly, you aren't fighting against Earth," Lar said. "You are fighting our goddess. Choose wisely."

Ehmach straightened at last. Lar's breath caught in his chest. How had Sophie done that? And how would the queen react? Ehmach stared at them for a few long moments, then struck her wristbands together. The projection from Cygnus-Prime vanished.

Chapter Twenty-Two

Sophie's chest rose and fell in gasping breaths. Her eyes were wide and the skin of her back prickled like she'd come too close to a live wire. She had attacked the Cygnian queen. She didn't even know *how* she'd affected the woman or King Korvin. Sophie's spine plates—or whatever they were—crackled with wild energy.

"That didn't go well." Lian shrugged when everyone turned to look at her. "What?"

"That is the biggest understatement in the universe." Sophie's heart was pounding. What had she done?

Lar stood close, his concern for her stretching out from their bond. "Are you alright?" he asked.

"I don't know," she said. "I've never been more scared and angry. They were threatening my entire planet."

Lar pulled her against his chest and wrapped his arms around her. His warmth coursed through her, along with his own spark of energy. It doused the maelstrom within her, bringing a kind of balance. She took a slow breath and let it out, then another. Gradually, her racing heart calmed, his steady beat calling hers back to a cadence that didn't feel like it was about to burst out of her chest.

"Give them time," Kral said. "They'll see reason, eventually."

"And if they don't?" Bron asked.

"They won't put our people in more danger of extinction," Kral said. "They know the Vegans will defend Earth, and even our fleet can't stand against them."

"Not if they're acting alone, but what if they get help?" Becca's voice was low and calm, but Sophie heard the strain in it. "Is there any chance they'll join the Tau Centauran Assembly?"

"No." Kral shook his head. "If they move against Earth, they'll be on their own."

As the adrenaline in Sophie's system faded, the weight of what she'd done became clearer. She had attacked the leaders of an entire planet of epic warriors. Ehmach thought Sophie had led Lar to break his vow, and that Earthlings were dangerous. She had pushed their people closer to war.

"Please tell me it's not my fault if they do," Sophie said, her voice quivering.

"Hey." Becca strode over and put her arms around Sophie's shoulders, hugging what she could reach within Lar's protective embrace. "Whatever decisions they make are on them, not you. We all make our own choices—and deal with the consequences."

"Yeah, but I attacked them," Sophie said.

Becca shook her head. "It was an accident. You didn't

even know you could affect them. They were holograms, for crying out loud."

"They might not see it that way," Sophie said.

Dorn spoke up from his place by the door. "They might not care."

Everyone turned to face him. Sophie peered out from between Becca and Lar.

"What do you mean?" Lar asked.

Dorn raised one shoulder in a shrug. "Ehmach and Korvin think we're on the brink of extinction. That they went to the High Council for help shows how desperate they are. If they're pushed too far, they might decide it's better to go out fighting than wait for time and age to take the last of us."

Sophie's heart rate picked up again, and her stomach twisted and roiled. The Cygnians were so close to finding hope for all their people. They couldn't give up now. She sensed Lar's unease grow, but there was no doubt alongside it. He must believe Dorn was right.

"That's... But... You..." Sophie's brain reeled, addling her speech. "She can't attack Earth. We're here. Your soulmates are here. Maybe all the soulmates for the remaining Cygnians. If they go to war with us—"

"They'll never learn the truth," Dorn said.

Kral strode to the center of the room and slashed at the air with his arm, his claws flashing in the light of the crystalline chamber. "Then we show it to them. We make them understand that our future is with Earth, working together as allies. As equals."

Becca nodded. "We have to give them hope again."

"That's easier said than done," Sophie said. "Especially after what I did. I ruined things."

Lar held her closer, his presence bolstering her and soothing some of the searing anxiety burning through her. If the Cygnians attacked Earth, Sophie would never forgive herself, no matter what anyone else said.

"I'm not so sure about that," Bron said. "In fact, you might have opened up an entire universe of possibilities for us all."

Bron was looking at some kind of holographic display. Sophie pulled away from Lar, though she kept a tight grip on his hand as she led him closer to Bron. The hologram showed a silhouette of a human-looking female made up of glowing light with streaks of silver coursing through it. Waves of every shade of blue ebbed and flowed through her form, like swaths of cobalt oil moving through dark blue water. Electric-blue energy rippled down the silhouette's back, rising and ebbing as spine plates. The energy went deeper than her spine, a network of light filling her entire body. Was that Sophie?

Bron pointed at something, then angled his head toward Rom.

"What does this look like to you?" Bron asked.

Rom pushed away from the wall where he was leaning

and joined Bron. The others came nearer as well. Lar kept Sophie tucked against his side as she clung to his waist. From the nearer vantage point, she was even more sure it was a silhouette of herself. But what was all that blue energy? She hated admitting it, but she looked pretty bad-ass in the hologram—like she'd stepped straight out of a sci-fi movie.

Power flooded up through her arm in the image, her hand curled above her as if grabbing something. At first, nothing was in her grip, but then another silhouette formed. Ehmach. The Cygnian queen was a darker and more uniform navy blue. The energy coming out of Sophie's hand connected them, lighting up the other woman.

More shades of blue flowed into Ehmach's form, with the same swirling eddies and sparks of silver. A few seconds later, Korvin's silhouette joined them, beginning as solid bright sapphire, then morphing into swirls of every shade of blue imaginable—all lit up by lightning strikes of silver coming from Sophie.

Rom swore under his breath. "Cygnus-X, that looks like blue space."

"What's blue space?" Sophie asked.

"It's a different level of our universe," Bron said. "Humans would probably call it another dimension."

"We drop into it whenever we need to travel between solar systems," Rom said. "Space isn't the same there, and you can cross immense distances in a relatively short amount of time."

"So, you guys can teleport?" Sophie asked.

"Not quite," Rom said. "It can still take a while—and it requires a ship."

"Blue space transit engines are huge," Tarn said. "Aside from living quarters, most of the space within the *Arrow* is taken up with the blue space engine."

"What exactly are we looking at?" Kral pointed at the display.

Bron ran a hand over his beard, his brow furrowed. "It appears as though Sophie reached through blue space and somehow connected her energy with Ehmach's. When Korvin touched the queen, he was affected as well."

Nuar let out a laugh. "That's ridiculous. No one can do that."

"Is it ridiculous?" Lian turned to him. "When I was kidnapped, you said you found me because our souls were connected and you sensed me."

"A soulmate bond is between two unique beings," Tarn said. "Their souls are one and the same and can't be truly separated by any distance."

"Yeah, but how does that work?" Lian asked. "Nuar said the connection of our soulmate bond led you guys to me. And you've all talked about being connected through your prism bonds. There has to be some kind of mechanism that it works through. What if it goes through blue space?"

"That doesn't make sense," Nuar said. When her gaze turned into a withering glare, he quickly amended his statement. "I mean, I don't think it works quite that way."

"No one truly knows how prism or soulmate bonds work," Bron said. "Lar has more knowledge now than even our elders do."

"What do the elders say?" Becca asked.

"That the Maker returns our souls when a Cygnian is born," Tarn said. "The soul divides itself into two, with the other half waiting for another body to be born for it so that they can find each other and enjoy their lifetime together. There have been so few births, our priestesses assume that the other halves of the souls were lost."

"The Unmaker told me she is also the Maker," Lar said. "And that she believes the other halves of our souls have traveled to Earth. Is it possible they used blue space to do so?"

"We don't really understand how blue space works, either," Bron said. "We only know how to use it for our travels."

"How does that affect what happened between Sophie and Ehmach?" Rom asked.

Sophie's mouth was dry, and her heart pounded in her ears. She licked her lips and swallowed, trying to push out the words. "Because blue space might not just connect soulmates."

Lian stared at her for a few moments, then nodded. "Some humans believe that there's an energy flowing through the entire universe that connects us all."

"Blue space links everything physically," Becca said, her gaze distant as she thought things through.

"What if it also links things on an energy level?" Lian asked. "What if it connects our souls? Not only soulmates, but everybody."

The room spun around Sophie. She held on to Lar as her mind reeled. He squeezed her closer against his side, holding her tight. The idea that she could reach out and electrocute her enemies without even being near them was absolutely terrifying. Not just because she didn't know how to control it, but because… it tempted her.

She *wanted* the power, wanted to protect the people she loved, to protect her planet. But who was she to mete out justice that way? How long would it take for the line to blur or for her to make a mistake and 'punish' the wrong person?

"It sounds like we're missing a hell of a lot of data," Becca said. "We need answers."

"What do you suggest?" Kral asked.

Becca's brow furrowed. "Would the Vegans know more?"

"Undoubtedly," Bron said.

"We can't bring them into this mess." Kral held up a hand when Becca looked ready to argue. "I know you think Cygnians need to work on requesting help."

Becca crossed her arms over her chest. "No, I think *you* need to work on asking for help."

Kral let out a sigh. "This is a difficult situation. If the Vegans decide that Cygnus-Prime is a threat to Earth, they may go on the offensive."

Sophie felt as though ice filled her veins. It took her a moment to realize that the fear was being amplified by Lar's. The idea terrified him. Were the Vegans really that powerful? She had thought things couldn't get any worse, but everything was getting more complicated and out of control.

"That would suck," Lian said. "But I don't think the Vegans would do that. The ones I've met in Harbor have been nice."

Becca softened her voice—and her stance—as she reached out to Kral, her hand resting on his arm. "We need their help. We have that mystery box that won't open, a bunch of pickled Tau Ceti floating in jars having who-knows-what done to them, a death platform that vaporizes whatever you put on it, a mad scientist doing experiments on his own people, a shapeshifting asshole running around making trouble for everybody, and at least several missing Earthlings—including one who's part of our family."

Sophie's stomach churned hearing that awful 'to-do' list repeated and the reminder of Hayley. Becca had a stronger grasp on everything that was going on than

Sophie expected.

"Did Tobek go over all that with you?" Sophie asked.

Becca shrugged. "That, and we did a little recon with him. You guys were... busy... for a while."

Sophie's cheeks heated. Lar's spine plates rose above her arms. The warmth he sent through their link had nothing to do with embarrassment. Tingles spread through her belly and a growing fire lit within her chest. He stared down at her, his golden eyes glowing bright, silver flickers dancing in their depths.

"Stop trying to distract me," Sophie murmured.

"I'm just reminiscing," he said. "When I decide to distract you from these troubles, you'll know."

She had never seen someone pull off a better smoldering grin. The promise in that smile filled her mind with her own newly made pleasant memories. It would be so easy to lose herself in him again, to find a private room on the ship and shut out everything they faced. Lar bent down and kissed the top of her head, sending encouragement and love flowing through their bond. She gave him a quick squeeze, then forced herself to stand straighter at his side. There was no hiding from this. They needed to confront their problems head-on. With Lar at her side, she could do anything.

"Okay, so, focusing," Becca said. "If approaching the Vegans formally is out, what about informally? Do any of you have a Vegan friend who might be able to help us?"

"Buddy does," Rom said. "I think her name is Cyan."

"My brother is friends with a lizard person?" Becca said.

Rom shrugged. "He's friends with all kinds of people. His sandwiches are spectacular."

Sophie actually managed a little laugh at that. She and Becca shared a look. Their brother's cooking was amazing, but knowing that aliens were eating his subs was... weird.

"We'll have him call Cyan and ask for assistance," Kral said. "Discreetly."

"It will be tricky to keep this communication secret, since he's involved with the Coalition's chief engineer," Lar said.

"We don't have to tell him what it's really about." Becca turned to Kral and said, "We talked about asking the Vegans for help when we were ready to have kids."

Kral's eyes pulsed a bright orange. His spine plates rose, and the temperature in the room must have spiked ten degrees. Even with Sophie's nascent connection with the prism, she felt the surge of longing that blazed through each Cygnian warrior at the mention of having kids. Her eyes filled with tears from the intensity of their wish for children—until Kral's desire hit the edges of her awareness. His claws extended and his fingers flexed, reaching for Becca. Sophie suddenly felt a lot more guilty about what the others must have sensed while she and Lar were 'bonding.'

Becca held up her hands and stepped back. "Settle down, we're not there yet. But it's a good cover story for why we want to meet with her and why we want to keep it quiet."

"We shouldn't lie to the Vegans," Tarn said.

"It's not a lie." Sophie rested her hand on Lar's stomach and turned to him. "I want a ton of kids. Like a *ton* of them. The sooner we start, the better."

This time, Lar's spine plates snapped up. A low rumble vibrated out from his chest, resonating in her bones in a way that made heat explode deep in her belly. She gasped, her skin prickling as his desire washed through her, her own spine plates flaring to life behind her.

"Knock it off," Becca yelled. "We don't have time for that."

Right. Plus, they were in a room full of people. Sophie shook herself and backed up a step, though the look she and Lar shared kept the fires within her smoldering.

Becca let out a disgusted sigh. "Lar, you're the communications guy on the ship. Send a message to Buddy asking for Cyan's contact information. Tell him it's regarding 'physical compatibility issues,' and I guarantee he will not ask more questions. We're his sisters, after all."

"I'll take care of it immediately," Lar said.

"We need to meet with her on Earth first, though," Sophie said. "It wouldn't make any sense to have her meet us here, and we can't leave this place unprotected."

Becca nodded. "That's a good point. Kral and I will go to Earth to meet them."

"Let Lar and me do it," Sophie said.

Becca raised an eyebrow. "Why?"

"I need to see Dash," Sophie said.

She was sure that Lian was keeping Dash safe, but since neither Ed nor Dash seemed to be on the ship, Sophie guessed they were back on Earth with Lian's family. Guessing wasn't knowing, and now that Sophie had a chance at being certain her dog wasn't a shapeshifting alien, she wanted desperately to give Dash a big hug—and a bigger apology.

Becca rolled her eyes. "You and that dog."

"Becca..." Sophie pushed all of her grief, fear, confusion, and hope into the word.

If they met with Cyan on Earth, Sophie could ask her about how to scan Dash to make sure she wasn't a Scorpiian. Sophie was desperate to see Dash and make amends for neglecting her over the past few days. The idea filled her with hope that she would be able to bridge the strange and amazing future she was heading into with Lar and with her previous life on Earth. Sophie's heart was in her throat.

Becca opened her mouth as if she was going to argue, but then let out a sigh and nodded. "Okay. You can go."

Chapter Twenty-Three

Once more, Lar stretched next to Sophie within his shard, but this time, there was no tension or strain in keeping themselves apart. She pressed her body against his, one arm draped over his back as she propped her head up with the other, her elbow bent and her palm buried in her lustrous brown hair. She watched him silently as he piloted them out of the Ceres base and programmed the shard to fly them to Earth.

The trip would be an excellent opportunity to discuss everything that had happened between them recently. Then again, thinking of having her close in the shard and being away from Ceres and the rest of the prism... Perhaps Lar would not program the most direct course.

"Thanks for taking me back," Sophie said.

Lar looked over his shoulder at her and arched an eyebrow. "There is no need to thank me." He would do anything for her.

She leaned closer, running her hand along his side and grinning. Waves of sensation washed over his skin and his spine plates rose in appreciation. His cocks swelled beneath him.

"Maybe I *want* to thank you," she said.

He was very glad he'd set their course for a leisurely route to Earth—and that he hadn't bothered to put on a shirt before they left. He engaged the autopilot system, then rolled to his side. The moment there was room for her, Sophie wiggled closer and wrapped her arms around his waist.

Warmth spread through him, his muscles heating beneath her touch. He pulled her against his chest, then leaned in for a deep, claiming kiss. Her fingers traced along the sides of his spine, tantalizing him with their proximity to his spine plates. The hum of electricity filled the small space as they paused.

"Is it safe for us to do this in here?" Sophie said breathlessly. "It's a little cramped, and we do light things up."

Lar smiled, kissing the nape of her neck. "Shards are very durable."

"I need to wear more dresses," she said.

"Dresses?"

His translation session described the word as a sort of overly long, flowing tunic. He didn't see how that would help, until Sophie leaned in and nipped his ear, whispering, "With nothing underneath."

A rumbling growl of approval vibrated through him. The thought of being able to drive himself into her whenever he wished made his cocks swell further. Heat tore up through his body, suffusing his chest. He pushed himself up so that he could grab her thigh, pulling her fully beneath him. As soon as he did, she wrapped her legs around his hips, gripping him with surprising strength. Sophie moaned in pleasure as his shafts rubbed against her core through their clothing. Her tunic inched up, exposing the warm skin of her belly to the tips of his crowns protruding from his waistband. He left a trail of need on her skin where he stroked her.

"I need you naked, Sophie," he said. "I need to bury myself inside of you."

"Then I'm going to need a little more room to work."

She unhooked her legs and rolled to the side when he rose above her, ducking beneath his arm. She kicked off her shoes, then shimmied out of her jeans and tossed them aside. The shard was spacious enough for her to sit up, but Lar could only prop himself on an elbow while helping with the laces of her tunic.

As he loosened the ties on her back, he watched the lines of blue light pulsing through her spine in sync with the beating of their hearts. She pulled the tunic over her head and he reached out to stroke the skin above her spine. She gasped, supporting herself against the wall of the shard. Her spine plates emerged, rippling along her vertebrae like waves, trails of their tingling energy twining around Lar's fingers as if trying to pull him closer.

"Mate," he said.

She turned, eyes smoldering with need, and launched herself at him—again, with surprising strength. Was she still using her wristbands to augment her abilities? His thoughts scattered as her soft lips claimed his and she pushed him onto his back, straddling him. He reached between them, clasping a breast and rolling one of her nipples between his fingers. She moaned against his mouth, her smooth tongue darting in to explore him.

She trailed the backs of her fingers down his abdomen, playing with his muscles and tracing their lines. His breath stuck in his chest as a fire lit along his nerves stronger than a solar flare. She drew her fingertips along the waistband of his jeans and he moaned as she reached his thick lengths jutting out from them. His cocks jerked in response to her touch, straining against the frail Earth fabric.

Deftly, she undid the fastener, then grasped his primary cock, squeezing him hard and pumping her hand along his shaft. His nerves flared to life beneath her ministrations. She spread his jeans wide, pushing them down his hips to gain more access. Her need flowed into him through their bond—a need that mirrored his own. He wanted her to straddle him, to bury him as deeply within herself as she could. Instead, she slid down his torso and wrapped her lips around his secondary cock.

Pleasure surged through him, threatening his self-control. Arcs of electricity licked the crystal ship, buzzing and snapping around them. Waves of iridescent colors rippled over the walls, absorbing the energy they emitted. Sophie kept moving on his primary cock, squeezing and stroking. Her lips tightened over his crown, her tongue passing over his most sensitive skin in patterns that pushed him to the brink of ecstasy.

She released his primary cock and grasped the secondary, giving it her full attention. She wrapped both hands around him and pumped her hand fast and hard. His back arched as a guttural roar broke from him, his cock releasing itself in her mouth as she matched his thrusts until he was spent.

His mind was still spinning as she crawled on top of him and slid her slit over his primary cock, renewing the erotic energy coursing through his body. She was wet for him, her core ready from their recent foreplay. The moment their bodies aligned, she pushed herself down, taking him in deep. She tightened her sheath, moaning with pleasure as she rocked her hips above him, sliding him almost out of her body, then crashing back onto him. Lightning arced from her spine to the walls of the ship. The same energy pulsed through him, sparking along his nerves as she led him to the brink once more.

Unity with her was beyond his greatest dreams.

He felt himself swell, filling her. Her core was so tight, so perfect. He arched his back so that he could reach up and take one breast in his mouth, flicking his tongue across her nipple and then sucking it hard. She gasped, her sex pulsing around him.

He thrust up into her, harder, faster, meeting each gyration of her hips. Throwing her head back, she screamed his name as he pounded into her. Her release pulled him into his own. He emptied himself into her, jets of his seed shooting into her body as pleasure as blinding as the light they emitted racked through him. He kept thrusting, her hips firm in his grip, his cock throbbing within her as her own body gripped him tight. Spent, she collapsed on top of him, her hair feathering over his chest.

In a gasping voice, she said, "Well, we certainly made that work."

"Yes." He took a few panting breaths as he calmed. "I don't think I'll ever look at this vessel in quite the same way again."

They both laughed, limbs tangled and warmth mingling in the space. Rainbows of light floated around them. Sophie reached out as if to touch one. Her finger passed through it.

"Did you mean what you said earlier?" He surprised himself with his question, though he knew it was rising to the surface of his thoughts. His chest tightened in anticipation of her response.

"I'm really chatty. You need to narrow it down."

"About children."

"Of course, I did. I talk a lot, but I mean what I say. I want a million children with you."

"That's quite a few to care for."

"Let me clarify. I mean what I say, but I exaggerate. A dozen should be fine. Not so many that we can't give them all attention, but enough to fill a house. An enormous house."

His hearts pounded. The idea of a home with her—a home filled with children—created such longing in his soul he could hardly bear it. The skin along his back prickled and his spine plates vibrated with such strength he wondered if they might break through the crystal beneath him.

"I guess we'll need a house first," Sophie said. "Could we settle in Harbor? Unless you want to live on Cygnus-Prime." A spike of anxiety passed through her. His hearts raced along with hers. "My family is really close, and I'd miss them if I didn't get to see them often."

"You needn't worry. We cannot live together on Cygnus-Prime. The gravity fields of my home system would crush you, and the radiation would be lethal."

"Oh," she said. "So, you don't mind settling on Earth, then?"

He laughed. "Anywhere you are is my home."

Her concern vanished as a flood of love rushed into him.

"You've earned yourself another kiss with that." She pushed herself up to kiss him again, gentle and lingering, then she rested her head on his shoulder as he traced a line up and down her back—not quite along her spine.

"Dash will love Harbor," Sophie said. "We can get her some sheep."

"I don't think I know what those are, but sure."

Sophie's laughter rang through the vessel, but quickly faded. A pang of longing and sadness rose in her, echoing through their link.

"What is it?" he asked.

"I'm still afraid," she said. "That I won't be able to tell who is real. Aside from you and the rest of the prism. I hate being wary of my own dog."

"We'll figure something out. Perhaps the Vegans know more of how to detect Scorpiians."

"I hope so."

Since Dash was in Harbor, that was where the shard was heading. Lar had asked Buddy to arrange for Cyan to meet them there. If they could determine that Dash was not the Scorpiian shapeshifter, perhaps they could bring the dog along with them when they returned to Ceres. Lar was certain that would please Sophie. The shard was small, but there was room for another life form. One thing he knew, though. If they added a passenger in the shard, he'd be setting a direct course back to the *Arrow* when they left Earth.

He held Sophie against his chest and allowed himself to bask in her warmth and love. They didn't know what awaited them on Earth. This moment of peace might need to tide them over for some time. He was determined to enjoy it.

Chapter Twenty-Four

Harbor, Kansas
Sol System - Planet 3
Earth:

Sophie's heart pounded as Lar piloted the shard into the Cygnians' hangar in Harbor. She had never met a Vegan, but they sounded so intimidating. She needed Cyan's help. This meeting had to go well.

The ship drifted to a stop, hovering several feet off the ground. Lar hummed a note that Sophie felt more than heard, and the floor beneath them swung open, becoming a ramp. Instinctively, she reached for the wall as she started to slide out, trying to find something to hold on to. She let out a squeal when Lar grabbed her waist as he slid past. He landed on his feet under the ship, keeping her upright and grinning down at her.

"That was... exciting," Sophie said, panting as she regained her balance.

"We Cygnians like to make an entrance."

He took her hand and led her toward the large open doors at the front of the building. Sunlight streamed into the space, reflecting off the shard and casting rainbows against the hangar's walls. Sophie craned her neck to look at them, letting Lar guide her forward.

"Wow, that is beautiful," Sophie said.

"Indeed."

She started at the high, unfamiliar voice, whipping her head around to see her first Vegan. The brilliant grass of the field around the star port spread before her, darker green trees swaying in the distance. Someone cleared their throat low to the ground, cutting into the chorus of cicadas. Sophie dropped her gaze. Her eyes widened, and she sucked in a breath. She stifled a squeal of excitement while her mind spun, processing the being in front of her.

Everyone was so in awe of the Vegans, Sophie imagined them as sentient raptors. Nothing like the being standing before her just outside the hangar. Nobody said they were *teeny* lizard-people. Teeny, totally adorable lizard-people. Sophie had already possibly caused one interstellar incident—she would not cause another. She pinched her lips together to keep from saying something she would regret.

Cyan couldn't be much over three-and-a-half feet tall, standing a bit hunched over. If she got down on all fours, she'd be a quarter of Dash's size and would look a lot like a cross between a giant-sized baby iguana and a basilisk lizard, complete with a row of long spines running down her back and most of her tail. Her scales gleamed emerald, and black stripes lined with beautiful, bright blue spread out from her spine, trailing along her sides.

The silver bands of her exosuit caught and reflected the light from the late afternoon sun, wrapped tightly around her arms, legs, neck, and tail and curving over her abdomen like another rib cage. The gold eyes in her round head glinted and she angled her neck in a reptilian manner as she regarded them, her wide mouth pulled in a frown and her tail swishing behind her in what Sophie was sure was agitation.

Cyan crossed her arms over her tiny chest. "I believe protocol dictates that you arrive and depart after dark."

"But the protocol can be deviated from in emergencies," Lar said. "Regardless, our cloaking device did not fail."

Cyan made a little clicking sound and frowned. "I suppose. But what is this emergency that is so important you took that risk? Buddy said you wished to consult on 'compatibility issues.' I cannot think of a related scenario that warrants breaching protocol, unless Kral and Becca or Nuar and Lian have... injured themselves." Her cheeks turned rosy, and she looked away.

So... cute...

Sophie's stomach filled with butterflies. She wanted to slap her hands to her face and let out a long, "Awwww," but was pretty sure Cyan wouldn't appreciate that. The Vegans were basically running around in the Land of the

Giants. Sophie didn't want to annoy the alien.

"There is more to our situation," Lar said.

"A lot more." Sophie snapped her mouth shut and pinched her lips between her teeth.

One of Cyan's brow ridges rose. "Are you... alright?"

Sophie nodded vigorously. Lar chuckled, his amusement fluttering across her awareness. She scowled at him.

"We have been through quite a bit in the last few hours," Lar said. "Sophie even more in recent days."

Cold spread through her stomach at the unwelcome reminder of her abduction, but she fought it off, focusing on Lar's comforting presence. She was a Cygnian warrior now. If a Tau Ceti tried to take her again, she'd unleash her new shock powers on them. The idea chased away the chill.

"I'm not the one who literally came back from the dead," Sophie said.

"What?" Cyan's eyes widened, and she took a few steps closer to Lar. "Cygnians crystalize upon death. It is impossible to recover from that."

"Nuar and Bron can provide you with data on the Earth treatments they used to reverse the crystallization process," Lar said. "But it was my soulmate connection with Sophie that enabled me to return to my body."

"You... returned." Cyan wrung her long, thin fingers together, her scales losing some of their luster.

"That's what we wanted to talk to you about," Sophie said. "At least partly."

"I believe the Maker changed us somehow," Lar said. "She told me she could use my connection to Sophie and the prism to—" He shook his head. "I'm trying to remember. What she said made little sense. Something about a game?"

Cyan's eyes widened, her pupils narrowing to the tiniest of lines. She took a few steps back, her tail thrashing behind her. The color of her scales morphed to a pale lime.

"The Cygnian Maker," she gasped. "You... You saw her? Spoke with her?"

"I did." Lar cast a glance at Sophie, his concern as obvious in his furrowed brow and tight lips as it was through the anxiety creeping along their bond.

"What—" Cyan swallowed hard. "What did she look like?"

"She was beautiful," Lar said. "A clear, crystalline blue, with tall antlers and four arms. Her eyes were every color imaginable."

His concern transformed to wonder as he spoke of the Maker, filling Sophie with the same warmth and awe. She wished she could have seen what he had, but then, now that she knew she had a Cygnian soul, she guessed eventually she *would* see their Maker. The idea was unsettling, especially given Cyan's reaction.

"Praxxa," Cyan whispered.

"Is that like… a Vegan swear word?" Sophie asked.

"What? Nothing." Cyan stood straighter, though her tail whipped around so strongly, her body vibrated with the movements. If this kept up, she was going to dislocate it.

Sophie knelt in front of the Vegan and used her calmest voice. "We don't want to upset you. We need your help and didn't know who else to turn to."

"I cannot help you with your Maker," Cyan said.

"But—" Sophie began.

"I *cannot* help you with your Maker," Cyan repeated.

"That isn't what we're asking for," Lar said.

"What do you expect me to do?" Cyan's eyes narrowed the slightest bit.

"The Maker did something to Lar and me," Sophie said. "His spine plates are still crystallized, and they have electricity running through them. And I have these."

She leaned forward, twisting so that her back was toward Cyan. How did Sophie summon her spine plates? She tried to think about how upset she'd been earlier when confronting Ehmach and Korvin, the first time the energy had appeared. Her stomach twisted, but her back didn't change. How upset did she have to be? She thought of Tobek shocking Lar. Tears filled her eyes, and she blinked them away. Still nothing.

"Dangit," she said.

"Dang what?" Cyan asked, her voice calmer. "What am

I supposed to be looking at?"

Sophie sighed. "I can't bring them out."

"Allow me to assist," Lar said.

He reached down and lifted Sophie to her feet, then spun her around and pulled her close, leaning in to kiss her. At first, all Sophie could think of was the pair of wide, golden lizard eyes watching them. But then Lar deepened his attentions, his heat and desire flowing into her, and her thoughts vaporized. Her toes curled and her skin rose in gooseflesh, energy began coursing down her spine.

"Cygnus-X what in the name of the Solar Cross has happened to you?" Cyan hissed in surprise.

Lar broke off the kiss, grinning. It took Sophie a moment to remember what was going on. The little lizard-person circling around them helped. Sophie turned and made shushing noises, checking to see if anyone had heard them. No one was within eyesight. As Sophie spun, Cyan followed, keeping her shocked eyes glued to Sophie's back.

"How did...? What did...? When did...?" Cyan stammered.

Sophie kept trying to turn to face Cyan, but the little lizard person matched her movements. Finally, Sophie broke out laughing.

"You're making me dizzy," she said.

Cyan stopped at last, placing her hands on top of her head. "This is unprecedented. Absolutely amazing."

Lar chuckled, the deep vibration reassuring Sophie. "We had hoped you could use your exosuit to scan Sophie and me to see how extensive the changes to our physiology are," Lar said.

"And, also scan Lian and Becca and see if anything's up with them," Sophie added. "The Maker hit all of us with some kind of silver light-ray."

"I... I cannot," Cyan said, shaking her head.

Sophie's stomach dropped. If Cyan couldn't help them, who could?

"What do you mean you cannot?" Lar asked.

"I do not even know where to start." Cyan was still wringing her hands, though her tail had slowed. Sophie felt awful to have upset her so much.

"How about with a simple scan?" Sophie suggested. "You can compare us to whatever the regular data would be for our people."

"No, it is not that," Cyan said. "You wish to keep this secret, and I truly understand why. But anything I scan with my exosuit is processed through the Vegan Life Ship's core processors, which all of us have access to." She blushed and looked at the ground. "Maintaining privacy has been an issue for me before."

"What did you do, then?" Sophie asked.

"I went to Rin for help," Cyan said. "He is a Coalition field medic and was of great assistance."

"We'd like to keep the Coalition out of this for now,"

Lar said. "But if you could use our technology and assist with analyzing the data, even that would be a great help. Your knowledge is invaluable."

Cyan made a series of disapproving clicks, her eyes narrowing further. At least some of the color was returning to her scales.

"It's just until we find out a little more," Sophie said. "Like I mentioned, there's... a lot going on."

"Beyond *this?*" Cyan said.

Sophie's eyes filled with tears. She blinked them away. If only this was the biggest thing she was dealing with. Life would be so much simpler. She squatted down, hugging her knees to her chest.

"Cyan, can I trust you?" Sophie asked. "I mean really trust you?"

To her credit, Cyan didn't reply immediately. She was thinking through her answer. Her eyes widened, and she cocked her head to the side in that distinctly reptilian manner. Her tail whooshed back and forth several times, then calmed. She turned and looked out at the green field across from the hangar bay and the town beyond the trees, dropping her hands to her sides.

"I will not endanger Earth," Cyan said. She turned to Sophie at last. "Nor my people."

"I would never ask you to," Sophie said. "But we need your help. Lots of people need your help, and we don't have anyone else to turn to. Kral's parents are becoming outright hostile toward us."

"Sophie." Lar gasped, a surge of unease traveling through their bond.

"If we can't trust her with that, there's no way we can trust her with the rest of it," Sophie said.

The skin around his eyes tightened, but he nodded. "Very well."

Returning her attention to the Vegan, Sophie continued. "I'm tangled up in a whole mess of stuff. Lives are depending on me, and I don't know what I'm doing. Please, I need your help."

Cyan opened and closed her mouth a few times. She looked back at the trees and took a deep breath, then let it out.

"You can trust me with your secrets, though I must tell you that I will share them with one other," Cyan said.

"Another?" Sophie said. "Who?"

Cyan's cheeks turned pink and the blue stripes that traced the black along her spine grew brighter. "Periwinkle. We do not keep secrets from each other. He is my boyfriend."

Sophie nearly lost her balance at the image of two adorable lizard people holding hands and staring at each other with the soft look that had entered Cyan's eyes. Maybe their tails would twine up in a little heart.

So... cute...

She did her best to hide her reaction. Behind her, she

sensed Lar's amusement—more toward her than the thought of the Vegan couple, probably. The tension within them both eased, reflecting through one another.

Sophie cleared her throat. "If you trust him, we'll trust him."

"Wait, is this the Vegan known as Peri who sometimes visits Harbor?" Lar asked.

"He is." Cyan straightened and puffed out her chest a bit. The green had fully returned to her scales.

"This is quite fortunate," Lar said. "I know him. Peri is an engineer. His help will be invaluable to us with... our investigations."

Cyan narrowed her eyes. "Just what have you both become 'tangled up in?'"

"A lot." Sophie shook her head and stood.

"We would like you to accompany us to the *Arrow*," Lar said. "We can explain more there."

"Where is the *Arrow*?" Cyan asked.

Lar and Sophie exchanged a glance, neither knowing how to respond.

Lar finally said, "Not... here."

Cyan narrowed her eyes further and let out a low hissing noise. It seemed more a sound of frustration than anger. She looked past them and said, "Well, we will not all fit within your shard."

"We thought you would pilot your own vessel," Lar said.

This time, the snort she let out was one of absolute frustration. She crossed her arms over her chest and said, "I am not permitted to pilot vehicles of any sort. Apparently, I am 'dangerous.'" She made sarcastic air quotes at that word, then crossed her arms again.

Sophie pinched her lips between her teeth to keep from laughing. What had Cyan done for which she was banned from piloting?

"Peri can assist," Cyan added.

"That is excellent," Lar said. "If you wouldn't mind, could you perhaps give Sophie's dog a ride?"

Sophie's heart lurched. She didn't want Dash to go with someone else. Sophie wanted to be with her. The main reason she insisted on being the one who met with Cyan on Earth was so Sophie could reunite with her dog. Her stomach churned as she thought of the rest of it.

And to find out if Dash really is Dash.

Cyan's face lit up and her eyes grew wide. "A dog? I would relish the opportunity to study this life form more closely. I am a xenobiologist myself."

"Then we are indeed fortunate," Lar said.

"Dash might be a little much for you to handle," Sophie said. "Border Collies have a lot of energy."

Cyan waved her hand dismissively. "My exosuit will assist me in handling her safely."

"Sophie," Lar said, stepping closer. "If we are to trust them, we need to *trust* them."

Cyan looked back and forth between the pair, but remained silent. He was right. Sophie needed to trust. But was she really ready to know the truth that scared her more than almost anything?

"Dash is one of the other things I need your help with," Sophie said, her voice small.

"Oh?" Cyan cocked her head to the side.

"Can you scan for life forms in this area?" Sophie asked. "Like every single known type of life form?"

"I can." Cyan nodded.

"So, like, Lyrians and squirrels and dogs and cats and Sadirians and Cygnians and Scorpiians..." Sophie tried to make the list as long as she could to hide the importance of that last alien sentient. It didn't work.

"Do you mean the Earth insect or the shapeshifters from the Scorpii system?" Cyan asked.

"The..." Sophie's throat was suddenly tight. She coughed to loosen it. "The second one."

"My exosuit can detect them." Cyan lifted her hands and spun in a slow circle. "We have increased security greatly since we learned of the Scorpiian Dean's presence in Harbor."

Lar reached out to rest his hand on Sophie's shoulder. She stood, then leaned her back against his chest. He wrapped his arms around her.

"Amplifying our scans for detection of pheno-adaptive life forms was one of the first things we did as part of those measures," Cyan said. "My scanners are only detecting wildlife from Earth in the surrounding area, aside from the staff in the command center of the spaceport we are—" She stopped when she looked up at Sophie, angling her head to the side and stepping forward quickly. "Are you all right?"

"No," Sophie said. "I'm not."

Cyan reached out and gently rested her fingers on Sophie's elbow. "These things that you are tangled in, I am guessing the Scorpiian Dean is involved?"

Sophie bit her lip and nodded.

"He's been targeting Buddy's family," Lar said.

"I had heard as much," Cyan said.

"I'm afraid…" Sophie blinked back the tears filling her eyes. Her stomach pitched and clenched. "I don't know who to trust, except Lar, the prism, and their soulmates. He told me Vegans can detect Scorpiians, so I figure Dean can't replace you, but I don't know who is themselves anymore. Anyone could be Dean. Even my dog."

"Sophie," Lar said, stroking her hair.

"What if he took her?" she said, the tears finally spilling down her cheeks. Her next words hollowed her out. "What if my dog isn't my dog and… What if Dash is gone?"

"Where is Dash now?" Cyan asked, her voice gentle.

"She's staying with Lian's friend Olivia." Sophie sniffed.

"I know Olivia," Cyan said. "She operates the library in Harbor. You have nothing to worry about. We scan the entire town for Scorpiians continuously. If Dash were not Dash, we would be aware of it."

Sophie clamped a hand over her mouth to quiet the sob she couldn't stifle. Dash was Dash. Her dog was safe—at least, for now. Sophie shook as a wave of relief passed through her body. She turned and wrapped her arms around Lar, burying her face against his chest as the tears wouldn't stop.

Ever since the Tau Ceti had abducted her, she'd been so worried about everyone she loved. Hayley was missing, Amy was hurt, Dash might not be Dash. The list kept repeating, over and over. Sometimes, Sophie thought it would drive her mad. But she had channeled her fear into training. She knew she had to stay focused to help protect people. Now she knew Dash was safe. It was 'one less thing' on an endless list of seemingly impossible tasks.

"You poor being," Cyan said. "You have been through a great deal in the past few days."

"There is more," Lar said.

Cyan nodded. "I feared as much."

Sophie couldn't bring herself to turn around. She clutched Lar tighter.

"Sophie was not the first Earthling to be abducted," Lar said. "Nor was Lian. Dean and the Tau Ceti have taken others—human and animal alike. We don't know where they are, why they were taken, or what has been done to them, aside from genetic engineering and perhaps cybernetic enhancements."

Cyan let out a low hiss. Sophie heard the air snap as Cyan's tail whipped back and forth again.

"If Earthlings have been abducted, we should reach out for help now," Cyan said. "The Elders must know or at least Earth's Department of Homeworld Security."

"They've been gone a long time." Sophie's voice was muffled against Lar's chest.

"If we move too quickly, we risk making things worse," Lar said. "Our enemies do not know that we're aware of what they've done. We must be careful not to reveal what we've figured out so far. That is why we need your help—to learn more before approaching others."

Cyan clicked a few times, but then patted Sophie's back.

"I will discuss this with Peri and your prism," she said. "But I will not endanger this planet or my people—and I consider Earthlings among them."

"We understand," Lar said.

"Sophie." Cyan's voice was so gentle. Sophie turned to face the tiny Vegan, pulling away from Lar a bit. When she did, Cyan took Sophie's hand in hers, the scales rough against her fingers. "We will get Dash and Peri and return to the *Arrow* with you. No matter what course of action we take, we will venture into this future together. I will do my best for you."

"Thank you." Sophie bent down and wrapped her arms around Cyan. The Vegan stiffened for a moment, then melted against Sophie, patting her back.

"Hmm," Cyan said, a soft chuckle to her voice. "I have often wondered what these felt like. I see why humans are so fond of hugs now."

Sophie stood and wiped at her cheeks. "Well, there's plenty more where that came from."

Cyan smiled and nodded. "Then let us begin."

Chapter Twenty-Five

The group headed toward Harbor's library after leaving the hangar, walking through the field where Lar had imagined his and Sophie's children playing. His hearts warmed as he realized that was now a possibility. He took in a breath to ask Cyan if she might be willing to help them sooner rather than later, but a burst of intense excitement from Sophie distracted him.

"Dash must be so full of energy," she said. "I haven't run her through any of her exercises in days."

"Exercises?" Cyan trotted to keep up, her body angled forward and her tail undulating behind her.

"Dash competes in agility challenges," Sophie said. "It's something Earthlings train certain dogs to do who have the proclivity. If Dash didn't have that outlet, she'd go crazy."

Cyan jerked her head back on her neck a bit—another reptilian mannerism. "Then you must certainly run her through these exercises as soon as possible."

Sophie laughed, her excitement growing even stronger as they neared the town. "I have a portable practice course at home that I take to the dog park with her sometimes."

She turned to Lar and asked, "Do you think we could stop by there and pick it up?"

"I'm not sure how much I can fit in the shard, but perhaps Cyan could help with this as well?" he said.

"Peri and I will take it," Cyan said. "His shuttle should have ample space, as he transports... various projects in it."

The way she looked aside and twined her fingers together made Lar wonder just what kind of 'projects' she was referring to. Perhaps this pair was an even better match for the needs—and methods—of his prism than he thought.

"Thanks so much," Sophie said. "Can you meet us at my house in Florida, then? I think we can get Dash that far."

An excited Dash and an excited Sophie sharing the shard with him... Lar hoped she was right. He chuckled as he imagined the chaos that was sure to ensue from the three of them cramming into the small space.

Cyan nodded. "I see no issue with meeting you there. Peri is aboard the *Reckoning*, and is most likely occupied at the moment, but we should be able to arrive shortly after nightfall."

"Great." Sophie's happiness warmed Lars' hearts.

"I'll send you the coordinates," Lar said.

"Thank you." Cyan bowed as they reached the edge of town. "I will prepare for our journey and see you soon."

Lar's chest tightened as Sophie bent down and hugged Cyan again. He had never seen anyone hug a Vegan before or seen them hug each other. The little lizard's cheeks pinked, and she patted Sophie's back. He let out his breath, relief washing through him.

"Such an odd custom," Cyan murmured.

"Let me know if it ever gets tiresome, and I'll stop," Sophie said.

Cyan smiled. "I doubt it will, but I shall keep that in mind."

She turned to Lar and took a somewhat jerky step forward, then extended her arms. Was she offering him a hug? Lar could scarcely believe it. He knelt down on one knee and gently put his arms around the little Vegan. Her chuffing laugh tickled his ear as she patted his shoulder.

"Such an odd custom," she said again, pulling back.

Lar rose to his feet. "I will not forget your kindness to my mate."

"And I will not forget that you promised I could spend time with your dog." She wagged a long finger at them, a wide grin stretching her lips as she turned and walked away. "Such a wonderful opportunity to study them. I wonder if they are as soft as they appear?"

"They're even softer," Lar called after her.

He was beaming when he looked back to Sophie. She threw her arms around his neck, laughing. Her joy burst through him, his hearts pounding with it, matching her beat.

"Thank you so much for helping me be with Dash."

"Of course." Lar held her tight, relishing the warmth of her love—both toward him and her dog. How happy would Sophie be when they were actually reunited? "We should go get her."

Sophie nodded, then grabbed his hand and pulled him down the sidewalk. He laughed again, his smile growing as her enthusiasm flowed into him during the short walk to the library. As soon as they arrived, Sophie rushed through the door.

"Dash?" she called.

For a moment, Sophie held her breath, eyes wide as she stared at the dark wooden bookshelves blocking their view. She clapped her hands to her mouth as the thudding of clawed feet came from one row, tears flowing over her cheeks. Dash ran around a corner and bolted toward them. True to her name, she was incredibly fast. She paused a short distance from them and put her nose to the ground, letting out a high whine and wagging her tail so fiercely that her entire body shook from it.

"Sweetie," Sophie said, dropping to her knees. "Come here."

Dash's ears perked up, then she practically threw herself into Sophie's arms. Lar had never seen a life form thrash around with such excitement and joy. Dash licked Sophie's face and neck—anything she could reach—her furry butt thudding into Sophie as she wagged her tail and Sophie hugged her tight.

"Oh, Dash," Sophie said, sniffing. "Who's my good girl? You are. You're the best doggie."

"I'm a little partial to Zorro, but Dash is cool, too." A feminine voice that Lar didn't recognize sounded from the shelves of books. It was followed by a beautiful Earthling with long, dark hair and brown skin. She wore a pale blue dress with thin straps on her shoulders and shoes that flapped beneath her feet as she walked.

"Olivia?" Lar asked.

The woman nodded and extended her hand, which he shook in the Earth custom. "You must be Lar. It's nice to meet you."

"And you," Lar said. "Lian speaks highly of you."

Olivia arched an eyebrow. "Are you sure it's the same Lian that I know?"

"I am." Lar laughed and Olivia joined in.

"She can be... prickly," Olivia said. "I'm glad she's finally found someone who can handle her. An entire group of someones, really."

"I think she's awesome." The fur on Dash's neck muffled Sophie's voice. She had buried her face in it.

Sophie leaned back for a moment, then showered Dash with a dozen kisses. The dog had the biggest smile, lying across Sophie's legs. Sophie's own happiness kept flowing into Lar, her relief and hope filling him. Lightness suffused Lar's body. He felt almost as though he could float upon Sophie's joy. It was like nothing he had experienced before.

"You'll probably think everything is awesome for quite some time after this reunion," Lar said, his voice breathless.

"Dash missed you." Olivia glanced over her shoulder at the two enormous dogs splayed out on the floor. "Zorro tried to keep her happy, but Ed wasn't much help." Lian's Saint Bernard looked up briefly, then flopped back onto his side.

"Dash wore them out, didn't she?" Sophie said.

Olivia smirked. "You could say that."

"I really appreciate you taking care of her." Sophie rose to her feet, though she kept one hand on Dash's head. "If we can ever return the favor, let us know."

"'We,' huh?" Olivia arched an eyebrow again. "I was wondering what was up with you wearing those Cygnian leathers."

"They're so cool, right?" Sophie spun around.

Lar tensed a moment, but Sophie turned so quickly and the room was bright enough that the glowing line down her spine didn't catch Olivia's eye. He was eager for them to return to the rest of the prism at Ceres, and imagined that Olivia might have quite a few questions if she noticed them.

"Very nice look," Olivia said. "It'll be all the rage

soon."

Sophie laughed. "I bet."

Lar hated to cut their visit short when the women seemed to be getting on so well, but it was almost sunset. "We should head back to the hangar," he said.

"That's a good idea." Sophie scratched behind one of Dash's ears. The dog leaned into Sophie's hand, mouth open in a radiant smile. "I can get Dash to run off some energy before we leave."

"Her leash is by the door." Olivia pointed toward the side exit that led to the community greenhouse.

As the four of them headed to the door, Lar couldn't help but think of how their adventure on Earth had begun —with Nuar wrecking the greenhouse while testing his strength against a Lyrian who lived in Harbor. It had not pleased Lian when the pair of aliens crashed into her greenhouse, destroying the plants she was carefully cultivating. She started off hating Nuar, but they had come so far since then in only a few days. Lar's chest felt overfull as he thought of their future with something that had eluded him for his entire life—hope.

"Here you go." Olivia picked up one of the leashes hanging by the door and handed it to Sophie.

"Thanks again." Sophie leaned in, but paused. "Do you hug?"

Olivia smiled and said, "Absolutely!"

The women laughed as they embraced, warming Lar's

hearts further. They settled so easily into each other's energy. Was it possible that perhaps Olivia had a deeper connection to their prism than just her friendship with Lian? Lar must arrange for her to meet the other Cygnian warriors to see if there was something to his thought.

Sophie stepped back and made a gesture with her hand toward Dash. The dog immediately sat down, staring intently at Sophie. Dash remained that way till Sophie had attached the collar.

"She understands you?" Lar asked, surprised.

"Of course." Sophie headed out the door, Dash walking calmly at her side, and Lar followed. "This is what I do. I'm a dog trainer."

"I did not know."

There was much for them to learn about each other. Lar was eager to know everything he could about his soulmate. Sophie beamed at Dash, laughing and smiling. Sensing her joy, he was grateful he could help them be together. Their bond was something truly unique and beautiful to experience. When they reached the edge of town, Sophie took off Dash's leash and gave a high whistle. The dog tore through the green field, running faster than a beryl beast. Any time she ventured too far away, Sophie gave another whistle, and Dash returned.

"No wonder you're already so good at activating different commands on your wristbands," Lar said. "It would seem you've trained Dash using a similar concept."

Sophie laughed and smiled at him. "I guess so."

Her smile hit him deep in his bones. His soulmate was so joyful. The most joyful being he had ever met. And she was his. She caught him staring at her and her smile softened as she tucked a lock of hair behind her ear.

"What is it?" she asked.

"I am just thinking that I am the luckiest sentient in the universe."

"Nope, that would be me." She turned to him and wrapped her arms around his neck, pulling him down for a deep, claiming kiss. When she was done, she left their foreheads resting together. "You came back to me."

Her relief poured into him, her lingering fear and strengthening hope rising and falling like Earth's tides. She had been through so much. He captured her lips again as the depth of her love opened up before him. He could fall through it forever and always know contentment.

He broke off the kiss and said, "I will spend the rest of my life making you happy. This is a vow I will never regret."

She laughed. "No more vows. We don't need them. We're soulmates, after all."

"Indeed, we are."

Dash came running up to them, leaping in the air and prancing back and forth. She seemed as happy as Sophie, though with more energy. The trip to their home would be interesting.

"Let's get that gear of yours," Lar said. "Dash will need something to channel all that energy into if she's going to be on the *Arrow* for any length of time."

"Probably so."

They walked across the field toward the hangar as the last light of the day faded. They piled into his shard, Sophie holding Dash close as he situated himself at the controls.

"You sure you're okay with this?" she asked, lying next to him after the ramp closed.

"Of course, I am," Lar said. "Dash is your companion. She's mine now as well, if you're alright with me thinking of her that way."

Sophie's eyes brimmed with tears again. "I'd like that a lot. We're a family now."

Again, his chest filled to bursting with warmth. *Family.* It was not something he expected he would ever have, aside from his parents and his prism. He would do everything in his power to protect them.

Dash settled on his other side, that huge, open smile still on her face as she glanced around. She looked as though she thought this was all a glorious adventure. Perhaps it was. The greatest of his life.

He piloted the shard from the hangar, activated the cloak, and headed toward Florida, grateful that the trip would be brief. Dash whined a bit as they gained altitude. Sophie stretched across Lar to comfort her. Dash tucked her nose between her paws and rolled over so that her back was against Lar's side. He chuckled, then reached down to scratch behind her ears, as he'd seen Sophie do earlier. Dash relaxed further against him, closing her eyes.

Her nap was brief, as Sophie's home was only a few minutes away for his shard. He brought the ship down in their backyard, keeping the cloak active and dimming the lights within. Before opening the ramp, he considered any other ways they might give away their presence, as they almost had during their previous visit.

"You okay?" Sophie asked. "You seem a little tense."

"The last time we were here, we didn't consider our actions carefully enough. The *Arrow* hovered over the house while we went inside to help Amy and look for you. We kept the cloak active, but didn't think to turn off the lights within the ship. When the access platform lowered, light poured out of it."

"Did anyone see?"

"Yes, but luckily the Sadirians have experience in covering up such events."

Lar wasn't sure how the Coalition had spun the story, but was glad they had kept most of the planet unaware that aliens walked among them. Once the populace learned that other sentients were not only visiting but making Earth their home, undoubtedly some would object to their presence. Lar wanted to raise his children here with Sophie. They must proceed with greater caution to preserve that chance.

"I can't imagine how they explained a bunch of hot blue guys strolling around our yard," Sophie said.

"We at least managed that." Lar struck his wristbands together and activated the hologram that would camouflage his appearance. Light washed over his body, making his skin appear dark brown and his braids nearly black. When Sophie stared at him for several moments without speaking, he asked, "What? Do I not look human?"

"You look human, all right," she said. "I was just thinking I'm going to have to fight other women off with a stick."

He laughed at the image. "They wouldn't stand a chance against you. And it would be completely unnecessary."

She smiled, but an underlying tension of her own rose within her. "I haven't been back since Norem's goons kidnapped me."

"You are safe with me. I won't let anything happen to you. And I scanned the house as we arrived. It's empty."

She nodded, though her unease remained. Lar wrapped his arms around her and pulled her close. Sophie burrowed against his chest. With a whine, Dash rose and clambered onto Lar's side, pushing her nose between them so that she could lick Sophie's face. Sophie laughed, the edge of her anxiety softening.

"Thanks, girl," Sophie said, rising to kiss the top of Dash's head and rub her neck. "Let's get this over with."

Lar hummed the note that lowered the ramp. Dash half slid, half ran down it, then leapt to the ground. She truly was an agile creature. Lar and Sophie slid down after her, landing on their feet.

"That really is fun," Sophie said.

He smiled at her and took her hand in his as they walked to the sliding glass door that led to the living room. The Tau Ceti triad who abducted her had vaporized the original door, but Coalition soldiers had replaced it. Soldiers Lar originally believed to be behind Sophie's abduction and Amy's injury.

Dean's plot to pit the Cygnians against the Coalition could so easily have worked. Dean was a nuisance that Lar tired of. His prism would find the Scorpiian and end him, but first, Lar needed to get Sophie back to the *Arrow*. Back where she was safe.

Lar used his wristbands to unlock the door and slide it open. Dash bolted over the threshold, running to jump up on the couch. Once Sophie and Lar were inside, he closed the door again, keeping the vast insect population at bay. Sophie crossed the room and turned on the lights. She glanced around the space, one arm clamped across her stomach. Her anxiety returned, prickling down Lar's back and making his spine plates try to rise.

"Someone cleaned up," she said.

"The Sadirians. They didn't know who might stop by and wished to make sure there were no signs of the struggle."

Sophie looked around the room, though she didn't seem to be focusing on anything. He had no doubt she was seeing the room as she last remembered it. Splintered furniture, books everywhere, and a toppled shelf resting on her little sister—who had been shot. Lar walked to Sophie and pulled her against his chest, holding her tight.

"It is done," he said. "Amy is healing. You are free."

"I know. It's just... It's a lot. There's so much going on, I don't know what to feel first."

"Feel me," he said.

She laughed, then sniffed a bit. "I don't know if you realize how that sounded."

"I meant feel my love for you." He leaned in and nipped her neck. "But if the other meaning would also comfort you, I'm eager to assist."

Her laughter grew. She wrapped her arms around his neck and pulled him down for a kiss. He was just turning her toward the stairs when a rattling noise came from the front door. Sophie drew back from his embrace and wheeled toward the sound, a mixture of excitement and fear threading through her.

"Oh shit," she said. "That might be my parents."

She straightened her tunic and brushed her hair back past her shoulders. What started as a quick glance at Lar turned into a long stare.

"I don't suppose you brought along a shirt, did you?" she asked, smirking.

Lar lifted his arms, then let them drop to his sides. "I did not."

"It'll be okay." Her smirk blossomed into a smile as she stood closer, taking his hand in hers and turning to face whoever it was. She took a deep breath, anticipation rising in them both.

The door opened and closed around the corner. Wheels creaked against the tile of the foyer and keys clattered as they landed on a surface, out of sight. Dash began to whine. She jumped to the floor and slunk across the room, pressing her body against Lar's legs when she reached them. She dropped her nose to the dark umber carpet, glancing furtively toward the entrance.

"That's weird," Sophie said. "Dash loves my parents. She only started acting that way recently around—"

A young woman's voice called out. "Hello? Is anyone home?"

Sophie's terror hit him a moment before a wave of rage that made his spine plates snap up. His hologram couldn't hide them once they left the projection field, especially with their crackling new energy. Sophie shook her head tersely at him and gestured for him to remain calm. When he saw who walked toward them, pulling a small, wheeled container behind her, his spine plates being seen became the least of his worries. Sophie turned to the newcomer and swallowed hard.

"Hayley," she said. "Welcome home."

Chapter Twenty-Six

Sophie wasn't a violent person. Mercurial, yes, but she'd never had a temper. Bonding with Lar had brought forward a part of her that only used to appear when she heard of people mistreating animals—a part that honestly frightened her. As Sophie looked at 'Hayley,' all she saw was Amy lying on the floor, blood and scorched flesh covering her shoulder. All Sophie remembered was Rixon and Jaxa jeering at her in her prison cell and the story of how their boss—the *thing* in front of her—had tried to kidnap a Lyrian child.

Now, this void fucking alien was trying to trick Sophie into thinking he was her best friend. Her best friend who was somewhere in the universe, afraid, alone, maybe hurt. Hayley had been out there for *months*. Knowing what Dean was capable of, she probably didn't think anyone was coming for her. Sophie's hands tried to curl into claws, but she forced them to stay relaxed, not to let him know she was on to him.

It was all Dean's fault. All their suffering. He was going to pay with pain and blood or... whatever flowed through his veins.

My Cygnian soul wants to rip this piece of shit in half.

She needed him whole. Or at least able to talk. Could Scorpiians talk if she ripped him in half?

'Hayley's' red hair was in her standard ponytail, tufts out of place after a day of travel. Her skin was even paler than usual, like it always was when she returned from a long trip. She looked back and forth between Sophie and Lar, one eyebrow arched and her lips pursed, as though she held back a knowing grin.

God, everything about Dean's performance was perfect. The expressions, the way he moved. The way he wore Hayley's face. Sophie couldn't stand it. But she had to, just for a little longer.

"I thought you weren't coming back till next week," Sophie said. That had been the most recent lie Dean had fed her.

"My project wrapped up early." Dean gestured toward Lar, his brow furrowing and a smirk hitching the corners of his lips. "Who's this?"

Sophie forced a smile onto her face. Her cheeks prickled and burned, but hopefully, Dean thought it was embarrassment instead of rage. She stepped over to Lar and hugged his closest arm.

"This is Lar," Sophie said.

Smiling at Lar was easier. Masking the fear tightening her throat and make her heart race, not so much. She wanted to kill Dean, but wasn't sure she would be able to, even if she knew how. Lar would try, though. Or at least, he'd try to help capture Dean so they could question him about what he'd done with her best friend. If Dean found out they knew he wasn't Hayley, what would he do?

"Wow." Hayley's eyebrows rose as she gave Lar an astonishingly convincing once-over.

No, not Hayley. *Dean.* This was Dean. How was Sophie still thinking of him as her best friend? He was so freaking good. Guilt tore through her. He had fooled her for too long.

Dean's smirk grew more pronounced. "It's nice to meet you."

He cast a meaningful look at Sophie, a look they had shared so many times—a look *Hayley* and Sophie had shared. Sophie's gaze caught on light reflecting from Dean's wrist. He was wearing Hayley's charm bracelet. Sophie had seen him take it off over the last few months. That was Hayley's actual bracelet. Suddenly, information wasn't all she needed from him.

Sophie forced herself to smile. Heart pounding and willing Lar to trust her, she squeezed his hand, then released it and stepped toward Dean. All the way toward him. Her stomach roiled as she lifted her arms to hug him, her skin crawling as if spiders scurried beneath. Her spine heated, but she tried to tamp it down, imagining an icy waterfall flowing down her back.

"I missed you," Sophie said, taking his hand in both of

hers—the one where he wore the bracelet.

"Aww," Dean said. "I missed you, too." He looked over at Lar and arched an eyebrow, then leaned in close. "But something tells me you kept yourself busy while I was gone."

Sophie let out a brittle laugh. "I did."

Dean laughed as well, but stopped, furrowing his brow as he looked at her, his expression dripping with concern. "What's wrong?"

"I just..." Sophie clasped his wrist right above the bracelet. "I really do miss you," she whispered.

She tore the bracelet off and leapt back, hoping to get as far from Dean as she could in case he attacked right away. It... worked. The room flew past her vision as she hurtled across it, slamming into the wall hard enough to crack the plaster. She landed on her feet, flailing to keep her balance as dust settled around her. How had she done that?

"Sophie." Lar was at her side in an instant, his hands on her arms to steady her.

"What the hell was that?" Dean said, green eyes wide with shock. "What... What is on his back?"

The fury that rose up in Sophie would not be denied. Zings and crackles sounded along her own back as her spine plates flared, heat scorching the wall behind her and filling the room with the scent of ozone. Streams of electric-blue energy wound down her arms, spinning around her fingers and sharpening into claws.

"Oh my God, Sophie," Dean said. "What happened to you?"

"Stop pretending," Sophie yelled. "We know who you are."

"It's me," Dean said, his eyes pinched with pain and concern. "Hayley."

"No, you're the *thing* that took Hayley." Sophie struck her wristbands together and hummed the note that extended their energy blade. More crackling sounded from her back, and she felt a wave of power ripple down her spine, all the way through her legs and into the floor. Smoke rose above her feet as the carpet smoldered beneath her. "And you're going to tell me where she is right now."

Dean was so good. His eyes widened and filled with tears, and his mouth dropped open. He took a step back, shaking his head in disbelief. He looked so much like Hayley. *Just* like her. For a moment, Sophie doubted.

Dash didn't.

Dean screamed as Dash leapt at him, sinking her teeth into his arm. Sophie's stomach lurched. Dash had never attacked anyone before. What if Sophie was wrong, and this *was* Hayley?

Then Sophie saw the blood. Silver blood.

"You stupid beast," Dean said.

He kicked at Dash, but she was too fast. All that agility training was paying off. Dean's arms turned entirely silver and lashed out like whips. Dash avoided them, but kept lunging in, snapping, yet never quite connecting. Sophie wasn't sure she could get in close enough with her sword without getting Dash hurt. With her terrible aim, she didn't dare try to blast him while Dash was constantly bounding at him. At least Dash was holding her own.

Lar moved to the side in her periphery, raising his arms as he flanked the Scorpiian. A blast of blue energy flew out from his wristbands, hitting Dean's shoulder. The tissue vaporized, leaving a dripping, silver hole. It quickly filled in.

"What did you do with Hayley?" Lar demanded.

Dean avoided another of Dash's attacks with some impressive agility moves of his own. Dash pulled back, snarling as she looked for an opening.

Dean kept an eye on the dog, but managed to sneer at Lar and say, "What *didn't* I do with her?"

His words struck Sophie harder than any blow could have. All the air seemed to rush from her lungs, and tears burned in her eyes.

"You son of a bitch." She rushed forward with her sword raised.

Dean flipped over a chair between them. Sophie was about to jump over it, but Dash was right there. She ran up the back of the chair and leapt at Dean. Instead of dodging again, he grabbed Dash out of the air.

"No," Sophie screamed. "No!"

Dean glared at her for a moment, then his face and body began to glow. Hayley's form seemed to dissolve as he dropped to the floor, coils of silver entwining around Dash. He glowed brightly, then the light dimmed, leaving Sophie staring at two Dashes. Two absolutely identical Dashes. They lunged at each other, biting fiercely and shaking their heads when they scored a hit. Sophie had seen some vicious fights before, but nothing like this. She had to do something, but she didn't know which dog to help. All she knew was that she had to stop them before Dash was hurt.

Sophie deactivated her energy blade, then reached for the closest dog. She tried to lift it off the other, using her foot to fend off its opponent. This could be Dean in her grasp or it could be Dash. Lar rushed forward and grabbed the other dog. Both wriggled in their arms, trying to get at the other. Sophie couldn't tell them apart. Dean was even an expert at pretending to be her dog.

"How do we know which is him?" Sophie yelled, heart hammering in her chest.

"Cyan said ultraviolet light might work," Lar said. "Unless Dean has found a way around it by now."

"Then use it."

He nodded, then pointed his arm at the light fixture above them. His wristbands must be active already. One note plunged them into darkness, and the next he hummed flooded the room with violet light.

"Black lights?" Sophie said. "Seriously, that's all it takes?"

The dog in her arms glowed a vibrant blue-purple. Sophie was so surprised, she almost dropped him. She tightened her grip instead.

"Your shields, Sophie," Lar yelled.

Oh shit. She hadn't activated them, and she was holding one of the most dangerous life forms in the galaxy. Two more silver whips grew out of Dean's back. One connected to the suitcase he'd wheeled into the room. The other stabbed toward her, slicing her side. She staggered back, dropping the shifting form she held. Her hand instinctively went to her stomach. When she drew it away, blood coated her palm, a line of silver charms resting across it. Hayley's bracelet, still in her hand.

"Sophie," Lar screamed. He dropped Dash, and both rushed toward her.

She expected more pain. Her Cygnian leathers were torn, and through the gap, she saw a long wound along her side oozing an alarming amount of blood. The waistband of her jeans was already soaked.

She would not let Dean stop her. They were going to find Hayley, and when they did, he would pay. The coward was running. Not toward the door, but up the stairs.

"We have to stop him." She took a step forward, but the room spun.

Lar suddenly had her in his arms. He did something

with his wristbands, something that burned against the throbbing pain in her stomach when he waved his arm over her injury. Behind him, she saw a streak of black fur launching itself up the stairs after Dean.

"Dash," Sophie yelled.

Lar's eyes widened as he saw the dog in pursuit. He lifted Sophie into his arms and sprinted to the stairs. The walls streaked by as he leapt to the next floor. Their house had a long hallway that ended in a window. Dean was running toward it at full speed. Dash was following him just as quickly.

"Lar," Sophie gasped.

He quickly set her down. The moment her feet touched the carpet, she leaned against the wall for support, willing him to keep after Dash. Another leap had him right at her dog's tail. Lar wouldn't have time to catch Dean and Dash both. Her heart caught in her throat as she wondered which he would choose.

Lar grabbed Dash, tackling her to the ground just as she was about to bite Dean's tail. The Scorpiian leapt up, his front paws hitting the window and shattering it. Glass exploded outward, clinking as it scattered on the walkway below.

Chapter Twenty-Seven

Sophie waited for the 'thud.' She wanted to hear Dean land on the stone walkway, preferably breaking some bones. Did Scorpiians even have bones? Instead, a glowing silver light rose in the sky, morphing into a bizarre pterodactyl with an arc-shaped head and long tail trailing behind him. The glow faded, and with two strong beats of his wings, Dean climbed higher and vanished.

Tears burned her eyes. Sophie pushed against the wall, keeping one hand on it to steady her as she walked toward Lar and Dash. She ignored the dark smear her hand left on the wallpaper and slid Hayley's bracelet into her front jeans pocket, then gently pressed against the wound on her side. Whatever Lar had done to it, the skin was rough and sealed. The pain had retreated to a throbbing ache pulsing through her abdomen. It didn't hurt nearly as bad as her heart.

Dean had gotten away, and now he knew they were on to him. How could she ever find Hayley?

Lar stood with Dash in his arms. The dog was whining and staring out the window. Lar's remorse touched at the edges of Sophie's mind, but she couldn't share it. He had saved Dash. All Sophie felt was gratitude as she limped toward him. He smiled at her gently and nodded, her gratitude reflected in his hearts. But only for a moment.

His wristbands started to emit a beeping noise. It grew louder and closer together.

"That doesn't sound good," Sophie said as she reached them.

Lar's eyes widened as a wave of terror flooded from him through their bond. He grabbed Sophie, holding Dash tight in his other arm. Keeping both of them close against him, he ran for the window and leapt. Sophie was glad that Dean had broken it already. It kept them from getting cut up as they sailed through the open space.

Her breath caught as her heart pounded, wondering what was going on. She knew something was happening. Something bad. The sound from Lar's wristbands had become a single, high-pitched keen. She felt him humming, the vibration carrying through his chest, but had no idea what controls he was activating.

Time seemed to stop for a split-second, then all hell broke loose as her house erupted in a ball of fire. They were still mid-air when the shock wave hit them, flames licking the air all around. The blast propelled them forward even faster—over the fence and into the neighbor's yard. They splashed into Mrs. Wilcott's pool.

The chlorinated water stung Sophie's eyes as she looked above them to see more flames spreading across the surface, along with bits of debris. The inferno dissipated, and Sophie kicked upward. Lar pushed her and Dash both above the water.

Sophie gasped and sputtered, pushing away the pieces of wood floating closest to her. Dash immediately began swimming to the edge of the pool. Sophie glanced around, but didn't see Lar as she treaded water. Where was he? There were lights in the pool, and when she looked down, she saw him standing below her. What was wrong that he wasn't swimming for the surface? Had he crystallized again?

Panic tore through her, icy and sharp. His eyes still glowed bright, and a faint outline of gold covered his body. What was going on?

She took a deep breath and pushed herself under the water. Hooking her arms beneath his armpits, she tried to lift him up, but it was like trying to move a boulder. Her side blazed with pain, but she didn't care. She had to get him to the surface.

He reached out and touched her cheek, smiling gently. He hadn't crystallized? Then why was he just standing there? He pushed her back to the surface, keeping his hands on her hips to hold her up, then walked toward the shallow end of the pool. His head quickly rose above the waterline.

As soon as she knew he could hear her, she said, "Lar, are you okay?"

"I'm fine. Cygnians can't swim—we sink. I was able to activate my atmospheric generator before we landed. The same shielding that assists us in surviving space can also help us under water or in many other hostile environments."

Her heart hurt from its thumping, and each beat sent a sharp spike of pain to the wound at her side. A wave of calm pushed its way into her mind, flowing into her through their bond. She wrapped her arms around his neck as he strode up the steps and back onto dry land. Dash was waiting, panting and whining at them.

"I'm so glad you're okay," she said.

Lar set her down, a scowl on his face. She wasn't sure what was worrying him until he tugged at the hem of her tunic.

Right. She'd been stabbed.

He hummed a few notes. The gold light encasing him vanished. Sophie vaguely realized that he was dry. That shielding was really handy. The second note he hummed activated the scanning function of his wristbands. A hologram of her stomach appeared a few inches above her body. The more the lights flowed over her, the more details filled in. The wound didn't look deep. It was a graze, really. Flashes of red showed both the slash on her side and the skin where Lar must have cauterized it.

"You may have scarring," he said. "I'm so sorry. I didn't know what else to do. Nuar will heal it better. He might be able to—"

"Don't worry about it." Sophie rested her hand on his cheek. "I'm the soulmate of a Cygnian warrior. It'll make a great story for our kids when they notice it."

Regret, guilt, and a host of other emotions were wreaking havoc on him. She could sense that he was trying to shield her from them, but failing.

"Hey," she said. "This wasn't your fault."

"I should have protected you."

"You did protect me. And Dash. Besides, we protect each other."

He nodded, but wouldn't meet her eyes. That was unacceptable. She gripped his face in her hands and pulled him in for a kiss. She poured all of herself into it, willing him to sense her relief that they were safe, the love that she felt for him—that was only getting stronger. Dean might have gotten away, but they would track him down. They would make him tell them what he'd done with Hayley. They were Cygnian warriors, dammit, and no Scorpiian would get the best of them.

"Ahem." Someone cleared their voice behind them.

They broke off the kiss and turned to see Cyan standing in the ruins of the fence between the adjoining yards. Next to her, another Vegan stared, open-mouthed, at the flaming remains of her house. The outline of his black stripes was a paler blue than Cyan's.

"We... have come to pick you up," Cyan said.

The other Vegan, who must be Peri, walked toward them, but kept his face angled toward the smoldering building.

"Yes, we… Um…" Peri began. He let out an agitated chuff, then lifted his arms toward the fire. "What happened here?"

"It's kind of a long story," Sophie said.

"I can imagine—" Cyan began, but then yelled, "Vapor pits!"

Peri's eyes widened as lights flooded the yard. The next second, he disappeared. Just vanished from sight. He could turn himself invisible? Cyan dropped to all fours and jerked her head side to side, as an agitated reptile might. Her movements made her look exactly like a giant iguana.

"Sophie?" A familiar voice spoke behind her.

Sophie plastered on a smile as she turned to face her neighbor, stifling what would surely come out as an unhinged laugh. How were they going to explain this?

"Hey, Mrs. Wilcott," Sophie said. "This is my boyfriend, Lar. We're kind of having a rough night."

Mrs. Wilcott was in a pastel, floral-patterned bathrobe, her thin white-blonde hair was up in rollers. Her mouth hung open as she stared past them at the burning house. Cyan scurried into the bushes, her legs moving awkwardly as she tried to keep to all fours. When she reached the fence line, she pushed herself upright and ducked out of sight.

"I think we had a gas main blow up or something," Sophie said. "Lar here needs to get me to a doctor so they can check me out."

"Indeed." Lar bowed slightly. "It was nice meeting you."

Mrs. Wilcott looked away from the burning house, her cheeks turning pink and her shocked eyes entirely focused on Lar. "Oh," she said, practically fanning herself. "Yes. So nice..."

Lar picked Sophie up and started carrying her to her yard. Sophie actually heard Mrs. Wilcott sigh behind them. Dash followed Lar close behind.

"Could you maybe call the fire department for me?" Sophie called over Lar's shoulder. "Thanks."

Mrs. Wilcott raised her hand in a half-hearted wave, then turned to stare at the flames.

Back in their yard, a small square of light led them to Peri's cloaked vessel parked on the ground. Cyan was next to it, flailing her arms and gesturing for them to get inside quickly. Dash ran in before them.

"We have notified the Coalition that there was another... incident," Cyan said. "I am sorry, but they had to know to ensure the blaze is controlled. The local fire department is also on its way."

"That is not my concern," Lar said, ducking low to enter the ship. "Sophie is injured."

He set her down on a soft couch that hugged half of the

circular ship. In front of it, a control panel took up the wall. It was straight out of a sci-fi movie, with glowing buttons and blinking lights. The only odd thing about it was the "chairs." Three branches grew from the floor, arcing near the controls. Peri was lying on one, his tail wrapped around it to keep himself stable as he worked. It was yet another ship that would be incredibly uncomfortable for a human to operate.

The interior was all white—the floors, the couch, the walls—everything except for the gleaming chrome control panels. The top of the ship was entirely transparent. When this thing flew, it would look like a flying saucer. Not one of the all-metal kind, but equally cool. It was plenty spacious inside, though Lar's head was close to brushing the clear dome above them. He hovered close, his brow knit with worry.

Sophie almost wished the dome wasn't clear. She had a superb view of Hayley's house burning down. With the help of the Vegans and Nuar, her body would heal quickly, but their home…

The second floor collapsed into the first. Flames flew up into the sky, a shower of sparks floating into the darkness before going out. She felt the heat through the still-open hatch. There was no coming back from this.

"I will tow your shard to Ceres," Peri said, "while Cyan tends to Sophie's wounds."

"Thank you," Lar said. He held her hand in his,

interlacing their fingers.

This was her future. *He* was her future. And when they found Hayley… she would understand about the house. Sophie knew with even greater certainty that none of them could ever go back to life as it was before.

Chapter Twenty-Eight

Tau Ceti Epsilon Base
Ceres Dwarf Planet
Sol Asteroid Belt:

Cyan stared intently at her scans of Sophie, her lips pulled in a frown. The holoprojections displayed system after system of Sophie's body in various levels of detail, translucent images of her spine, her injury, and other anatomical points of interest rotating slowly in the space before them. Lar sat by, his chest tight as he watched the Vegan work. Cyan didn't look happy. She kept making clicking noises that somehow sounded disapproving.

Had Lar inadvertently made things worse? Cygnians rarely became injured. All their warriors received basic medical training on how to assist other life forms, but after everything he had been through, he had a unique perspective on how limited Cygnian medicine was.

"I'm okay," Sophie said, sending reassurance through their bond. "You can stop worrying."

"I will always worry over you." Lar lifted her hand to his lips and kissed it. He turned to Cyan and asked, "Are you able to heal her injury better than I could?"

"Hmm?" The Vegan absently glanced at him. "I have already addressed her wound."

Lar let out a gasping breath. He lifted the hem of Sophie's tunic to find her abdomen completely smooth. There was no trace of any damage—at least on the surface. Sophie sat up a bit and looked at her side.

"Amazing," Lar said.

"When did you even do that?" Sophie asked. "I mean, I was all warm and tingly for a minute, but I thought that was just whatever you did to dry Dash and me off."

Cyan chuckled. "I find it best to be quick about such things. The wound was shallow and easily addressed. I am more concerned by the deeper changes to your genetic structure." She shook her head. "This should not be possible."

"What shouldn't?" Sophie asked.

Cyan moved aside as Sophie swung her legs over the edge of the couch and sat up. Lar scooted close to her, wrapping his arm around her and tucking her against his side. Cyan waved her hand, dismissing the holoprojection. She stared at them for several long minutes until Peri glanced away from his controls and said something in their sibilant language. Cyan narrowed her eyes and hissed at him, then turned back to Sophie.

"Your DNA has been altered," Cyan said. "You are no longer entirely human."

"I figured." Sophie shrugged. "Lar said the Maker changed us—the human soulmates—through our bonds."

Cyan's lip curled up in a sneer and shook her head. "No Maker can change already existent DNA. Not like this."

"You sound like you've had some experience with Makers." Sophie's curiosity flowed out to Lar. "More than some, actually."

Peri twisted further toward them, a series of hisses, pops, and clicks peppering his speech. Cyan's scales turned an even more vibrant green, the blue surrounding her black stripes becoming almost livid as she responded in kind. Lar didn't have to understand their language to know they were having an argument.

Cyan snorted a breath out through her nostrils, then said, "I have experience with a vast amount of genetic information. While genetic engineering can take place during a life form's gestation, once the being is born, it is not possible to manipulate it to this extent. Your DNA has been changed on a fundamental level to include a great deal of Cygnian material. Over half of it is affected."

"Gosh, I guess I should have a hard talk with my parents." Sophie smirked and arched an eyebrow. Cyan did not seem amused.

"The Maker said that Sophie and the other soulmates of our prism carry the other halves of our souls," Lar said. "She told me that their links allowed her to alter them."

Cyan let out another sneering snort, her contempt

palpable. "And I am telling you that she does not have that power."

"Should you not speak of the Maker with respect?" Lar said, keeping his voice carefully neutral.

Apparently, it wasn't non-confrontational enough. Cyan's eyes narrowed to the merest slits and her shoulders rose, her hands curling into curved crescents ending in very sharp claws. Her lips peeled away from serrated teeth that glinted in the ship's light. Her tail thrashed back and forth behind her, cracking the air like a whip.

Even more frightening, her exosuit expanded, covering parts of her body in armor. Sharp edges grew from it, along with glowing protrusions that looked very much like blasters. Lar's hearts pounded, drawing Sophie's along with them. He pushed her farther back on the seat, trying to get between her and the irate Vegan without being too obvious about what he was doing. He didn't want to agitate Cyan further. Sophie didn't stop him, her confusion and concern adding to his own.

"Cyan!" Peri yelled, leaving his perch and running to join them.

He grabbed Cyan's elbow and pulled her away, murmuring something in their language. Cyan shook her head, her exosuit retreating to its normal bands and her scales returning to their usual color. Her stance lost some of its menace as she straightened. She still didn't seem pleased. Lar doubted he would ever view any of the

Vegans in the same way again.

"I apologize," Lar said, even more cautious about his tone. "I meant no disrespect to you, as well."

"It is I who am sorry." Cyan bowed curtly.

"You really hate her, don't you?" Sophie said, scooting forward on the bench. "I mean, this is personal. It's like you've actually met her." When Cyan turned away, Sophie continued, looking back and forth between Lar and the Vegans. "I thought your Makers were similar to the religions we have on Earth, but the more I'm learning about this…" She shook her head, unease rippling through her. "I'm starting to think this is something else entirely."

Before Cyan could reply, Peri said, "We are arriving at Ceres. Perhaps we should all focus on that, since Sophie seems in good health."

Lar wished Cyan had responded before Peri interrupted her. They were speaking of his Goddess as if they *knew* her. But then, did Lar not know her now as well? What kind of entity was she? He would speak with Tarn as soon as he was able. Then perhaps they would try to gain an audience with Cyan—when their prism was nearby to lend support.

Peri returned to his perch, Cyan resting on another branch beside him, though she kept her hands away from the controls as he piloted them into the access tunnel that led deep into Ceres. The ruins were even eerier seen from the clear dome of the Vegan vessel. Patches of ice in intricate shapes extended from ductwork that had exploded, the fluid freezing at the cold touch of space. Scorched rock and melted metal were everywhere, the oppressive dark corridors chilling him.

"Queen Ehmach was very thorough in her destruction of this Tau Ceti base." Peri's neck craned around as he looked at the remains they were navigating.

As they rounded a sizeable chunk of debris, the *Arrow* came into view. The crystalline ship hovered near the spot where Lar had first crashed his shard. The milky-white light from its hull lit up the dark cavern, calming Lar's nerves.

"Your ship is truly beautiful." Only a slight hint of tension remained in Cyan's voice.

"I would like to speak with your engineers." Peri cocked his head to the side. "The ability to cultivate and control the growth of crystal at this level would be very helpful in my experiments. It would seem Cygnian technology has surpassed our own in this regard."

"I'll introduce you to Tarn and Bron once we're aboard," Lar promised.

Peri brought his ship closer to the *Arrow*. When he released the tow beam on Lar's shard, Lar remote-piloted it into its position on the Cygnian mothership using his wristbands. Peri flew his own vessel underneath the access hatch. The platform that detached from the ship to open the hatch already hovered a few feet above the ground. It was large enough to accommodate the small Vegan ship. As soon as they touched down, the platform rose, bringing them into the *Arrow* itself. They made swift work of their decontamination procedures and filling the space with atmosphere.

Within minutes, everyone was in the common room, Sophie hugging her sister and enduring an inspection that had Lar cringing in shame. The tear in Sophie's tunic did not go unnoticed, and Sophie quickly related everything that had happened to them. She even went back and filled in Cyan and Peri with what had come before.

"I'm sorry that I could not protect her better," Lar said, his throat tight as he looked at Becca.

"From what Sophie said, you got her out of the house before it blew." To his surprise, Becca approached and hugged him briefly. "Thank you for saving my sister."

Sophie leaned closer to Becca and said, "'And her dog.'"

Becca laughed. "And her dog."

"It would seem you have all been swept up in quite a complex situation," Cyan said.

"I know this might not seem important with everything else going on," Sophie cast a warm glance at Lar, "but we really do want help having kids. Eventually."

Lar could feel her nervousness. He shared it. They weren't just asking for help with creating families, but with making sure those families were safe from the threats presented by Dean, the Tau Centauran Assembly, and even Cygnus-Prime, if Ehmach did not see reason.

"If we can determine what Norem and Dean are working toward, it may assist us with locating the missing Earthlings," Kral said.

"Hayley is like a sister to me. We have to find her." Sophie wiped at her face where a tear had escaped.

Becca stepped toward Sophie, pulling her into a hug. "She's like a sister to all of us." Becca released Sophie and moved away, glaring around the room as if daring any of them to disagree. "And with or without anyone else's help, we're going to get her back."

"You are asking us to assist you in making your family whole." Peri's voice was solemn. "Both the one that exists now and the one that you have yet to create in the future.

"We are." Sophie nodded.

Lar wrapped his arm around her and tucked her against his side. Cyan stepped forward and took Sophie's hands in hers and stared up at them with her golden eyes. Lar felt a surge of hope. He didn't know if it was his or Sophie's. He did know that he was holding his breath and could not let it out until he knew their decision.

Cyan glanced at Peri over her shoulder. After a brief pause, he nodded. Cyan smiled and turned back to them.

"We will assist you," she said.

It was as though the weight of a planet had lifted from Lar's shoulders. He nearly sagged from the relief. Sophie dropped from his embrace, kneeling in front of Cyan and throwing her arms around the tiny lizard person. Everyone in the room gasped, staring wide-eyed and waiting to see Cyan's reaction.

All except for Becca, who hissed, "Sophie! Knock it off," in a low tone.

"It's okay." Lar chuckled. "They hug now."

Becca shook her head. "Only Sophie could manage this."

Sophie leaned back, but kept Cyan's hands in hers. "Thank you so much," Sophie said.

Dash ran up to the pair, barking and wagging her tail.

"Ah, yes," Cyan said, beaming at the dog. "I look forward to becoming better acquainted with you as well."

Sophie stood as Cyan turned her attention to Dash, scratching the dog behind her ears. Lar pulled his mate close and wrapped his arms around her.

"I will start with a thorough examination of the Tau Ceti soldier, Tobek," Cyan said, moving away from Dash. "Perhaps his anatomy will provide clues about helping the others."

"Great." Tobek looked less than enthused.

"Nuar can assist," Kral said.

Nuar nodded, then gestured to the hallway that would take them to the medical bay. Tobek and Cyan headed off with him, the female Vegan already asking a stream of questions.

"I am most intrigued by this 'platform of lightning-death,'" Peri said. "I wish to inspect it."

"Bron will take you there," Kral said.

"Just be really careful with it," Becca added.

"And don't touch it." Sophie's agitation spiked for a moment.

"Of course." Peri shook his head and grimaced. As he fell in step next to Bron, he asked, "Are they always this... interactive?"

"Always," Bron grumbled.

"That pair are going to get along famously," Becca said.

"Indeed." Kral turned back to the room. "I want the *Arrow* in top condition. We have many who would oppose us and few who would help."

Tarn and Rom nodded, then headed in different directions to their respective posts. Dorn had already slipped away.

"Well, we have an exploded house to deal with," Becca said. "We're working with the Department of Homeworld Security already. They've been watching the place since the prism's first visit."

"Thanks for taking care of it," Sophie said.

Becca squeezed her hand. "Any time." She turned to Kral and said, "Come on."

He nodded, then followed her from the room.

Sophie wrapped her arms around Lar's waist, burying

her face against his chest. He stroked her hair, sending soothing calm to her—as much as he could manage, with his own hearts so full of emotion. They had achieved many victories, but had more challenges before them.

"I can't promise that everything will be okay," Lar said. "But I promise you I will do everything I can to get Hayley back."

Sophie actually laughed a bit as she looked up at him. "And deal with all that other stuff? Our laundry-list is pretty long."

"There is… a lot. But we will get through it."

Dash walked up to them and sat next to his leg. He scratched the top of her head and she leaned against him, staring up at him with a broad smile. Sophie smiled at him as well. He sensed her growing resolve and the beginning of a tentative hope.

"Of course we will," she said. "We defeated the Unmaker. There's nothing we can't do together."

"Then let's get started." Lar took her hand in his and led her from the chamber. He didn't know what the future had in store for them. All he knew was that he would face it with Sophie at his side, their souls at last complete. The promise of that future was more than enough for him.

Dorn left the common room as quickly and quietly as

he could when Becca and Kral began giving assignments to the others. There was no assignment more important than the one he already had—protecting Amy. He slipped into the room set aside for her. Nuar had moved her from the portable stasis pad to the bed. She was still heavily sedated and wouldn't wake up for hours.

Dorn stood in front of the wall across from the foot of her bed. Locking his joints and muscles in place, he could remain there for days if needed. He hoped he wouldn't have to wait that long to greet her, to hear her voice. Seeing Kral and Nuar, and now Lar, with their soulmates, and how well they all fit together, Dorn was eager to finally meet his own.

She rested on the bed, her shoulder-length brown hair spread over her pillow and her chest rising and falling in shallow breaths. He had spent days with Amy, watching over her, but he'd never heard her laugh or seen her smile. He'd never listened to her speak.

What would she be like? The other soulmates were so well matched, he had to believe he and Amy would be the same. That didn't mean he knew what to expect.

She looked frail as she slept. For a moment, the image of how he'd first seen her crashed through his mind. He saw her lying on the floor, her shoulder a burned mess from the Tau Ceti's blaster, her heartbeat so weak, they could scarcely register it. Dorn's spine plates rose, claws pushed forth from his fingertips. He would surely crack his teeth if he ground his jaws any harder.

She is safe now. She is with me.

He repeated the mantra over and over, willing himself to calm. The other Earthlings had surprised all the warriors with their strength—of resolve and of spirit. His Amy would be the same, he was sure of it, and yet, he felt a fear unlike anything he'd ever known as he watched her rest. He could barely stand being separated from her for even a few moments. At times, all he could think about was that she had almost been killed before they had even met.

More than he wanted to destroy the person responsible, he wanted her to wake up. He wanted her to open her eyes and look at him and to discover every way that he could make her happy and give her whatever she needed. All *he* needed was for her to be alright. He watched the soft rise and fall of her chest, counting each breath. Each one brought her closer to him. He could feel it.

"Come back to me, Amy," he whispered.

She sighed in her sleep, stirring for the first time. His hearts beat faster, pounding in his chest. A furrow appeared between her brows. She must feel it, his excitement, his longing. He would not put that on her. Willing himself to calm, the cadence of his hearts softened into a beat that he hoped would lull her back to rest. She drifted further into sleep again.

He settled deeper into his stance, letting a trancelike state of watchfulness fill his mind. When she woke, he would be here for her, with whatever she needed to feel safe and whole. When she woke, he would be ready.

Epilogue

Tau Ceti Alpha-3 Base
Orion Nebula:

Soft strains of Brahms drifted through the corridors of Orion-Alpha-3. Unlike the Epsilon base, the walls here were a gleaming burnished gold, with streaks of red and blue light darting along control panels both to please the eye and report the status of various systems. The floors were gunmetal blue, polished to a high shine and spotless. Everything was spotless. Norem would have it no other way.

The few elite soldiers privileged enough to be assigned to his most secretive base knew better than to complain if they didn't like the music. They knew better than to complain at all. Everyone did. Well, almost everyone.

Mindy whined within her room, pacing along the transparent wall that separated her from the rest of Norem's office. Her white coat needed to be brushed, but she wouldn't let anyone near her. The last time he had tried had resulted in... an unfortunate interaction.

Norem leaned back in his heavily padded chair,

rubbing the fingers that he'd required to be grafted on to replace the ones she had bitten off. Perhaps Mindy noticed, because she paused to growl at him. He chuckled, rising from behind his desk and crossing to stand before her. Light shone from his highly polished Earth-style shoes as his feet sank into the plush burgundy carpet.

"I don't understand why you're mad at me," Norem said, the thick Southern drawl he'd picked up on Earth affecting his words. "You're the one who attacked me. I was just trying to be friends."

Mindy whined again, and turned to look at the enormous cylinder that dominated the wall nearest her room. Bubbles continually floated within the transparent material of the tank, catching the lights embedded in its top and bottom. Norem loved to follow their movement. Even now, he felt a peacefulness fill his chest as he took a moment to stare at his greatest creation, his prize specimen, the pinnacle of achievement in his already accomplished career.

"I know—you already have a friend." Norem ambled over to the tank and stared within it for a time. He looked over his shoulder at Mindy. "Lots of people have more than one friend. Hell, I've ordered every single soldier on this station to be as nice as they possibly can to you."

He shrugged, turning back to the tank. "I suppose that isn't saying much, since most of them are psychopaths by Earth standards." He chuckled, then glanced at Mindy again. "'Takes one to know one?' I might not be able to communicate mind-to-mind with you—yet—but I can figure out what you're thinking. I've been working hard to understand you this whole time. You're important to me. Both of you. Eventually, we're all going to be friends."

He tapped on the control panel attached to the side of the tank, checking the readouts. Vitals were good. Rejection was low and integration numbers were high. Brainwave activity was increasing. Everything was going perfectly.

He took a moment just to enjoy the results of his work, listening to the music and observing his creation suspended in the tank. An oxygen mask covered the bottom half of her face and sensors obscured most of the rest of it. Her hair floated around her head, darkened by the water, but with glints of red shining from the lights.

"The very best of friends," he murmured.

Her eyes snapped open, glowing with vibrant green light bright enough to illuminate the surrounding water.

"Hello, Hayley," he said.

—

Thank you so much for reading *Lar: A Scifi Alien Warriors Romance!* The adventures continue in book four in the *Cygnian 7* series, *Dorn: A Scifi Alien Warriors Romance!* Dorn has no idea how much of a handful he's dealing with. Amy is not to be toyed with—much like a certain kitten who lives on the *Reckoning* and is just as tired of not being taken seriously. That's right, the most mischievous of the Space Kittens, Queenie, will be showing up in Dorn and Amy's book, and you are not going to believe what she's been up to. Read on for a sneak peek of Dorn and Amy's adventure!

Dorn: A Scifi Alien Warriors Romance

Cygnian 7
Book Four

Chapter One

Amy stared up at a smooth white ceiling. Odd fragments of rainbows were flickering in her blurred vision. Her mouth felt as if she'd been drinking sandpaper smoothies and her head spun from the images of the strange memory-dream. Someone had taken her from her home. Men dressed up as characters straight out of a low budget sci-fi movie had attacked Amy and her sister, Sophie. Except they hadn't just been doing some kind of cosplay. They'd carried weapons. *Actual* weapons, capable of doing things no technology she knew of could do. No technology from Earth.

Was she seriously considering this? That aliens had abducted her?

Her heart raced, pounding against her chest in a punishing beat. Whatever was happening, if she was going to get herself and Sophie out of this, Amy needed to control her emotions and think clearly—to calm down and assess her environment and situation. Sophie would be hapless. It was up to Amy to save them.

Her left shoulder was strangely stiff and a constant current ran up and down her spine. The not-unpleasant tingling spread over her back and down her arms and legs. She twitched her fingers and toes unobtrusively to make sure she could move while taking in more details about her surroundings.

There were no tiles or overhead lights, though the room was brightly lit. She blinked repeatedly to bring her view into focus. The wall above her head was also white, with a monitor built into it, integrated so seamlessly that she couldn't see a gap around the edges of the screen. Various shapes in different colors pulsed, spiked, or faded in and out on its otherwise black surface. She had never seen a vitals display like it, but she would bet she was in some kind of hospital.

A wave of shivers passed through her like the ones she

would get when she'd been sick for a while and hadn't moved enough, but the stiffness in her shoulder warned her away from trying to rise. The shivers turned to tingling, the hair on her arms and legs standing on end and her spine becoming a racetrack for arcs like lightning along her nerves. What the hell was that? She blinked a few times to clear her vision, her eyes drawn to her left. Her heart picked up again, pounding against her chest as the tingling in her spine and skin intensified a hundredfold.

A man was standing near her bed. Or at least, a male... something. He looked mostly human, but his skin was the pale blue of a perfect spring sky. His eyes glowed vibrant green, the color so intense, it tinged his high cheekbones and strong brow. His hair was white, flowing around his shoulders, but with the bangs pulled back in a ponytail. Her 'abducted-by-aliens' theory was definitely gaining credibility.

From where she lay, he seemed impossibly tall. He must be pushing seven feet, if not more. Cords of muscles stood out on his arms, shoulders and jaw. His cheekbones were chiseled perfection. The tight, white leather pants he wore clung to muscular thighs thicker than her waist. He wore a sleeveless tunic of matching material that laced up the front, giving her a tantalizing view of sculpted abs and a chest she wanted to turn into a cheese tray.

Was she still dreaming? This guy was too gorgeous to be real, her reaction to him too visceral. Her hands curled, the skin of her fingertips tingling and her palms itching with the desire to touch him. She would pull his hair loose and run her fingers through it, then figure out how to untie those laces on his shirt as she kissed the curve of his lips. The curve that was deepening as he smirked at her as if he was privy to some secret that amused him.

His smile hit her like a nuke going off in her nether regions. More of her skin broke out in goosebumps. Stiff shoulder or not, she wanted to get up and throw herself at him. She mercilessly clamped down on the urge.

What the hell was going on? Had someone drugged her? Her mind was clear, though. Then again, drugs would explain the pale rainbows she was still seeing floating in the air, especially around the blue giant. They faded the longer she stared at him.

She must still be dreaming. Or maybe hallucinating. Except the weirdness started long before waking up here— back at her house when those three guys showed up in silver catsuits and shot her with a ray-beam. Her heart picked up at the memory, her chest tightening as the recent fear came back full force. The giant's pale white eyebrows pulled together, the corners of his eyes pinched with concern. The emotion emanated from him like a palpable thing—yet another form of hallucination? He reached for her with his huge hand, fingers outstretched. The tips of his nails were sharp like claws.

Somehow, she knew his touch would be gentle, his

hands strong and warm. He would hold her close and protect her. No one would ever hurt her again. The pull toward him was so strong, her entire body tingled with it. Her core tightened and wave after wave of goosebumps spread across her skin. If she let herself fall toward him, into him, they would share a bliss unlike anything she'd ever experienced. All she had to do was let go.

Right before his hand touched her shoulder, she flung herself to the side, rolling off the bed and landing in a crouch. She leapt back, needing more space to maneuver, and ended up in a fighting stance, feet set wide, her arms up and ready to defend herself. The light in the room caught and reflected off of two shimmering wristbands made of a substance that gleamed like chrome, but with some kind of transparent crystal-like material coating it. Lights of every color dotted their surface in a complex pattern that made no sense. Her eyebrows lifted as she quickly looked them over, trying to find a hinge or a keyhole or any way to remove them. There wasn't so much as a seam where someone had welded them together on her forearms.

"Amy."

The blue giant's familiar voice coursed through her like the vibration of a plucked guitar string, starting in her feet and thrumming its way all up through her body. The same voice as in her dream. A jolt of energy seared her spine, electric arcs of pleasure zinging along her arms and legs.

She didn't know her name could sound so sensual, so full of need. Ever so briefly, she closed her eyes, fighting off the sensations, trying to tamp them down. She finally gave up, settling instead on ignoring them and glaring at the threat before her.

She swallowed hard. "And you are?"

His perfect lips quirked up in a half-smile that sent more heat pulsing through her. In that low, rumbling voice, he said, "Dorn."

"Just Dorn? No last name?"

"Dorn is the first, last, and only name I was given."

"Fair enough. Speaking of gifts, care to tell me about these fancy handcuffs?"

His brow furrowed, and his smirk faded. "Those are wristbands, not handcuffs."

"Potato, po-tah-to."

He cocked his head to the side, brow slightly furrowed. They probably didn't have potatoes where he was from.

"If they aren't cuffs, then tell me how to take them off," she said.

"You need to wear them for your protection. They're a gift, not a means to control you."

"Can you use them to control me?"

His lips parted briefly, then he snapped his mouth shut.

She snorted. "And there's my answer."

Dorn stepped around the bed and she backed away further. Damn, he was huge. She had felt better when there was at least something between them—a bit of cover for her to hide behind when this situation inevitably went pear-shaped. As he lifted his hands, she noticed he was wearing wristbands that looked exactly like hers. Briefly, she wondered if he was in the same mess that she was. They could band together and fight off the bad guys, rescue Sophie, and escape back to Earth, where Amy would show him her appreciation by—

She shook herself, forcing her attention back to the reality of her unbelievable situation. That was a complete fantasy. She wasn't a daydreaming romantic like Sophie, who fell for any hot guy that caught her eye. Wait...

Amy glanced back at Dorn's wristbands. She had seen something similar recently. A friend of their older brother, Buddy, had crashed family dinner only a few days ago. Kral. He was as tall as Dorn and even more thickly muscled—and he'd worn the same style of wristbands, only without the flashy colors. Kral hadn't been blue, but who knew what these guys could do with their advanced technology.

Her stomach tightened as she realized Becca might be in as much danger as Amy and Sophie. Kral had been extremely focused on their eldest sister. But he was a friend of Buddy's, and Buddy was extremely overprotective of them all—especially Amy. He wouldn't bring someone dangerous into their lives. Then again, Kral's presence had agitated Buddy. He was desperate for

Kral to leave. There was more going on with that dynamic than Amy could sort out at the moment.

She couldn't make decisions based on hopeful speculation. No. Dorn knew what was going on and was part of it. Amy's family was in danger. She needed to see him as an enemy, not a potential date. Whatever he did to make her want him so much, she needed to fight it with everything she had.

—

This adventure is just ramping up, and I can't wait to share more of the Cygnian warriors' stories with you, continuing with *Dorn: A Scifi Alien Warriors Romance*.

If you want to learn more about Lar and the other Cygnian warriors' universe, you can check out *The Department of Homeworld Security* adventures. Many of the novellas have been collected in the first two series omnibuses, *The Department of Homeworld Security Omnibus 1* and *The Department of Homeworld Security Omnibus 2*. Or you can pick and choose with the individual novellas.

I'd love to keep in touch. Join my newsletter at sendfox.com/cassandrachandler to hear about all the adventures happening in Cassland. And if you enjoyed this book, please consider leaving a review at your favorite book review site. I'd really appreciate it—reviews help readers and authors alike!

Thank you for reading *Lar: A Scifi Alien Warriors Romance!*

Cassandra Chandler

About the Author

USA Today Bestselling author Cassandra Chandler uses her vivid imagination to make the world more interesting, spawning the ideas she turns into her enthralling Science Fiction Romances and darkly evocative Paranormal and Urban Fantasy Romances. Fast-paced and funny, lighthearted or dark, her stories will introduce you to characters you'll fall in love with and worlds you long to explore.

www.ingramcontent.com/pod-product-compliance
Lightning Source LLC
Chambersburg PA
CBHW071215250626

47159CB00001B/319